P9-BZR-226

"Donna Alward has become a shining star . . . Fans of Brenda Novak and Robyn Carr are going to simply adore."
—*Fresh Fiction*

"This story of loss, family love, and the power of friendship is one anyone will love to be a part of. The emotions that *Summer on Lovers' Island* brings out is amazing."
—*Romance Junkies*

"I loved everything about the sleepy little town of Jewell Cove. I recommend this book to anyone that loves a great second chance at love story set in a small town."
—*Harlequin Junkie,* Top Pick

"Wonderful, witty, and memorable . . . readers will love discovering the richly layered stories and enticing secrets residing in Jewell Cove."
—*New York Times* bestselling author Shirley Jump

"Donna Alward writes warm, memorable characters who spring to life on the page. Brimming with old family history, small-town secrets and newfound passion, you'll want to pack up and move to Jewell Cove, Maine!"
—Lily Everett

"Old family secrets, a bitter tragedy, and a restless spirit add mystery and an eerie touch to this compelling story that is steeped in small-town New England flavor so rich you can taste it and beautifully launches the author's new series."
—*Library Journal*

Somebody
Like You

DONNA ALWARD

St. Martin's Paperbacks

This is a work of fiction. All of the characters, organizations, and events portrayed in this novel are either products of the author's imagination or are used fictitiously.

SOMEBODY LIKE YOU

Copyright © 2017 by Donna Alward.

For information address St. Martin's Press, 175 Fifth Avenue, New York, NY 10010.

ISBN: 978-1-250-09264-9

Our books may be purchased in bulk for promotional, educational, or business use. Please contact your local bookseller or the Macmillan Corporate and Premium Sales Department at 1-800-221-7945, ext. 5442, or by e-mail at MacmillanSpecialMarkets@macmillan.com.

Printed in the United States of America

St. Martin's Paperbacks edition / February 2017

St. Martin's Paperbacks are published by St. Martin's Press, 175 Fifth Avenue, New York, NY 10010.

10 9 8 7 6 5 4 3 2 1

CHAPTER 1

Every single terra-cotta pot was smashed.

Laurel Stone blinked quickly, annoyed at the sting at the back of her eyes as she stared at the mess. She was angry. Furious. Most people would rant or turn red in the face. But not Laurel. When she got mad, she angry-cried. And right now she was so infuriated that she could barely see through the hot tears.

She'd come in early to do some watering and deadheading before starting the weekly stock order, but discovered the gate hanging limply from its hinges, its lock busted. She immediately took out her cell and called the cops, working extra hard to keep her voice from shaking. Falling apart was not an option. She'd made it through a lot of life changes lately and had kept it together. This time was no different.

Now, as she waited for the police, she swiped at her face and bit down on her lip. It was only six thirty in the morning and she hadn't even had her first coffee yet. The brew sat cooling, forgotten in her ladybug print travel mug.

Normally she hummed away to herself, unwinding the hose in the cool morning air. Not today. Today she had to deal with the fact that crime actually happened in quiet, idyllic Darling, Vermont.

And that left her shaken.

The Ladybug Garden Center was her pride and joy, her foray into building a new life for herself. There'd been little incidents in her first few weeks of opening, but she hadn't thought much of them. The parking lot had been messed up a bit where someone had pulled doughnuts with their car. Two lilac bushes from the bed by the store sign had been stolen. She'd sighed at the inconvenience, but chalked it up to simple mischief.

This time the intent was obvious. Deliberate. And it felt personal.

All the pottery was in shards on the floor. Six-packs of annuals had been pushed off their tables, spilling dirt and crushed blossoms. Hanging baskets had been carelessly dropped, so that the planters cracked and split. Tomato and pepper plants were strewn everywhere, broken and wilting. The lock on the little safe had been smashed, and they'd taken the small amount of money set aside for a float.

Laurel was sweeping shards of pottery into a dustpan when she heard the gritty crunch of tires on gravel. She stood up and braced her hand on her hip as the cruiser crept slowly up the drive and into the parking lot. Might as well get the report over with, and then get on with the cleanup and the call to the insurance agent.

The cruiser door opened.

Damn, damn, damn.

She'd forgotten, though she wasn't quite sure how she could have since Darling was such a small town. Aiden Gallagher. One of Darling's finest, complete with a crisp navy uniform, black shoes, and a belt on his hip that lent him a certain gravity and sexiness she wished she didn't appreciate.

The last time she'd seen Aiden, she'd been home from school, barely twenty-one, and he'd flashed her a cocky take-a-good-look grin, all the while parading around the Suds and Spuds pub with some girl on his arm. Not that she'd expected any other sort of behavior from him. But still. Ugh.

Aiden approached the gate and she took a deep breath. He was a cop answering a call. Nothing more. And that was how she'd treat him. She definitely wouldn't acknowledge that they'd known each other since they were five years old. Or that he'd once had her half-naked in the back-seat of his car.

"Laurel," he greeted, sliding through the gap in the fence. "Looks like you've had some trouble."

She would do this. She would not cry again, especially not in front of Aiden. She had too much pride.

"A break-in last night." She opened the gate a bit wider so he could get through. He passed close by her, his scent wafting in his wake. She swallowed. After all these years, he still wore the same cologne, and nostalgia hit her right in the solar plexus. He took off his cap and she saw his hair was still the same burnished copper, only shorter and without the natural waves, and his skin showed signs of freckles, but nowhere near as pronounced as they'd been. He wasn't a boy any longer; he was a man.

He looked over his shoulder, his gray-blue eyes meeting hers.

Definitely a man.

"Wow." He stopped and stared at the carnage. "They made a real mess. Was anything taken?"

She shrugged, focusing on the issue at hand once more. "Inventory-wise, I won't know until I get things cleaned up and do a count. But I doubt it. The float for the cash is gone, but that's only a few hundred dollars. Mostly they just made a mess."

Laurel bent over and righted a half-barrel of colorful begonias, purple lobelia, and million bells. Her gaze blurred as she noticed the crushed, fragile blossoms and pile of dirt left on the floor.

"Laurel?"

She clenched her teeth. If he saw her with tears in her eyes . . . today was upsetting enough without adding humiliation to the mix.

"Laurel," he said, softer now. "Are you okay?"

"I'm fine." She bit out the words and pushed past him, going to the counter area. She could stand behind it and the counter would provide a barrier between them. "You don't need to worry about me, or take that soothing-the-victim tone. What do you need for facts?"

She sensed his withdrawal as he straightened his shoulders, and she felt momentarily sheepish for taking such a sharp tone. But she was angry, dammit. Hell, she was angry most of the time, and starting to get tired of hiding it with a smile. This was truly the last thing she needed.

"Do you have a slip or anything with the amount of the float?" Now he was all business. It was a relief.

She took a piece of paper from beneath the cash drawer in the register. "This is our rundown for what goes in the float each night. It's put in a zip bag in the safe. Like a pencil case."

He came around the counter, invading her space, and knelt down in front of the cupboard. "This is the safe?"

"I know. It's not heavy-duty . . ."

"It looks like they just beat it open with a hammer."

Great. Now she was feeling stupid, too. "It's Darling. I didn't expect something like this to happen here."

He stood up and gave her a look that telegraphed "Are you serious?" before stepping back beyond the counter again. "Something like this happens everywhere, Laurel. What, you didn't think crime happened in Darling?"

Well, no. Or at least, not until today. The fact that she'd already come to this disappointing conclusion, and then he'd repeated it, just made her angrier.

Coming home was supposed to be peaceful. Happy. The town was small, friendly, neighborly. Even after years away, many of her customers remembered her from her school years and recalled stories from those days. Darling even had a special "Kissing Bridge" in the park. There were several stories around how the bridge got the name, so no one really knew for sure. But the stone bridge and the quaint little legend to go with it brought tourists to the area and made Darling's claim to fame a very romantic one. In a nutshell, those who stood on the bridge and sealed their love with a kiss would be together forever.

She should know all about it. Her picture—and Aiden's—hung in the town offices to advertise the attraction. Just because they'd only been five years old at the time didn't make it less of an embarrassment.

"I'm not naïve," she replied sharply. "Is there anything else you need or can I get back to cleaning up?"

"Can you think of anyone who might want to give you trouble? Someone with a grudge or ax to grind?"

Other than you? she thought darkly. This was the first time they'd actually spoken since she'd poured vanilla milkshake over his head in the school cafeteria in their senior year. "No," she replied. "I can't imagine who'd want to do this."

"I don't suppose you have any video cameras installed."

She shook her head, feeling inept and slightly stupid. Maybe she was a little naïve after all. She hadn't lived in Darling since she was nineteen—nine years. Things had changed in her absence. New people, new businesses.

"I'll have another look around. It looks like a case of vandalism more than anything. Probably some teenagers thinking it's funny, or after the cash for booze or pot, and smashed some stuff for show." His gaze touched hers. "Kids can be really dumb at that age."

Her cheeks heated. He hadn't had to say the actual words for her to catch his meaning. "You never know. They might have been dared to do it. Or some sort of stupid bet."

He held her gaze a few seconds longer, and she could tell by the look in his eyes that he acknowledged the hit. He'd kissed her because of one of those bets . . . more than kissed her. They'd been parking in his car and he'd rounded second base and had been headed for third. And then she'd found out about the wager and lost her cool. Publicly. With the milkshake.

The only thing she regretted was saying yes to going on that drive in the first place.

"So you still haven't forgiven me for that."

Laurel lifted her chin. "To my recollection, you haven't asked for forgiveness."

Aiden frowned, his brows pulling together. "We were seventeen. Kids. That was years ago."

Which didn't sound much like an apology at all.

"Yes, it was. Now, I have a lot of mess to clean up. Is there any more information you need or are we done here?"

He stared at her for a long minute. Long enough that

she started to squirm a bit at his continued attention. Finally, when she was so uncomfortable she thought she might burst, she turned away and retrieved the broom and dustpan from where she'd left them.

"Do you want some help with this?"

She didn't want him to offer. The idea of spending more time with him was so unsettling that she immediately refused. "No. Don't you have to get back to work? Besides, I have someone coming in at eight. You go do what you need to do, Officer Gallagher."

"Officer Galla . . . oh, for Crissakes, Laurel. Is that necessary?"

She pinned him with a glare. He was standing with his weight on one hip, accentuating his lean, muscular physique, one perfect eyebrow arched in response to her acid tone.

She wasn't the kind to hold a grudge. Not generally. Heck, she'd forgiven Dan months ago, and that was for something far bigger than a silly teenage bet. Why did Aiden get under her skin so easily?

Maybe it was because he'd been so callous, even after the fact. If he'd shown any remorse at all . . . but he hadn't. He'd taken the paper cup the milkshake had been in, and fired it across the cafeteria floor before charging out. And he'd never once spoken to her again.

Until today. And despite the change in circumstances, she felt much the same as she had that night in the backseat of his car. Out of her depth, over her head, and at a distinct disadvantage.

She looked away. "Sorry. I just want to clean this up and get ready to open."

She picked up the broom and began sweeping the little bits of broken pots and dirt into the dustpan. She saw his shoes first; big sturdy black ones that stopped in front of her. Then his hand, warm and reassuring, touched her shoulder. She'd been rude and brusque, and he was being kind. Damn him. Emotion threatened to overwhelm again. Couldn't he see that gentle compassion was harder for her to handle than cool efficiency?

"Are you afraid to stay here alone this morning?"

He throat tightened. "No, of course not."

"I'm on duty until this afternoon. I can check in from time to time."

"I'm fine." She looked up at him and set her jaw. "I can take care of myself. I'm a big girl."

He stepped back. "All right. But if you think of anything or anything else happens, call right away."

"Okay."

She kept sweeping and listened to his footsteps walk away across the concrete floor. The building always smelled delicious thanks to the flowers, but this morning the scent was even more pungent because many had been crushed and mangled. She sighed and rested her weight on the broom handle. He was just doing his job. And she was pissed off—at the state of the garden center and the fact that the one person in Darling she didn't really care to see was the one who'd been sent to help.

"Aiden?"

He turned when she called his name, but his expression was neutral. She wished she could be that way. Unfortunately she always seemed to wear her emotions all over her face.

"Thanks for your help this morning."

He nodded. "Just doing my job."

He walked to his cruiser and got in while Laurel stood there with a flaming-hot face. Once he'd turned to exit the driveway, she kicked a plastic bucket that had been abandoned in the middle of an aisle, sending it spinning away with a loud clatter. No sooner had she decided to extend an olive branch than he came back with a line that deflated any sort of possibility of amity. He was just doing his job, like he'd do for anyone else. She was no one special. Never had been. The knowledge shouldn't have cut, but it did.

Anyway, the bigger issue was the problem at hand—getting the store ready to open in just a few hours. The Ladybug Garden Center was her baby now. She'd invested all of herself into it, and she was determined to see it succeed, not only this spring and summer but into the fall and winter. In order for that to happen she would have to take steps to ensure this sort of thing didn't happen again.

Just as soon as she cleaned up the mess.

And stopped thinking about how Aiden hadn't changed that much, either. In good ways and in bad.

CHAPTER 2

Aiden stripped off his uniform, leaving the clothing trailing behind him as he headed for the shower. It was only mid-afternoon; he'd worked the early shift and could still enjoy what was left of the spring day. He stepped out of his underwear and left it abandoned on the bathroom floor as he flicked on the shower and waited for the water to get hot.

Law enforcement in a small town was a blessing and a curse. He blew out a breath and stepped under the spray.

Today's agenda had included a few traffic stops, a drunk and disorderly, and a homeless man hovering outside a store, being a nuisance. He'd known as soon as dispatch had called that it was George. No one knew George's last name. He didn't seem to have any family, and most of the time he lived in the shelter in town. Everything he owned was in a backpack that looked as though it had been through the war. Occasionally, George would hitch a ride to Montpelier and drift around there for a while, but then he always came back. He was completely harmless, often hungry, sometimes dirty.

Today he'd been sitting on a bench in the shade, not really disturbing anyone. But Mrs. McKenzie who ran the dry cleaners didn't like him loitering around. What Aiden figured she needed was a good dose of compassion.

He'd talked to George, then he'd taken him to the goodwill and helped him pick out some new clothes. All told, the jeans, T-shirt, and secondhand sneakers had cost about ten bucks. Then they'd made a stop at the General Store where Aiden bought him a sandwich, a Coke, and an apple, as well as new socks and a pair of fresh underwear. Hopefully, when George went to the shelter tonight, he could have a hot shower, clean clothes, and a decent meal.

Those calls were hard, and sometimes annoying, but Aiden at least felt like he was making a difference. He scrubbed vigorously at his hair, bubbles splattering on the walls of the shower. Unlike how he'd felt answering the call at the Ladybug Garden Center. Laurel had been . . . well, the same old Laurel he remembered. She'd been upset, but not too upset to look down her nose at him. For a minute he'd almost felt sympathy. Concern. But then she'd opened her mouth and it had become really easy to stick to business. God, but she was prickly.

Unfortunately her looks did not match her temperament. She was as beautiful—no, more so—than she'd been in high school. The girlish curves had turned into an alluring, womanly figure, discernible even beneath the shapeless golf shirt. Her hair was the same rich brown, and her eyes . . . he'd always been a sucker for her eyes. Blue, with a hint of violet in the right lighting that contrasted with her creamy skin and dark hair. Seeing her again had sucked all the wind out of his lungs. Not that he'd let her see that.

The spray sluiced away the suds in his hair. Why

couldn't he stop thinking about her? It was probably because she'd shown no hesitation in reminding him about their past. And his behavior. He certainly wasn't proud of it, but they'd been seventeen. Everyone was an idiot at seventeen, weren't they? Wasn't there a statute of limitations or something about that?

Wait until she found out what the town council was planning. He'd already been approached by someone in the tourism department. Laurel had only been back in town a few weeks, since the garden center opened for the season. They probably hadn't asked her yet. After this morning's reception, he was pretty sure what her answer was going to be.

Dressing up in a wedding gown and kissing him on the stone bridge? Hah. She couldn't even look at him without her mouth tightening up like a chicken's asshole. There was no way she'd agree to recreating the picture that had been taken of them when they'd been all of five years old. They'd been ring bearer and flower girl at a wedding, and the picture of the two of them had been adopted as the promotional photo for the town's famous Kissing Bridge. Cute back then, he supposed. Embarrassing as hell now.

He still took his share of grief for it. People had long memories, and the milkshake incident had been a sensation. The flip-side of small-town living: everyone delighted in everyone else's business.

He stepped out of the shower and toweled off, efficiently pulling on underwear, a pair of board shorts, and a T-shirt. He didn't do a thing with his hair besides run his hand through it and give it a shake, sending droplets of water spattering onto the mirror. A quick application of deodorant and he was done, taking a spare five seconds to hang up his towel.

"Yo, bro. You beautiful yet? I need to take a leak."

Aiden grinned. His slightly younger brother, Rory, must have finished work early today. The two shared the apartment, which was essentially the upstairs above the veterinary clinic. Rory got the rent cheap for being the "on-site" vet. Perks of being the newbie just out of vet school. "Something wrong with the clinic bathroom?"

"Naw." Rory looked up as Aiden entered the kitchen. Rory was already halfway through a beer. "I'm clocked out for the day is all. Last appointment cancelled."

"Does this mean you're cooking?"

Rory chuckled, shouldering his way past Aiden. "I can. Unless you want to go to Mom and Dad's."

Aiden didn't. News of the robbery had spread through town and he was sure his parents had heard. They'd have questions, not just about the robbery but also about Laurel. "I'd rather stay here. I can cook if you don't want to."

"Oooh, frozen pizza. Again."

"I can make more than frozen pizza." Aiden went to the fridge, considered the beer, and grabbed a soda instead. Somehow he just wasn't in the mood.

There was silence for a second as Rory headed for the bathroom, then a loud curse. "Shit, your shorts are on the floor. Gross."

Aiden laughed. He'd been in a hurry for the shower, but he deliberately left stuff around just to spool his brother up. Rory was such a damned neat freak. He needed to relax once in a while. The fact that he'd knocked off work was definitely unusual.

In the end, the choice for supper was taken out of his hands. One phone call and a not-so-subtle guilt trip later about how they never made time for their mother anymore, and both boys headed to the family home.

The Gallaghers lived just outside Darling, on a couple of rolling green acres dotted with tall maples and oaks. The house was huge by modern standards: only twenty years old but built in that old-fashioned colonial style so popular in New England. The front faced the dirt drive, but the back had a huge deck that overlooked the lake. Aiden sometimes wondered why his parents kept it, now that all six of the kids were up and grown. Only the twins lived at home, and even then only part of the time. It was a lot of house for two people, and so much work.

But as he and Rory drove up in Aiden's truck, he understood. It wasn't the kind of property—or home—that a person could turn their back on easily.

Claire's car was in the yard, Cait's wasn't, and neither was their older sister Hannah's. Ethan's SUV was though, and Aiden could hear screams and giggles coming from the backyard as he and Rory got out of the truck.

Rory grinned. "Ethan's here with the boys."

The oldest child of the family, Ethan was the only one of the Gallaghers to get married, much to their mother's dismay. Ethan was only thirty-two and already a widower, left to raise his boys on his own. As a firefighter working shift work, their parents helped out as much as they could.

"Uncle Aiden! Uncle Rory! Come play soccer with us!"

Ethan's son Connor came running, his five-year-old legs churning and his coppery hair flopping over his forehead. His little brother Ronan toddled behind, curls bouncing, trying desperately to keep up. Aiden remembered the feeling well. He'd done his fair share of chasing after his brothers when he was little. Particularly when they didn't want him to follow.

They followed the boys to the backyard, where a rousing game was already in progress: Connor and Gramps against Ronan and Ethan. Rory and Aiden made it three on three and the competition was on for real, along with some trash talk that was cleaned up due to the presence of the boys. Aiden had scored on his dad and was doing a victory lap of the yard when his mother, Moira, stepped outside and called everyone in for dinner.

"Wash your hands," she commanded, as she shooed them inside, each of them easily a foot taller than she was.

"Yes, Mom," Rory said, dropping a kiss on her cheek.

Dinner was a far cry from dry pizza. His mother had baked a ham, made whipped potatoes, vegetables, and fresh rolls. Aiden was just slicing into a fat slab of maple ham when his father, John, piped up, "Heard there was some trouble in town today. At the garden center. You know anything about that, Aiden?"

It felt like the ham in his mouth expanded as he tried to chew. He nodded as he forced a swallow. "I was on shift and answered the call. I think it was probably some teens acting out. Mostly it was just stuff smashed up."

Moira frowned. "Poor Laurel. She just got that place up and running."

"They only took the float."

"But all that stock." Claire sighed she buttered her roll. "That can't be cheap to replace. And her sales will take a hit in the meantime."

Claire was studying marketing in college and had a summer internship working for the town. Aiden looked at his little sister. She was growing up so fast. Today she was dressed in navy trousers and a neat little shirt with her hair up in a bun of some kind, every inch the professional.

"Yes, but it's Darling," Rory commented easily. "People will buy from her just to show their support."

Ethan hadn't said anything. He was busy trying to keep

the boys' food on their plates and in their mouths and not on the floor.

Moira eyed Aiden keenly. "So, how is she?"

He shrugged. "Upset. About what you'd expect."

"That's not what I meant. How does she look? I haven't been in to see her yet. Is she as pretty as ever?"

Aiden raised an eyebrow. "I didn't notice. I was, you know, doing my job."

Ethan finally laughed. "Right. As if. Laurel Stone has turned your crank ever since you hit puberty."

"I'm twenty-eight. Puberty's a few years ago, thanks." Aiden shoveled up some potatoes. He hated that his brother was right. He'd noticed her in sophomore year when they had math together.

Something about her had been familiar. They'd become friends, but he'd been too scared to make a move. Then, on a cold January afternoon, they'd been out skating with a group of friends near the Kissing Bridge. Laurel had mentioned that she was in the town photo, and it all seemed to click.

"Seems to me the feelings weren't returned," Rory added, breaking into Aiden's thoughts. "She did dump a milkshake over your head."

It hadn't been Aiden's finest moment. He'd been a jerk. And he'd been sorry, though she wouldn't listen to him. If she'd just talked to him, in private, he could have explained it all. Instead she'd made sure he was completely humiliated. There'd been no hope for them after that. Even if he'd put away his pride for two seconds, it had been guilt that kept him silent. He'd wronged her and deep down he knew it.

"Vanilla," Aiden confirmed, grinning. He wouldn't let them know how much it bothered him. Probably because history had repeated itself with Erica. Only in that case it hadn't been a milkshake. It had been his truck, and a rather sharp set of keys. Straight down the side of his custom paint job. He was no good with women, that was for sure. And he wasn't too great at learning his lesson, either.

"Well, it's a shame. She's been through quite a bit, you know."

"She has?" Aiden hadn't heard much. Just that she was back and that she'd opened the garden center. He tried not to listen to office or lunch-counter chatter. That type of gossip was one of the few things he didn't like about living in a town this size. Everyone made everything their business.

"She's newly divorced. Only married three years. You remember their wedding, don't you? There was a picture in the paper. They got married at that big hotel in Montpelier. They met in college and she interned at his accounting firm, if I remember right."

Today she'd been in jeans, rubber boots, and a T-shirt. Aiden tried to think of her in office dress and it didn't compute. She'd always been an outdoor girl. Jeans and ball shirts watching baseball games . . .

"And now her husband is getting married, again. To one of the partners at the firm." Moira leaned forward, her voice lowered. "The partner's name is . . . Ryan."

Claire rolled her eyes. "Oh for Pete's sake, Mom. You don't have to whisper. You can say the word *gay*."

"Well, maybe, but you have to admit it's a little strange, considering he was married to Laurel first. That's got to be a tough situation."

He felt sorry for her . . . and then knew that she'd hate being pitied.

"Well, no matter what's happened to her personal life,

whoever broke into the store really did a number on it. There was dirt and pots everywhere." He chewed another piece of ham and swallowed, then shrugged. "I know we got into our fair share of trouble, but if we'd pulled something like that, Dad would've kicked our asses."

"You got that right," John replied, sending his sons the evil eye. It was hard to take the big Irishman seriously, though. His rust-colored eyebrow did this funny lift when he was teasing, and his eyes twinkled.

Rory laughed and reached for the bowl of carrots. "And there's the big crime story for the month. Some kids roughed up some flowers and took a hundred bucks."

"And I'm glad." Moira looked over at Aiden. "I'm okay with Aiden's job not being all that dangerous. I'd worry too much."

"Like you do with Ethan," Claire said.

"Like I do with all you kids," Moira corrected, frowning. Aiden knew she wouldn't say so in front of Ethan, because he already put too much pressure on himself. They all knew Moira worried. Ethan was a firefighter and a dad. He had his sons to think of.

So Aiden kept quiet. If he responded, the guys would start their usual teasing about being a small-time cop in a small town. The jokes could go on for hours. Not that Aiden was really looking for adrenaline-pumping danger, but there were definitely days he wished he felt more effective. And if he brought up the subject of civic duty, they'd haze him even more.

So he sat with his mouth shut for the most part, covering his mood by putting on his devil-may-care face.

When the meal was over, Aiden helped clear the table with Claire, while Ethan took the boys for a bath, and Rory and John went out to the shed to have a look at John's latest woodworking project—a quilt chest for Moira.

Moira worked around the kitchen, packing up leftovers for Rory and Aiden to take home. "This will keep you boys fed for a day or so, anyway," she said, snapping the lid onto a plastic dish of leftover potatoes.

Aiden laughed. "Mom, seriously, we can feed ourselves."

"Not like your mother can."

He put his arm around her. "Well, duh." He grinned. "I appreciate it, I really do. But I'm a grown man. I do my own laundry and everything."

She looked up at him, her blue eyes soft with affection. "I know you are, and you do. But I'll always be your mother. Same as I am with all you kids."

The sound of squeals came from upstairs and they both smiled.

"How's he doing?" Aiden asked, letting go of his mother and reaching for plates to load in the dishwasher. Claire had gone back to the dining room to tidy the table, and it was just the two of them now.

"Ethan? Oh, he's muddling through. Doing better."

"But?"

"But he's moved from sad to grouchy. He's . . . he doesn't smile. You know?"

Aiden nodded. "I'll see if we can get him to come out with us soon."

Moira stopped what she was doing and faced Aiden, her expression sad and serious. "You and Rory . . . you have this singles club thing going on, and Ethan's past that now. But he can't stay alone forever. If you can get him to go out with you, do it. I'll keep the boys."

"I'll talk to Rory. I think we're both off this Sunday. If

Ethan's off shift, maybe we can hang out. Play a round of golf or something."

Claire came back in, a dishtowel over her shoulder and the salt and pepper shakers cradled in her hand. "You two look awfully serious."

"Just talking about Ethan, that's all."

Claire opened a cabinet and put the shakers inside. "Nothing's wrong with Ethan other than he needs to get laid."

"Claire!" Moira sent her youngest daughter a dark look. "Things are definitely not that simple."

She shrugged. "All I'm sayin' is that he's thirty-two and has a lot of responsibility. Add that to a really long dry spell . . ."

"I'm not having this conversation with my children," Moira muttered, and started some water in the sink to wash the pots and pans.

Aiden started laughing. They'd had this kind of conversation many times over the years, though Moira tried to keep it on the polite side of vulgar. But no topic had ever been off limits. As kids, that had been both wonderful and horrifying, depending on which side of the conversation they found themselves.

"Sex isn't everything, sis." Aiden reached for the dishwasher soap and filled the reservoir.

Claire stopped short and gaped at Aiden. "When did you get to be all fuddy-duddy?"

He shut the dishwasher door and hit the start button. "Oh, I don't know. I guess I must have grown up. But only a little. I've got a ways to go before I get to be as big of a stick-in-the-mud as Ethan."

"Aiden," Moira said quietly.

Ethan stood in the doorway to the kitchen, Ronan in his arms, the young boy wrapped in a hooded towel.

"E, I'm sorry, man. I didn't mean that." Aiden struggled to take his foot out of his mouth.

"Don't worry about it," Ethan said, and disappeared around the corner again.

But Aiden had seen the look on his brother's face. A mask of indifference, but a glimmer of hurt, too.

For the second time today, Aiden felt like a screwup. He'd always been known as the goofball, the kid not to be taken seriously. Ethan had become a firefighter, settled down, and had kids before he'd turned thirty. Rory spent eight years in college and had the beginnings of a great career. Hannah had gotten her business degree and now ran her own real estate agency. The twins were the babies of the family, a bit spoiled, and took their share of ribbing about it. It wasn't that his family didn't have expectations; they did. It was more that Aiden was always seen as the joker, the single guy, the one who liked life unencumbered.

He was the jock who'd taken Laurel Stone out on a locker-room bet and who'd never dated anyone for longer than six months. And he suspected that if he ever expressed his dissatisfaction with that image, no one would believe him.

"Nice work," Claire said quietly, and being chastised by both his mother and his baby sister put his teeth on edge.

"I'll go after him," Aiden said, his heart heavy.

CHAPTER 3

Laurel had worked all day at the garden center, cleaning up, dealing with the insurance company, doing inventory, and ordering new stock. It didn't make sense that she'd feel like spending the evening in the garden at home, but she did. She'd dealt with paperwork and customers all day. Right now she was getting her hands dirty, using the physical labor to work out her frustrations. Her arms ached from working with the tiller for the last hour, turning over the earth in the patch that would be her vegetable garden. She rubbed her hands on her jeans and then picked up a shovel and put it in her wheelbarrow. A load of garden soil and a load of compost had been delivered yesterday. She'd spread it, mix it in, and let the earth sit for a week or two before starting to plant.

She was about halfway through the compost pile when the back gate creaked. Laurel looked up and saw Willow Dunaway, owner of The Purple Pig Café, gliding through the gate with a yellow tote bag on her arm. Laurel looked down at her dirty jeans and sighed. Willow, even when she was rushed on the job, always managed to look airy and graceful. Laurel just felt dirty and clunky, especially now.

The two had been friends in high school, but had lost touch over the years. Now that Laurel had moved back, they'd connected over raspberry tea and chocolate scones at the café. They'd recently begun chatting about gardening and food production, since the café specialized in local, organic ingredients. Truth be told, the company tonight was a welcome surprise. Laurel could use a little of Willow's serenity.

"You didn't get enough of dirt and plants all day?" Willow asked, plopping down on the grass beside the wheelbarrow.

"I needed something more physical to work out my frustrations," Laurel admitted. She leaned on the handle of the shovel. "What brings you by?"

Willow's normally serene face wrinkled into a frown. "I heard about your troubles. Wanted to see if you're okay."

"I'm okay, I guess." Laurel tried a smile and swept her hand out toward her garden-in-progress.

Willow patted the grass beside her. "Come and sit down. You'll feel better. Connect with the earth for a bit instead of beating the hell out of it."

Laurel grinned. Willow was such a free spirit. Tonight she wore navy leggings and a tunic-style flowy shirt with a mandala stitched into it. Her face was devoid of makeup, dotted with a few natural-looking freckles and dominated by eyes the color of bluebells. Instead of twenty-eight, she looked about eighteen. Right down to the little purple and pink streaks in her hair, just on one side. She was very different from the preppy, type-A overachiever girl Laurel had known in high school, and Laurel silently admitted to herself that she liked the new, more relaxed version of her old friend. Tonight Willow brought with her the soothing scent of lavender.

Laurel sank to the ground and crossed her legs, rounding her shoulders and exhaling. "You're right. It does feel better."

"If you're that tense we could run through a meditation."

Laurel laughed. "I think I'm fine, Wil. Thanks, though. It's been a hell of a day."

Willow reached into her tote bag. "I figured as much so I brought this." She pulled out a bottle of wine and a couple of little glasses. "Sulfite free and organic."

It had a twist top so there was no need for a corkscrew. Willow opened the bottle, let it breathe for a moment, and then poured a healthy amount into each glass. The red liquid looked purply-black in the fading light, and the pungent scent was sharp and fruity. Laurel took a sip and sighed happily.

"See?" Willow laughed lightly. "Cheers."

"We're toasting? My business was vandalized and robbed." Laurel rolled her eyes. "Maybe we can toast to this day being over."

"Or we can toast the fact that you're okay and everything else can be replaced," Willow said. "Or that a day that started so badly is ending with a glass of wine with a friend."

Laurel's heart warmed. "I'll drink to that. Thanks, Willow."

"You're welcome. Now, fill me in. Any idea who trashed the place?"

Laurel took a longer drink and then shook her head. "No, not yet. The police think it's probably kids. I'm not sure if that makes me feel better or worse. I'm just . . . frustrated. I just got the place set up and open, you know?" She'd sunk her savings into buying the business, and taken out a healthy loan, too. She tried not to let that fact scare her, but it was a heavy responsibility just the same. "They seem to think it's just random. Not anything personal against me. But it feels personal. I'm trying to be analytical, but dammit, it hurts. It feels like kicking me when I'm down."

Willow nodded. "I can understand that. Look, Darling tends to be quiet, but it's different than when we were teenagers, Laurel. A bit bigger. And kids . . . I don't know. They seem to have too much time on their hands." She turned her glass around in her fingers. "I see a bunch after school, though the ones who're loud and obnoxious don't tend to be the herbal-tea-and-organic-cookie type, you know?"

Laurel laughed. "We were ever like that?"

"Of course not."

And then they both laughed softly. Willow had been top of her class in English and History. She'd served on every charity committee going and played in the school band. Laurel had always pegged her as a bit high strung, but not so much now. Both of them had been certain they knew everything and had the world by the tail.

Now Willow practically exuded calm and wisdom. And Laurel . . . well. She'd done everything on schedule. Gone away to school, got her degree, got a job, got married. The perfect life that saw her divorced at twenty-seven and with a mountain of debt. It was fairly humbling. Lessons had been hard to learn, but she'd come away stronger.

"You've owned The Purple Pig for what, a year now?" Laurel asked. "And here I am trying to make a go of a garden center. This isn't how we envisioned our lives, is it?" She looked over at her friend. "Not quite a decade since we graduated and look at us. Single and struggling as small business owners, working sixty-plus hours a week."

A shadow passed over Willow's face. "We didn't have life by the tail like we thought, did we?"

"Not quite. Know what, though? I don't think I'd change it." Laurel knew her life hadn't been perfect, but it had been good just the same.

They drank quietly for a minute or two. Laurel kept waiting for Willow to ask about Dan. She'd told Willow the basic truth the first night they'd hung out since her return. That Dan had come out and was in love with one of the partners of the accounting firm.

"You know Aiden's a cop in town now, right? You'll probably run into him now and again."

Just the mention of his name sent a flare of heat down Laurel's body. She wished she could credit her reaction to the wine, but she couldn't. Neither could she stop the strange feeling of anger that sparked whenever she heard his name.

"What brought him up?" She kept her voice casual.

"Just thinking about high school." Willow's laugh floated on the evening breeze. "Gosh, did you ever get him good. I think of that every time I see someone with a milkshake."

Laurel gave the obligatory chuckle, but truth was, she had fancied herself in love with him after nearly two years of friendship. His careless actions had given her hope and made her stupid teenage heart expand like it was giving off those little heart-shaped bubbles in cartoon pictures. And then reality had crashed down on her. He'd made her mad, he'd humiliated her, but he'd also hurt her deeply. Aiden Gallagher had caused her first broken heart.

"Actually, Aiden was on duty this morning."

Willow sat up straighter. "Why wasn't that the first thing you told me instead of waiting until now?" She put her hand on Laurel's arm. "What happened? Did he apologize? He's cute, isn't he? I think he's even better looking than he used to be."

"Then you should date him," Laurel replied caustically. "I'm definitely not interested."

"I repeat, what happened?" Willow grabbed the wine bottle and refilled their glasses. The evening was getting cooler as the sun went down. Laurel hugged her knees closer and studied her glass.

"Nothing. He took the details from me and went back to work."

"Oh." Willow sounded disappointed. "You're sure that's all?"

"I'm sure."

"Boring. No sparks? No laughing over days gone by?"

This time Laurel laughed. "God, no. I think we're still in the stay-out-of-each-other's-way place."

"He's still pretty sexy, though, isn't he?" Willow wiggled her eyebrows, and Laurel laughed.

"Okay, fine. He's sexy as sin, is that what you wanted to hear?"

"I know. All that muscle and stuff packed into the uniform and his eyes . . . he's got bedroom eyes. They're so blue. And he's a ginger."

"Gingers don't have souls," Laurel stated, giggling a little. The wine was getting to her.

"Oh, even you don't think that's true. You have a thing for redheads. Dan was one too, wasn't he?"

The easy question slammed into her. Did she have a thing for gingers? Wasn't that embarrassing! "Dan's is more strawberry blond."

"Right." Willow laughed. "Of course it is. Anyway, I just wondered if he'd said anything. He's single, you know."

"You won't step on my toes if you're interested," Laurel replied, though the idea of Willow with Aiden didn't seem to fit. Willow was too sweet, for one.

"I'm not. I'm happy just going on as I am right now." Willow smiled and held her glass out as she pushed herself to her feet. "Much as I love being connected to the earth and all, the ground's feeling cold and damp. Mind if we go inside? We can polish this off, complain about how becoming a grown-up hasn't lived up to our expectations, and then go into work a little extra tired tomorrow."

"Sure. I've got some chips in the house I think."

"Eew."

Right. Willow didn't let junk food pass her lips. "Crackers and hummus?"

"Getting better."

When Willow reached for her bag, Laurel saw a little tattoo on her wrist. But before she could ask about it, the back gate opened again. "Hello?"

Willow tapped her shoulder. "Laurel. Speak of the devil."

He was sex on a stick in his uniform, but in board shorts and a T-shirt he was equally devastating. His burnished hair was tousled and he had the beginnings of a stubbly beard. The relaxed pose set her pulse racing. She really wished it wouldn't do that. Aiden was not the sort of guy she needed.

"I'll take a rain check," Willow said, low enough that only Laurel could hear. "Though I'll want details."

"There won't be anything to tell," Laurel muttered back, scrambling to her feet, trying not to spill the wine left in her glass. "Your glass, Willow . . ."

"You can give it back to me later. Keep it. You might need the wine." Willow winked at her, which only annoyed Laurel more. She was not interested. Full stop.

"Hey, Aiden," Willow offered on her way through the gate. "Nice evening, isn't it?"

"Sure is."

Willow waved her fingers as she passed through, the only farewell Laurel received. Pasting on a polite smile, Laurel turned her attention to Aiden. "Can I do something for you?"

"Well, now, that's a loaded question." He smiled, a little dimple popping in his cheek. Laurel resisted the urge to roll her eyes. He was so obvious.

He stepped inside her backyard. "I was out at Mom and Dad's for dinner. The garden center came up in conversation, and I decided to stop by on my way home. See how you made out today."

Laurel wasn't sure if she should be perturbed or touched. His consideration was sort of nice, but it also seemed a bit presumptuous. "And you just happened to know my address?"

For a flash, he looked uncomfortable. Then he smiled again. "Okay, so you caught me. I had to look it up."

"Great police work," she said, lifting her glass to take a drink of wine.

He shrugged. "I 411'd it on my phone. No big deal." He met her gaze. "If you want me to go, I'll go."

She did and she didn't. Yes, because seeing him was plain weird and made her feel like an awkward teenager again. But no, because it really was kind of nice of him to look in on her. They weren't kids anymore. Maybe they could get along. As adults. Just because she was back in Darling didn't mean they couldn't leave the past where it belonged. She should be over it by now.

"It's okay. You want some wine?" She held out the bottle, then realized she didn't have another clean glass.

His grin widened. "You're sharing?"

She tipped the bottle and splashed a little more into her glass. What the hell. It had been a crazy, stupid, seesaw of a day. Then she held out the bottle again and gave it a wiggle with her hand, as if to say, "Take it."

He did. And then he lifted it and took a drink straight from the bottle.

"Classy," she remarked.

"It's not like you offered me your fine crystal," he replied. He looped his fingers around the top of the bottle and took a step closer, so they were only a foot or so apart. "I usually tell people it's not good to bring work home with them. In your case I'd make an exception. This is quite the yard."

She looked around. The tiller was still out, half the garden soil was distributed, nothing was planted. A small greenhouse sat in the south corner, where she'd started tomatoes, peppers, lettuces. It was too early to have many of her annuals out, though her perennial beds were coming along. Another six weeks and things would look very different.

"I bought this place because it came with three-quarters of an acre. Enough for me to have a vegetable garden in the back and flowers in the front."

"So the garden center is a labor of love for you."

He walked along the perimeter of her tilled earth, taking his time, pausing to sip from the bottle again. Laurel didn't want to notice the way his jeans fit his ass, but she couldn't help it. It was hard to ignore a man so nicely proportioned, after all.

"It really is. I had a smaller garden where I lived before. It was nice, but I felt a little cramped there."

"In Burlington, right?"

"Just outside. We commuted in."

We. She hadn't meant to bring up Dan. It was just easier if people didn't ask a lot of questions.

He turned and faced her. "*We* being you and your ex, right?"

She nodded, felt her face heat. *Please don't ask.*

"And you bought the center and moved back home. A fresh start?"

"You could say that."

He smiled then. "Are you glad to be home, Laurel? Or does it feel like a consolation prize?"

His question hit her square in the chest, stopping her breath for a split second. How very insightful of him to ask. Was it a consolation prize? She didn't want to think so. It was more complicated than that. And she wasn't unhappy. Not really. It was all in how she chose to view it. She could feel sorry for herself or she could see this as an opportunity for a new start, to reinvent herself and be even stronger.

She'd married Dan right after graduation and had joined him at the firm directly after. It hadn't been a mistake, exactly, but she'd be lying if she didn't admit she enjoyed her new freedom and autonomy.

"My marriage didn't work out," she said quietly. "So my life's switched course. I get to choose that course, Aiden. There's no consolation prize in that." And maybe someday she'd absolutely believe it.

Quiet settled over the yard. The sun was down now and most of the birds had quieted, though the odd mourning dove could still be heard cooing somewhere close by. Laurel shivered a little. The air had cooled and now that she wasn't shoveling dirt, there was a bit of a chill that settled on her skin. Still, she didn't want to invite Aiden inside. That would be a "friendly" move, and she was aiming more for civility.

"And what about what happened this morning?" he finally asked, holding out the bottle and adding a little more to her glass before taking another swig. "Is everything okay at the Ladybug?"

She laughed. "It sounds funny when you call it that." Funnier than it should, and she giggled again. Damn. She should have sent that wine with Willow . . .

He chuckled in reply, the sound low and alluring in the twilight.

"Everything is fine," she answered finally, letting out a sigh. "My mom and dad stopped in this morning and helped me clean up the mess. I've been in touch with the insurance company and reordered stock and bought new locks for the gate. And a new, heavier-duty safe, you'll be glad to know."

"Good."

"With a lot of the stock within the fence but outside the building, a security system didn't seem overly practical. But starting tonight we're going to have it better lit. Maybe it'll be a deterrent." She finished what was in her glass. "I guess I idealized what it would be like coming home. That Darling was perfect. Idyllic." There was that word again. Maybe part of the problem was that she set her expectations just a little too high.

He didn't reply so she offered a little smile. "Reality strikes again, huh."

He shrugged. "It's still a good place to live. Sometimes I wonder what it would be like to work in a place where I really made a difference, you know? It's pretty low key around here."

They'd ambled back toward the gate. How had that happened? Laurel realized they were nearly shoulder to shoulder and actually having a conversation. Today really was turning out to be the strangest day.

"You'd rather be a cop somewhere bigger? More dangerous?"

He shrugged. "It's not the danger, or even the excitement. But more a sense that . . . maybe there's a greater need somewhere else."

She looked over at him. In high school he'd been a bit of a joker. He'd played ball in the summer, hockey in the winter, and was part of the ski club. His GPA had been okay—he'd worked at his schoolwork just enough to pull off respectable marks. He'd had a much more active social life, Laurel remembered, and had always been invited to parties. She'd been quiet, studious, and as friends they'd been a bit mismatched.

Her memories didn't quite mesh with the man standing in front of her now: a civic-minded public servant.

"Laurel?"

She stopped and looked up at him. Even in the dark, she could see the earnestness in his eyes. He'd always been attractive in a roguish, atypical sort of way. Not the tall, dark, and handsome type, and not the All-American blond and blue-eyed preppy kind of guy. More of a rough-and-ready scrapper with an impish smile and a gleam in his eye. The gleam was missing now, and the smile replaced with a sober expression, which only served to highlight the crisp outline of his lips. Laurel swallowed. This had been the problem all along, hadn't it? From the time she was fifteen, she'd had a "thing" for Aiden. Maybe she didn't have it any longer, but memories were powerful things. Sometimes the body remembered what the heart would rather forget.

"About what happened in senior year . . . I'm sorry about that."

Holy shit. An apology at long last. It didn't make her feel better, though. She knew it should and it didn't.

"I should never have gone with you," she admitted. "I was gullible."

"No. You trusted a friend." He put the empty bottle down on the grass and reached for her arm. His fingers tightened around her forearm and a little swoop of something skittered through her stomach at the touch. "It wasn't you. I did want to be with you. It wasn't because of the bet. It's just that . . ." He looked away and heaved a sigh. "Okay, look. I know I had a reputation when I was in school. The truth was, I liked you and never asked you out because I was afraid you'd say no. Until the guys made me a bet. It was stupid, I know. But it was the only way I was able to get the guts up to ask. It seemed . . . I don't know, easier, when it was about a team bet and not about real feelings."

He'd really cared about her? She clenched her teeth together. That actually made it worse. It might have been better to think he hadn't considered her feelings at all, because this way he'd willingly humiliated someone he cared about.

"Wow, Aiden. If that's how you treat your friends . . ."

"Hey, I was an idiot. If I'd been smart, I would have said

I'd lost the bet and let it drop. But I was there with the guys, and they were being pushy, and I found the story just coming out. They said no one would tell and that it would stay within the team."

She took a step back. "But someone told their girlfriend, who told someone else, and I ended up finding out because I could see people looking at me and whispering and I had to ask what was going on." The embarrassment still burned. Worse, when she'd found out the truth she'd had to keep all her emotions locked up. No crying, no hysterics, no acting like her heart was crushed. She'd had to grin and bear it like it meant nothing. Just like she had with the divorce.

She wouldn't tell him how hurt she'd been, because she had a scrap of pride left. Even after all that had happened in the last year, she still had a teensy bit of pride.

"I was seventeen, Laurel. And I liked you and I was an immature guy who did everything wrong."

Not everything, Laurel thought. He'd known what he was doing in the backseat of his car. She'd considered letting him be her first, but in the end she held back. Things had gotten hot and heavy and . . . real. Her heart ached a little just thinking about it. Ten years. High school had been ten years ago. But she still remembered feeling beautiful and desirable and alive in his arms.

He'd destroyed that memory, and the hope that had gone along with it. And it had been a long time, but not so long that she couldn't still feel the hurt of that seventeen-year-old girl. Perhaps it was even more raw now, after the end of her marriage. That feeling of being the center of someone's world . . . she'd felt it twice in her life. And both times it had been a lie.

"Let's just forget about it, okay? It was a long time ago."

"And we're adults now."

"Yes," she said, "we are." So much had happened since those days. Sometimes it was hard to believe.

"So we can be friends?"

Ugh, he would ask. And how could she say no? Refusing would either make her look like a bitch or, worse, like what had happened still mattered. She smiled weakly. "Sure."

The silence that followed was awkward. She hadn't sounded sincere and they both knew it. Why was she letting it bother her so much? They were at the gate now. The buzz from the wine made her head light, made her body a little bit floaty. She was such a lightweight when it came to alcohol. He was waiting, his hand on the top rung of the fence. They were close enough now that she caught his scent, the fresh shower smell of him mingled with spring grass and evening air.

"Laurel?"

Oh, the way he said her name. His voice was deeper now, husky with a little bit of grit. She looked up into his eyes and held her breath. Was it her or were they swaying closer to each other? She looked over at his hand on the fence, remembered the feel of it on her skin, how even at seventeen it had felt capable and . . . right.

She let out her breath and stepped back, bent over to pick up the abandoned wine bottle. "Friends," she repeated as she stood. "I think we'd better just leave it at that."

Aiden cleared his throat. "Right. Well, I'm glad we cleared the air. And glad you got things straightened out at work."

"Thanks for stopping by."

Funny how a conversation could go from intensely intimate to stilted in just a few seconds.

"I'll see you around."

He opened the gate and it creaked behind him. As he walked away, Laurel closed the latch. One, she was going to have to lubricate that gate so it wasn't so noisy. And two, they definitely hadn't cleared the air between them at all. If anything, it had all just become more muddled.

CHAPTER 4

The Darling Chamber of Commerce met once a month for breakfast. The meeting generally rotated venues each month, reserving several tables at a local eatery or a meeting room at one of the businesses. For the month of April, however, they were meeting at the town hall in the boardroom.

Laurel dressed carefully for the event. As a new business owner, she wanted to create a good impression among her peers—many of whom she'd known as a kid and who had many years of business experience compared to her "youthful enthusiasm." Before entering the venerable brick building, she smoothed her hands down her white skirt and checked the buttons on her blouse. She'd tamed her blunt-cut, shoulder-length hair into a bun, hoping it looked like one of those deliberately messy topknot things. She rounded out the ensemble with a pair of pristine-white heels that she hadn't worn since her days with the firm.

One big inhale and exhale, and then she put her hand on the door and swung it open.

Darling, as a town, had incorporated in 1827. But before then, since before the revolution, it had been a village surrounded by farms and rolling forests. There was history here, particularly in the old building that had withstood not only the years but a fire at the turn of the twentieth century. The lobby-type area boasted plank-width hardwood floors and lots of rich cherry in the counters and desks. An elevator had been installed for accessibility purposes, but altogether the sturdy and slightly scarred interior gave visitors a sense of stability and gravitas. When she'd been younger, she'd loved the sight of it.

Now she found it more than a little intimidating.

Darling used its history to its advantage in attracting both residents and tourists. Tourism was big business with the proximity to lakes, golf courses, skiing, and nearby cities. Many of the businesses catered to that seasonal traffic, while others were more specifically geared to residents. Laurel hadn't been sure what to expect at the monthly breakfast, and she was surprised to see at least twenty-five people already milling about the boardroom, hovering mostly at the coffee station set up on one side.

She looked up at the wall behind the pastry table. There, in all its glory, was The Photo. Her cheeks heated as she remembered standing close to Aiden just a few nights ago. In the photo they were five. It was a candid shot taken by the photographer at Laurel's Aunt Susan's wedding. Laurel and Aiden were standing on the Kissing Bridge, her basket of flowers in one hand while Aiden held the other. Her dress was long and white with a pale green sash, and he wore an adorable black suit. They were leaning toward each other, their eyes closed and lips touching.

It *was* adorable. Or it would be, if she weren't in it. But both their parents had given the town permission to use it.

As a result the photo appeared not only in the boardroom but also on town promotional materials.

"You haven't changed a bit."

Laurel turned to see Sally Ingram looking up at her. Sally had to be in her sixties now, but her wrinkles were hidden behind expertly applied makeup and her hair was the color of summer wheat. At barely five feet, Sally was a little powerhouse of energy.

"Hello, Sally." Laurel smiled. "And I've changed quite a bit. I can't believe that picture is still up here."

Sally tittered. "Of course it is. The Kissing Bridge is our main attraction."

"I figured it would have been replaced by now," she remarked.

"Oh, maybe it will. I hear there's a refresh happening in the town tourism campaign. Something about pushing the fall months and the colors and whatnot." Sally looked sharply at Laurel. "Speaking of colors, you should come into the spa and let us put some foils in that hair of yours. It could use a lift."

Great. She'd already been feeling insecure about how she looked, but she'd been satisfied when she left the house this morning. Now she was back to square one, and resisted the terrible urge to raise her hand and touch her hair. "Maybe I'll do that, Sally. Work's keeping me quite busy right now, though. Spring and all."

"Yes, I heard about your little trouble." She tsked and shook her head. "Though I did hear that Aiden was the officer on duty. You two have some history, if I remember correctly." She winked at Laurel. "Oh look, there's Owen Hardcastle. I've been meaning to speak to him about some renovations. Enjoy the breakfast, dear." Sally turned to leave but at the last minute spun back and put her hand on Laurel's arm. "Oh, and it's good to have you home again."

That was all it took for Laurel to feel the warmth of homecoming that she'd been missing. Sally's comment about her hair was an occupational hazard; no different than if Laurel had suggested someone plant some hostas around their flowering crab or add creeping phlox as ground cover for their perennial beds. And the comment about Aiden was typical too; not much was missed in a town this small. Determined to keep her chin up, she made her way over to get a coffee, and then grabbed a plate and added some strawberries and an apple Danish to it before finding a seat.

The hour went quickly and Laurel focused on not dropping anything on her white skirt while chatting to other business owners in the community. All had heard about the break-in, and several mentioned needing to stop by for planters and baskets for their storefronts in the next few weeks. It was mainly a social hour, and a chance for people to catch up on different things happening in Darling. Graduation and wedding seasons were starting up, and much of the conversation was dominated by the rush on flowers, hairstyles, photographers, and catering.

When Laurel had nearly finished her second cup of coffee, the mayor, Brent Mitchell, stood up at the front and tapped a microphone to see if it was live. When the tap echoed hollowly through the room, he cleared his throat.

"What's happening?" Laurel leaned over and whispered to her table companion, a middle-aged man who'd recently opened a new law firm off of Elderberry Drive.

"Whoever hosts the meeting gets the mic," he whispered back.

She sat up again and crossed her left leg over her right. Folded her hands in her lap. It hadn't been so bad, the social hour. And in another thirty minutes she could head home, change into jeans and her golf shirt with the Ladybug crest, and head to the greenhouse.

The mayor greeted the group, spoke briefly about moving from the winter months into spring, a new year of tourists and plans to re-energize a "buy local" campaign. He welcomed new members—including Laurel, who smiled weakly and gave a little wave—and then began his spiel about the new promotion plan for the town.

Laurel had started to tune him out a bit and was wondering if she could possibly sneak out unseen, when the words "Kissing Bridge" and "famous photo" reached her ears.

She snapped her eyes upward to stare at Brent, only to realize that tens of pairs of eyes were focused solely on her. Because she was in that damned photo.

"Laurel, we all know how cute you are in that photo. We'd like to update it this year, though. You don't mind, do you?"

Have that picture disappear? Not have a reminder of Aiden in her face every time she saw a Darling brochure or rack card? "Of course I don't mind," she replied, smiling. "I think it's a great idea."

"Terrific. Someone in the office will be in touch with you about it, then."

He moved on while Laurel considered his words. In touch with her? The only thing she could think of was that her parents had signed a release and maybe she needed to do something with that. *Show me where to sign*, she thought, her lips twitching just a bit. She'd be glad to be done with it.

When the meeting broke up, Laurel made her way across the room as quickly as possible, stopping to offer tidbits of conversation as she went. Chatty was great, and she really did want to take part in some of the spring and summer promotions coming up, but she was on the e-mail list. Right now she just wanted to get back to work.

Finally she was outside again, in the fresh air and sunshine. She gave her shoulders a quick roll and adjusted her purse strap before walking toward her car, her heels tapping on the paved parking lot. The emergency-services building was next door. On this side, the building was small and compact, with a small public entrance and a line of parking spaces along the edge where the cruisers waited for officers. The other side of the building was big, brick, and housed the two firetrucks owned by the town, as well as the Chief's van and the ambulance.

A cruiser drove in, parked, and the officer got out just as Laurel reached her vehicle.

There was no reason at all for her pulse to skip, or for the weightless, giddy feeling that swirled about in her stomach. Just because it was a police officer didn't mean . . .

And then he turned around. Even in his uniform, and a pair of aviators shielding his eyes, she knew it was Aiden. It was in the build. In his stance. And . . . in the stupid way her body was betraying her right now.

He lifted a hand in greeting, and smiled. The power of it was like a punch right to her gut.

She raised her hand and returned the greeting, and there was a moment of hesitation. She wasn't really thinking of going over there, was she? Talking to him? A memory flashed; the way he'd looked at her the other night in the dusky twilight, standing by her gate, smelling like sin and his voice soft and low. She saw the holster on his hip;

wondered if he had a bulletproof vest under his shirt, and found herself stupidly turned on by the idea.

She dropped her hand and pressed the key fob to open her door. No, she was not going over there. She wasn't going to say hello or watch as he slid those sunglasses off his eyes and looked down at her.

Instead she got into her car and put the key in the ignition. That damned photo of them was going away for good, wasn't it? And so should they. Nothing had really changed. She didn't like him, didn't trust him, and wasn't interested in romance. This physical . . . aberration that kept happening signified nothing. It was just that. Physical.

She backed out of the parking spot and glanced over at the police station lot. It was in her line of vision, after all. It wasn't like she looked *on purpose*. Aiden was gone, probably inside. And that was it. Photo retired, they'd moved on, end of story.

Somehow it didn't feel as satisfying as it ought.

April rolled on and turned into May. Laurel put in long hours at the garden center, with new stock arriving every day. She hired two university students for the summer, and once she had them trained on cash and basic upkeep, it freed up a lot more of her time to do admin and arranging. With the risk of frost waning and spring in full swing, it seemed every business owner in town was after urns, planters, baskets, or annuals for window boxes. And that didn't include the residential customers. In a town like Darling, keeping yards at a certain standard was a given. Right now her shrubs and perennial stocks were diminishing at an alarming rate. It was great for her bottom line, but she was exhausted. She was considering going to see Sally at the shop, not for foils but to get her hair cut short, just to cut down on maintenance time.

She arrived at work on a Saturday morning to find graffiti on her fence.

The fencing around the perimeter of the shrubs and trees was metal, but by the front signage there were two sections of six-foot wooden fencing. Each section was now painted with black spray paint. One side had a crudely drawn penis. The other a pair of breasts.

Anger rushed through her as she stared at the lewd pictures. A lilac bush, okay. A break-in for the cash box? Maybe it was random. But things continually happening to her? Bullshit. Someone was taking their shots and she was mad as hell about it. She felt . . . violated.

She whipped out her phone and called her dad first thing, asking if he could pick up another gallon of the paint they'd used and a roller. Then she looked up the main number for the police station. She didn't want to use 911; this wasn't an emergency. But it needed to be reported. The incidents kept happening and it was time something was done about it.

A female officer answered the call, arriving on scene thirty minutes later. In the meantime, Laurel had draped a few tarps over the offensive paint and had gone about the business of getting ready to open. Staff gave her a wide berth as drawers and doors slammed. When the police arrived, she took off the tarps. The officer merely sighed.

"Well, I don't know if it's a good thing or a bad thing to tell you that this isn't the only penis we've found around town," she said.

The dry delivery had Laurel laughing despite herself, possibly from a little relief. "So I shouldn't take it personally?"

The officer—her tag said Holbrook—shrugged. "Added to the other incidents here? It wouldn't surprise me if it ended up being the same person. But since other properties have been hit in similar ways, I don't think it's vindictive. They didn't get caught the last time, there are no cameras here, and you have this lovely big canvas right out front."

"Maybe I should have rethought the fence."

Then she got angry all over again. Why shouldn't she have the fence? She'd done nothing wrong here. She certainly hadn't issued an invitation. "You say it's not vindictive, but this keeps happening to me. Something's got to be done to stop it. All this damage is costing me money."

Her outburst didn't seem to affect the officer at all. "Let me take some pics for the report, and then it's all yours."

By the time they were through, it was nine o'clock and time to open. Being a Saturday, business was brisk. Her dad dropped off the supplies and offered to stay to help cover the tagging, but with the heavy shopping traffic, Laurel decided to wait until things died down. For now the tarps covered the tags, and she'd focus on her customers. Otherwise her anger would get the best of her and that was bad for business. By six p.m., things had slowed considerably. Laurel had been going flat out for ten hours, stopping for only fifteen minutes to run to The Purple Pig for a sandwich. Her stomach growled, her feet hurt, there was dirt beneath her nails and she really, really wanted a shower and a glass of wine—in that order. Laurel had just dragged out the hose to water the fruit trees when a half-ton truck drove into the lot and parked in an empty space.

The driver hopped out, and her heart slammed against her ribs as she immediately realized how she must look. Dirty jeans, mannish golf shirt that did nothing for her figure, scrubby ponytail through a Ladybug Garden Center ball cap, and probably smudges of dirt on her face and arms. Not that she was trying to look nice for Aiden or anything, but it *was* him getting out of the truck, looking sexy as hell in faded jeans and a T-shirt that stretched across his chest and shoulders.

She could pretend she hadn't seen him. Resolutely she turned on the hose and started watering the apple trees.

"Hey, Laurel," he called out, and that erased any hope of avoiding him.

She turned off the hose and faced him. "Aiden. What brings you by? Looking for a shrub or tree or something?" *Keep it businesslike*, she reminded herself. The last thing she needed was for him to know that he had the ability to fluster her.

"I heard about what happened."

Of course he had.

"Don't even. I'm still pissed."

"I know it's not what you needed. Did Crystal tell you that you weren't the only one hit?"

Crystal must be the officer from this morning. "She did."

"Well, that must make you feel better."

She stared at him. "Better? Seriously? Since I opened a month ago, I've had to have the driveway re-graded, I've had to replace shrubs that were stolen from out front, deal with a break-in and vandalism, and now tagging. Trust me, Aiden, the only thing that would feel better is if you actually did your job and found out who was doing this."

She turned the hose back on.

He waited. He waited a long time. Several seconds, maybe thirty. Which was really not that long at all but definitely felt that way. She was watering the third tree when he sighed. "You're upset."

"No shit, Sherlock."

He met her gaze, and his eyes were soft, even though she'd basically just accused him of not doing his job. The understanding she saw there made her stomach churn. She didn't want to lash out, but that was what she did when she was hurt. Angry.

Stopping by was kind and thoughtful. She kept trying to make him out to be a bad guy, and he kept being nice. It definitely made it difficult for her to hate him. Particularly since her biochemistry betrayed her at every turn. Even now, when she was utterly preoccupied with the day's events, she seemed to notice everything. His hair, his eyes, the breadth of his chest, the armband tattoo that looked like some sort of Celtic braid, peeking just below the hem of his T-shirt sleeve. The shape of his lips . . .

He muttered something that was as creative a curse as she'd ever heard, and sounded suspiciously Irish. She couldn't help but laugh, and tried to clamp her lips shut again. But not before he saw and heard, and his eyes took on an impish gleam.

"You're not fine. You're tired and upset and rightfully so. You're also just as stubborn as you always were." He put his hands on his hips. "I take it you're not adverse to help, just help from me in particular."

Her face heated. Dammit.

"Maybe this could be my penance," he suggested, giving her a quick grin. And she wished she could take him seriously, but he always seemed to be teasing. It was one of the things she'd really liked about him and hated at the same time. Particularly now, when she wanted to be, if not mad, completely unaffected. And she wasn't. He was trying to cajole her out of her mood and it was working.

"It's Saturday night. Don't you have a hot date or something?" She turned on the hose again. Focused on the large plastic pot holding a cherry tree.

"Nope. Free as a bird."

Dammit again.

"Come on, Laurel. Peace offering. Manual labor for you to stop hating me."

She glanced over at him. "Why do you care so much?"

He was quiet for a moment, and to her surprise the teasing expression left his face. After a while he answered, his voice a little lower. "I don't know why I care what people think so much. I always have. I don't like anyone to be mad at me. Maybe it has something with being one of the younger siblings in the family. I don't know. I just know that I don't like it that you're still so angry." His intense blue gaze locked with hers. "It's starting to become a personal mission to win you over. To atone for past sins."

"Good luck," she said dryly, more touched than she wanted to admit.

His boyish grin was back. "Come on, Laurel. You know you can't hold out forever. You think I'm hot." He had the audacity to wink at her.

She rolled her eyes.

"You do. You have a thing for gingers. And you have to admit, I grew up kinda good." His hands were still on his hips and he tensed his muscles so that his shoulders and chest tightened beneath the thin T-shirt.

"I think you're a bit taken with yourself, to be honest," she replied. And tried not to smile. She didn't want to be charmed, but he was incorrigible.

"Laurel."

Damn, his voice was all silky-smooth now. "Yes, Mr. Narcissist?"

"You know damn well you want to hate me and you can't. Besides, I saw your face just now. Maybe if I took off my shirt . . ."

"Would you like to go somewhere private to be with yourself?" she asked, biting the inside of her lip. She shouldn't be enjoying this so much. And she wouldn't be, if she thought he was serious. But he was teasing her. Like he used to do when they were friends. And today . . . she swallowed against a ball of emotion. Today she needed a friend, and all she'd had were well-meaning customers.

She looked over at him. "Jeez, Aiden. You're looking a little flushed. I think you could stand to cool off." And before he could reply, she flicked her wrist and aimed the spray of the hose right at the center of his chest.

The abrupt shock on his face was gratification enough, but then he grinned and reached to take away the hose. She danced away, still spraying him, admiring how the shirt now clung to his skin and the little droplets lit up his face and hair. A laugh bubbled up through her chest and out her mouth as she darted around the trees, dragging the hose with her. But there were too many pots and not enough room to maneuver and within seconds he caught her, wrapped one strong arm around her and wrenched the hose away with the other, spraying her in the process.

Cold water dripped from her nose, down her neck, over her bare arms. Aiden held her close against his body, close enough she could feel the hardness of his muscles, and thrilled at it. Their breaths came fast, their chests rising and falling with both laughter and the exertion of the struggle over the hose. But it was the way he was looking down at her right now that made her feel as if the lack of air was strangling her lungs. All it would take was the tiniest move and he'd be kissing her. Her gaze dropped to his lips—he'd always had fine lips—and she swallowed, nervous and scared at her reaction and turned on as hell.

She looked up, which was a mistake. Because he was staring at *her* lips. And his arm tightened just a little bit at the hollow of her back. Oh God . . .

A car horn honked and Laurel jumped back. He let her go, but the gravity of the moment remained.

"I've got to put this hose away."

"Don't you want to finish watering first?"

"Oh. Right."

He'd stepped back, too, but that didn't do Laurel any good because now she could see how much she'd soaked his shirt and despite backing off, he still looked damned delicious.

She picked up the hose.

"You're painting after close, aren't you?" he asked.

"What makes you say that?"

He grinned then. "Because you're not the type to let it go. And if you do it after close, your customers won't have to see."

It was disconcerting to know she was such an open book.

"Okay, yes. My dad dropped off a gallon of paint and a couple of rollers earlier today. It won't take me long at all."

And if she had to do it in the semi-darkness, she would.

"Let me give you a hand. It'll get done twice as fast and you'll get home that much sooner. How long have you been here, anyway?"

It was after seven now. Eleven hours. And she was damned hungry.

"Oh, long enough. Let me finish this and I'll get you the stuff."

"Good. And I'm going to change my shirt."

"You have clothes?"

"I always keep my gym bag in the truck."

Of course. Those muscles didn't just appear on their own, did they? She started watering the trees again, surreptitiously watching through the branches as he strode to the truck and reached in the back for his bag. She was pretty sure her mouth dropped open a little as he stripped off his wet tee and threw it inside. His Irish roots kept him pale and dotted with a few freckles, but there was no denying the physique. Holy hell, was that an actual six-pack?

She imagined running her fingers down over those taut ridges and gave her head a shake. Granted, she and Dan hadn't had sex during the last eight months of their marriage and there hadn't been anyone since. But to get this distracted by Aiden flipping Gallagher? She needed her head examined!

Watching him put on the dry shirt was nearly as entertaining as watching him take the other one off.

Once he'd locked the truck again, she shut off the hose and used the reel to wind it up. Then she went behind the counter and fetched the paint, stir stick, rollers, and trays that her dad had left behind while her remaining employee, Jordan, covered the store. Before she went outside, though, she grabbed a crappy windbreaker from the tiny storage closet. The water from the hose had chilled her now, and the spring evening was cooling. She also wouldn't care if she got a little paint on it.

"Okay, let's see the damage," Aiden said, taking the gallon pail from her as they walked to the front sign and accompanying fence sections.

She pulled off the first tarp and knew it was stupid to blush and feel embarrassed, but she did all the same. Two perfectly shaped breasts with round nipples stared back at them.

Aiden laughed and his eyebrows went up. "Well."

"The other side is better."

She peeled that tarp off too. When she glanced over at Aiden, he wore a contemplative expression. "I might be wrong, but I think the proportions are off."

She couldn't help it. She finally laughed. Really laughed, right from her belly and up through her chest until it echoed on the air. It really was funny. Annoying, but funny. And looking at it now she could see he was right. The size of the genitals was disproportionate. "They do say size matters," she gasped, giggling some more.

"I wonder if we could use the depiction to profile the perpetrator," Aiden mused, and it only sent her into more giggles. "Maybe he's got . . . delusions of grandeur."

"Stop," she begged, grabbing at the tarp, preparing to fold it, still chuckling.

"So you do know how to laugh," he said, grabbing the other corners of the tarp and meeting her hands in the middle.

"Of course I do. I've just been busy, that's all."

"I thought you were pissed at me, the way you left Town Hall the other day."

"Not mad. Just unsettled." It was only a half-truth, but then it was only a half-lie too.

"You looked good, all dressed up." He picked up the other tarp and they folded it together. His fingers brushed hers as they met in the middle again, but she quickly let go so he could finish folding it into a square.

"Thanks. Chamber of Commerce breakfast."

He looked down at the gallon of stain. "Uh-oh. You

wouldn't happen to have a screwdriver around, would you? Or a paint-can opener?"

"Hang on. There's a screwdriver inside."

When she came back, he'd unwrapped the paint trays and rollers and had the stir stick ready to go. She popped the lid off the can and he gave it a stir, then scraped the stick off on the lip of the can and poured a generous amount in each tray. "You take one side, I'll take the other?"

"Sure."

"Dick or boobs?"

She burst out laughing again. "Oh, I'll let you choose."

"I've always been more of a breast man." He grinned at her, then picked up the roller and began covering it with stain. She did the same, but her smile faded as she focused on the job. Yes, Aiden was a boob man. Her former husband hadn't been. And she didn't hate Dan; she didn't. Still, she'd be lying if she said it hadn't been difficult, dealing with the shock and subsequent divorce. It was like the world had shifted beneath her feet, plunging her into an alternate reality. Just because she didn't hate him didn't mean she hadn't felt angry and betrayed. To make matters worse, they'd all worked in the same office. The unorthodox love triangle made things just too awkward for everyone.

Leaving had been the best choice. And she was glad she'd moved back to Darling. But as she looked over at Aiden, she realized that it wasn't just his past behavior that had caused her to put up barriers. It was a very real fear of not trusting appearances. She'd been burned too many times thinking things were one way when they were really another.

Aiden looked completely relaxed as he rolled paint over the black markings. Maybe he was just here as a Good Samaritan. A good neighbor. An old friend. It was a weird headspace to be in: one part of her didn't trust him or appearances, and the other part didn't trust her own perspective, knowing it was skewed from experience. Which was right?

She went to work on her section of fence, content to work in the silence. Laurel could hear the peepers in the ditches, chirping restfully. Bit by bit she began to relax, working the muscles in her arm and shoulder up and down as she painted. Aiden refilled her paint tray without speaking; she murmured a thanks as eight o'clock rolled around. "I'll be back in a minute," she said, and went to tell Jordan to go home and to shut the door but to leave it unlocked as she'd secure everything when she left.

And then it was just Laurel and Aiden, finishing up the painting, listening to the odd car go by, the wind in the new leaves, the fading call of birds.

"I think that's it," he said quietly, putting down his roller. "You might need another coat, but it's too hard to tell right now with the light."

She swiped another few stripes and finished her side as well. "I'd still have half of it to do if you hadn't stopped by. Thank you, Aiden."

"You're welcome."

She felt marginally guilty for how she'd treated him the last few weeks. "No, I mean it. I've been short with you, and you haven't done anything to deserve it."

He busied himself pouring stain from the tray back into the pail. "If you really want to say thanks, I haven't had dinner yet."

She wanted to, if having dinner together was what he was suggesting. And that wasn't something she was happy about. "Um, it's been a long day and I'm dirty and tired."

"How about a pizza? I'll even stop and pick it up. You

can go home, have a shower or whatever, and I'll bring pizza over and there's no muss, no fuss."

It sounded so damned good. She was starving. And pizza was her absolute favorite, not that she'd let him in on that tidbit. "Just pizza."

"Of course." He put that innocent look on again. The one she didn't quite trust.

"This is not, and in no way can be construed of, as a date."

He stacked the dirty trays. "Of course not. Do you have a sink or set tub where we can clean these?"

Maybe she was building things up in her mind.

"Yes, inside at the back."

"Let's do that first."

So they went inside in the quiet, and washed out paint trays and rollers and left everything to dry and then locked up the store—after Laurel had taken the deposit out of the new safe—and went to their respective vehicles.

"See you in twenty or so," he called to her, one foot in the cab of his truck.

Not a date, my ass, she thought, sliding in behind the wheel. Everything about it felt like a date. Everything. And she had no idea what to do about it.

CHAPTER 5

Papa Luigi's Pizza was the best pizza in town. There were a few other chains that had set up shop, but Papa's was independently owned, made their own crust and sauce, and had that little extra something. Never mind that "Papa" was one of Aiden's oldest baseball buddies. Luigi was really Lewis. And he'd gone to culinary school after graduating.

Aiden ordered a large works with extra cheese. If he remembered right, Laurel wasn't a picky eater and pizza was a particular fondness of hers. While he was waiting, he popped over to the market and picked up a bottle of wine—after the other night he assumed she preferred red—and went back for the food. He passed the time chatting with Lewis, then snagged the box and headed to her house.

For the second time in about a week. Hmmm. Maybe she didn't consider this a date, but he'd bet twenty bucks that if he asked his sisters if pizza and wine at a woman's house constituted a date, they'd say yes.

A date with Laurel Stone. Damn. They'd gone on a date before that had ended with him perilously close to losing his head *and* his virginity.

Tonight, when he'd grabbed the hose from her, he'd felt the same excitement and uncertainty. Good thing that car had honked, or he might have kissed her. She really would have given him hell then.

The porch light was on at her house. He held the pizza and wine and rang the bell, hoping he'd given her enough time to shower. The house wasn't big, but not small either, a cozy two-story with gray siding and faux brick accents. The railing was painted white and there were new shrubs and some sort of leafy plant along the front of the house and along the walk. As he rang a second time, he wondered how she'd managed to move, take over a business, and put her own personal stamp on each location. It had to have meant some extraordinary long days, and his respect for her went up another few notches.

She opened the door. Her scent hit him first, something light and floral and feminine that reached in and twined its way around his senses.

"I'm starving," she announced. "Come in."

Her hair was wet, the shoulder-length strands more of a walnut brown than her regular, ordinary shade. She wasn't wearing any makeup, and she definitely wasn't in date night clothing. She had on a pair of pink plaid pajama pants and a pink T-shirt.

She looked perfect. Comfortable, relaxed, approachable . . . soft. He toed off his sneakers, left them on her front mat, and followed her into the kitchen.

"What kind did you get?" Laurel took the pizza box from his hands and plopped it down on the table. When she peeled back the lid she gave a blissful sigh. "Oh my God. That's an everything pizza from Luigi's."

"I hope you like everything on it. I seem to remember you aren't a picky eater."

"This is my favorite pizza ever." She reached for plates and plunked them on the table, adding a stack of napkins. "I discovered it when I came home for a weekend a few years ago. Whatever Lewis puts in his sauce, it's amazing."

"I got wine, too," he said. "The other night you had red, so I picked up a bottle. I thought you might need it after your long day."

"Bless your heart." He smiled. She actually looked like he'd given her a cherished gift. "Earlier I was thinking all I wanted was a shower, a glass of wine, and some food, and now here I am with all three. I'll grab a corkscrew."

No mention of any company in that trio of items, but that was okay. For a few minutes they loaded plates and she got glasses while he uncorked the merlot. When she moved to pour him a glass, though, he shook his head. "None for me, thanks. I'm driving."

She hesitated. "Of course. Sorry."

"Don't be. I'd probably be below the legal limit with a single glass, but I'm a cop. I don't chance it."

Of course, he only lived a twenty-minute walk away. Darling was pretty small when all was said and done. But he doubted she'd want his truck parked out front all night. They'd barely brokered a truce. Rumors would not be welcome.

She took her glass and plate of pizza, and led the way into the living room. It was a cozy spot. Her furniture didn't seem new, but it was comfortable, and there was a small coffee table and one end table. She had a big bay window at the front with wide-slatted blinds offering privacy or letting in sunlight. There was a gas fireplace and a small entertainment center with a television, cable box, and DVD player. No stereo, he noticed, or bigger speakers. All in all, it seemed rather minimalist. Other than a few potted plants, the room was devoid of any real decoration. No pictures on the wall or knickknacks like at his mother's. It was cozy, yes, but something was missing. It was missing anything that really said *Laurel.*

He took a bite of pizza—it really was amazing—and watched as Laurel took a long drink of wine, a huge bite of pizza, and then let out a sigh and closed her eyes.

At least he'd done something right.

She opened her eyes and smiled at him. "Thank you. This is awesome."

"You're welcome. Your house is nice." *Great conversation, butthead*, he chastised himself. It was as if he had no idea how to talk to nice Laurel instead of prickly Laurel.

"I haven't really had time to make it my own yet. Just moved in some furniture." She nibbled a piece of pepperoni. "Dan kept the house, actually, and it seemed stupid to take stuff just because I could. It was always more his house than mine anyway. He was living there when we got married."

A whole speech about her marriage. Aiden looked longingly at the wine, feeling he might need it if things got too in depth about her divorce.

"You didn't split it down the middle? Sell the house and stuff?"

She shook her head. "Naw. He bought out my half of the house, which was my down payment for here. My savings went into the business. Dan wouldn't have let me struggle. He's a good man."

Dan sounded like a paragon. Aiden decided he didn't like him already.

"You didn't want the house? Didn't want to stay in Burlington?"

She'd taken another healthy sip of the wine, looked over at him and shrugged. "It was too weird. We worked at the same firm and so does Ryan. Once the news broke, it was awkward as ass."

Eat your pizza, he told himself. *Don't ask too many questions.*

"What about you, huh? No girlfriend for a Saturday night, so you're forced into spending the evening painting over lewd graffiti?"

He thought about his ex, Erica. They'd dated for quite a while after high school. Erica had been a year ahead of them in school, but that hadn't mattered after graduation. He'd lost "it" with her. And she'd been fun. Right up until the time he'd turned twenty-one, she'd been twenty-two, and they'd been together nearly three years. She didn't want it to be fun anymore. She wanted it to be permanent and he simply hadn't been ready to settle down.

He'd also thought, quite mistakenly, that being honest about his feelings was the best approach. Boy, had that been a miscalculation. She'd only gotten more clingy. She'd started planning their future, what sort of house they'd have, how many kids . . . He'd taken the coward's way out. Not his finest moment.

"Not lately, I guess," he replied. "I haven't had a serious girlfriend for a while."

Laurel chuckled. "Have you ever had a serious girlfriend?"

Meaning she considered him incapable of being serious. Her and everyone else. Between the milkshake incident, and then the public blowout with Erica, he'd established a rep for himself in Darling. It sucked that that sort of thing followed a person.

"I dated someone for a few years."

At least she looked surprised. "What happened?"

"She wanted to get married. I wasn't ready."

"Oh."

"I was twenty-one. That's pretty young."

And she'd married this Dan guy at that age, maybe twenty-two. Maybe girls were just ready faster than guys. Since then he'd gone out with women, sure. He wasn't a monk. But he'd always kept things light and casual. No one had ever knocked his socks off enough to make him insensible. To make him do something stupid and impulsive.

"And no girlfriend since?"

"No one serious."

He folded his thin crust in half and took a big bite, wanting to change the subject. Why had he suggested this again? Well, he'd always found Laurel pretty in a simple, uncomplicated kind of way. And he supposed there was an element of challenge in it, too. There was something to be said for winning over someone who'd sworn to hate you forever.

It was more than that, though. He'd seen the fragile look on her face earlier, when faced with her business being attacked yet again. He'd heard her laughter as she wielded the hose and it had lit something inside of him. And when they'd almost kissed . . .

He looked over at her, all soft and relaxed and pretty and wondered if she'd still taste as good as she had all those years ago. Wondered if there'd still be that sense of girlish shyness in her kiss, or if she kissed like a woman who knew what she wanted.

He shifted on his chair. The challenge was suddenly becoming very real and he wasn't sure what to do next. His first urge was to kiss her and see what happened, but he figured he'd get a smack on the cheek for that. Maybe he should just get out. He could make his apologies and say he had to work in the morning and that would be that.

But Laurel deserved better from him. And if he wanted people to take him seriously, he might start by not behaving with a frat-boy move.

He chewed and swallowed. Laurel reached for the wine bottle and refilled her glass, then settled back on the sofa to tackle her second piece of pizza. "What about you, Laurel? Have you dated since the divorce?"

She shook her head. "Naw."

And then she picked up the wineglass and took a long drink. Like three swallows' worth.

"Touchy topic?"

She licked her lips as she put down the glass. "You've heard rumors, right? I'm sure you must have. Darling hasn't changed *that* much."

He was walking into dicey territory, so he proceeded with caution. "About the reason behind your split? Yeah, I heard."

She nodded, staring into her glass. "I figured. I try to ignore the talk, but I know it must be happening." She smiled sadly. "It's probably the one downside of coming back home. But there are a lot of good things, too. I'm starting to get better at weathering the storm."

Which meant that at some point she probably hadn't been good at it.

"Did he break your heart, Laurel?"

She didn't answer right away. Then she let out a sigh and nodded. "Yeah. He did."

She'd loved him, then. Really loved him. Aiden had the awful urge to plow his fist into something. On the heels of the impulse came the very real guilt that he'd once hurt her, too. Yes, they'd been young, but it was a tender age. Wounds went deep. Watching his little sisters grow up had been illuminating in that regard.

"What happened?"

She pulled her knees into her chest. "He shouldn't have married me in the first place. He was lying to himself and to me, too. Things hadn't been quite right between us for a while. I couldn't quite put my finger on it, and I thought we were just drifting apart, you know? That maybe it was work stress. Or that we'd moved past the honeymoon stage and we'd work it out." She looked over at Aiden and shook her head. "I was a bit naïve where my husband was concerned. He started going out for drinks with Ryan. I thought they were just buddies, and that maybe Dan needed someone to talk to." She gave a bitter laugh. "Joke was on me at the end. Dan came out, and now he and Ryan are a thing. A serious thing."

"Holy shit."

She smiled ruefully. "Right?"

"And you still get along?"

"Once he told the truth, he was very open with me. We were friends, too, Aiden. And he really, really struggled."

"That tells me about him. Not about you." He was surprised when she blinked quickly several times. Was she crying? He didn't see any tears on her cheeks, but she was definitely struggling. "Forget I said that," he offered, wondering how the hell he'd got himself into such a heavy, emotional conversation.

Because it was Laurel. And because, long before he'd hurt her, they'd been friends.

"You know, everyone always talks about Dan, and Dan's decisions, and Dan's struggles. Other than my mom, I think you're the first one to ask about me."

Her voice cracked at the end and he wondered if he should go to her. Sit beside her and put his arm around her, but she didn't seem to want to be coddled. Everything he'd seen so far showed that she was determined to stand on her own two feet. He couldn't blame her.

"Yes, it was hard," she stated. "But we didn't have to worry about children or custody or any of that stuff. I honestly, truly, wish him the best."

"But?" Again, it was about Dan. He frowned. "You don't have to self-edit with me."

Her gaze touched his. "You never used to be this astute."

"I used to be seventeen. No one's astute at that age." He tried a smile, because she looked so sad.

"Dan made mistakes. Lots of them. His intent was never malicious. It's not hard to be civil because I don't hate him. But . . . you're right. I felt . . . feel . . . betrayed. Hurt. Stupid for not seeing it. I was really, truly in love with him. When someone walks away, it hurts. Negativity is not helpful. So I try to focus on moving on instead."

"Like with the garden center."

"Exactly." She turned the glass around in her hands. "And so when that starts falling apart . . ."

"It's not just business. It's personal."

Her shoulders relaxed. "I'm glad you understand."

Aiden felt very humbled. "You are way more forgiving and generous than I would be in the same situation."

"The best thing I could do for Dan was let him go. And really, it's not like we'd be able to salvage our marriage.

That's a pretty irreconcilable difference." The corners of her mouth turned up slightly.

"And so here you are."

"Here I am," she agreed.

And damned if where she was didn't seem a little too lonely. Especially for someone like her, who'd always seemed to have her shit together.

He wiped his hands on a paper napkin. "So, does this mean you've forgiven me, too?"

She laughed then, lightening the atmosphere a little. "Well, I've just given you the sordid details of my failed marriage, so I suppose it means I must have."

"Good. Because I really am sorry, you know. I was a teenager and an idiot. I deserved that milkshake over my head."

Laurel had put her plate and glass down on the table. "I'm sorry I did that," she whispered. "I was just so . . ."

"Mad?" he supplied.

"Hurt," she corrected, and her voice was soft with honesty.

Aw, man. Angry he could handle. But for her to come right out and say that he'd hurt her . . . that was worse. "Hurting you was the last thing I wanted to do. Believe me. I liked you, Laurel. I liked you a lot."

Her gaze touched his. There was never any artifice in her eyes, he realized. Laurel wore her heart on her sleeve. It had been that way in high school, the other morning when she'd barely held back tears after the store had been robbed, and moments ago when she'd spoken about her husband. Right now he saw hurt and betrayal in the blue depths, as well as something else he couldn't quite define that made him want to put his arms around her and hold her close.

But doing that would be a dumb move. So he dragged his gaze away from hers, put his hands on his knees, and stood, reaching for the dirty plates. "I should really get going, let you get some sleep. Besides, I have to work in the morning."

"Of course." She got up and wobbled a bit; the wine had hit her more than either of them had thought, and he reached out with his free hand and steadied her.

"Oopsie doodles," she said. "I must be extra tired."

His fingers squeezed her arm. "You okay there?"

She nodded, looked up, and he forgot all about the plates in his hand and tomorrow's shift and Dan and anything else. His chest tightened as he struggled to find something to say or do that wasn't kissing her. Because that's what he really wanted. He wanted to see if her hair was as soft as it looked and if the intoxicating scent came from her hair or her skin or both; he wanted to taste her lips and the tang of wine that clung to them, feel her body against his like he had earlier tonight only alone where he could take his time and memorize every inch.

Holy shit, he thought, for the second time tonight.

Instead he let go of her arm, took the dishes to the kitchen, went directly to the front door and started putting on his shoes.

"You'll call if you need a second coat of paint, won't you? I'll give you a hand."

"Sure." She'd followed him and was watching, a dazed look on her face.

"Thanks for the pizza."

"Um, you bought it, remember?"

"Oh. Right." He'd lost his head, there was no doubt about it. "Well, see you around, Laurel." *You're such a chicken shit, running away.* The condemnation sounded in his head, but the truth was he wanted to kiss her and it scared him to death.

"See you around."

He opened the door. It opened inward, and she put her hand on the edge of the door as he stepped out onto the tiny landing.

"Good night," she whispered.

He took one last look at her lips, so pink and plump and achingly sweet. "'Night . . ."

She moved back. And the door was almost closed when he ignored every rational thought and pushed it back open again, stepped inside, and gathered her up in his arms.

She let out a surprised cry as he kicked the door shut behind him, then pressed her against the bare wall of the entry. Her breasts heaved against his as she struggled for breath, and he met her eyes for an instant, demanding permission, knowing he would not proceed without it. Her tacit response was to lick her bottom lip, a move so innocently sensual he wasn't sure she even realized she'd done it. And then her body melted against his, just the tiniest bit, and he lowered his head and captured her mouth in a kiss.

It was fevered, fast, and all-consuming. The heady fragrance from earlier wrapped around him, drawing him in, clouding his head with her feminine scent. But that was nothing compared to the soft fullness of her lips, the way they felt against his, the way she tasted, like woman and wine. Her arms twined around his neck, holding him close as a soft sound escaped her throat.

He cupped his hands just below her bottom and lifted her up, and she automatically wrapped her legs around him as their hips pressed together. He braced her against the wall and rubbed against her, pelvis to pelvis, nearly losing his mind at the sensation. There was something so natural, so . . . earthy about her that he craved. Maybe it was the complete lack of artifice. All he knew was that Laurel didn't need makeup or sexy lingerie or any other feminine trappings to make her desirable. Their clothes were on but their passion . . . it was naked. Raw, elemental, real.

And grown-up.

He gentled his kiss slightly, taking it deeper, slower, yet no less hungry. Her hands slid through his hair, her nails raking along his scalp and sending shivers down his spine. He let go of her with one hand, and slid the other over her breast, feeling the hard tip through both her bra and the cotton shirt.

This was different, he realized, and doubt snuck past his libido. He'd wanted this. She'd wanted it to, if her participation was anything to go by. But that didn't make it right. Or smart.

And yet he wasn't ready to let her go. Ten years ago she'd told him to stop and he had, and he'd driven her home, and smiled, and kissed her good-bye, and then collected on his bet. He wouldn't make such an immature mistake this time. There was no bet. No dare. Just need.

She unwrapped her legs from around him and her feet slid to the floor. Aiden ran his hands up her arms to her face, and cupped her jaw in his hands, still kissing her. He touched his lips to the tip of her nose, her eyelids, the crests of her cheeks, before settling back on her mouth again. God, that beautiful, mobile mouth that had the ability to make him forget all rational thought.

"Mmmm," he murmured against her mouth. "Laurel . . ."

"Shhh." The kiss was fully broken now, and she'd dipped her chin so he couldn't look into her eyes.

He put his finger beneath her chin and lifted it. His body was so hard and tense he felt like a string on a bow, pulled tight, desperate for release. But this time he ignored himself and focused on her.

"Look at me," he said quietly.

She did, and her cheeks flushed an adorable shade of pink. She was embarrassed? Oh my. What would she have been like if they'd actually gone to bed?

The idea wasn't helping deflate the situation at all.

"I said all the wrong things last time. Did all the wrong things. And I know you're probably in no place to start anything and I'm probably the last person on earth you want to start anything with. But Laurel? What just happened was just about perfect. You're just about perfect. And I'm gonna go now before I have the chance to mess anything up."

He stepped away, just a bit, but then leaned in and pressed a kiss to her forehead. "G'night."

This time when he slipped out the door, he closed it behind him and walked to his truck in the darkness.

CHAPTER 6

Sunday night marked the weekly dinner at Laurel's mom and dad's. While the Ladybug was open, she set her Sunday hours from ten a.m. to four p.m., so she'd at least have a shorter day. Working seven days a week was going to take a toll, probably sooner rather than later. But things would slow down in September, and she could rest then.

Right now she carried a bag of rolls and a premade Caesar salad from the grocery store—her contribution to dinner. Her mom would have made a homemade meal, but Laurel simply didn't have time to put together something elaborate to take with her.

Jennie Stone opened the screen door and smiled, and Laurel felt a lot of her tension melt away. "Mom. I hope I'm not late."

"It's barely five. There's time. Come in and sit down. Was the store busy today?"

"Insane." Laurel stepped inside the bungalow and unless her nose was deceiving her, there was apple pie for dessert tonight. Her stomach growled. She'd managed a bowl of cereal at nine, and a few slices of leftover pizza around one, but she'd spent a few hours unloading a shipment of bagged mulch by hand and she was starving.

Her dad, Mike, was out on the back deck, standing at the grill. "Hey, Pop," she called out, while putting the grocery bags on the kitchen counter.

"Hey, sweetie."

She opened the sliding door and went outside, stopping to plop a kiss on his cheek. "What's cookin'?"

He lifted the lid. "Your mother got me one of those beer-in-the-butt things," he explained, grinning from ear to ear. "I'm trying my first chicken on it."

Sure enough, a roasting chicken sat on a beer can, which was held in some sort of metal bracket. It smelled scrumptious.

"Looks good."

"Thanks. You want a beer?"

She shook her head. "You got anything fizzy? Soda or something?"

"Check the fridge."

She went inside to check for a can of soda and let out a sigh. There really was no place like home. Not that she'd wanted to live here. She drew the line at that, and she was more than happy to have her own house on the other side of Darling. Still, when she and Dan had been living in Burlington, they'd often made the drive on Sundays to have dinner with her folks, and it gave Laurel a feeling like not everything had changed in the last year.

Her mom had just put carrots on the stove and was peeling potatoes when Laurel went in. "You want any help, Mom?"

"You've worked all day. Go sit on the deck and put your feet up."

She retrieved the soda and kissed her mom's cheek on the way by. "Thanks for dinner. Is Ben coming?" Ben was her little brother and worked in the governor's office. She didn't expect an affirmative answer; Ben was even more of a workaholic than she was. The last time they'd all been together as a family was New Year's Day.

"I doubt it. He was down in DC last week. You know your brother."

Yes, she did. And she loved him. But he was on a fast track. It was hard for Laurel not to feel like she was moving backward instead of forward with the recent changes in her life.

She put her feet up as ordered and sucked back most of her soda, the fizzy carbonation easing her thirst. Her dad tended the chicken and they talked about the garden center, the graffiti, and the changes that had happened to Darling over the years. Dinner was nearly ready when her cell rang, the tune of "Ladybug Picnic" chiming through the quiet. Mike raised an eyebrow, making Laurel laugh as she reached for her phone, but her smile faded as she saw Dan's name come up.

He rarely called her; it must be something important.

"Excuse me, Dad."

She clicked on the answer button as she descended the back steps. "Hello?"

"Hi, Laurel. It's Dan."

"I know. Can you hang on a sec?" She worked her way around the corner of the house to the front yard, where she'd have at least a little bit of privacy. There was a big rock beneath a maple tree, and she went there and perched on it. "Okay. What's up?"

"I have a favor to ask. But before that, how are you? Are things okay with your family? The business?"

Sometimes she wished they hadn't stayed friends. A clean break might have been less complicated. Certainly it would have made it easier to move on. But then she knew he was asking because he genuinely cared. "I'm actually at Mom and Dad's now, for Sunday dinner."

"I miss those."

Uncomfortable silence. A snippy remark came to her mind but didn't pass her lips. She wondered if last night's confessions had anything to do with today's impatience.

"And the garden center?"

She crossed her legs, tucking them up beneath her on the boulder. "It's really busy. And we've had a few problems. A break-in and some graffiti."

"That's awful!"

She wanted to agree, but pride had her brushing it off. "Oh, you know, it comes with the territory." She remembered looking over at Aiden last night, in his T-shirt, spending his hours off helping her paint. And then the feel of his body crushed against hers . . .

It was really weird to be thinking about that while talking on the phone with her ex. She shook away the image and focused on Dan's voice.

"I'm sorry. You're probably busy enough without the added stress."

She sighed. "Well, yes. But you know Darling. People chip in to help. If anything, the break-in drove even more traffic to the store." That was her. Focusing on the positive. She put her free hand to her forehead. God, even her thoughts were sarcastic today.

"I'm glad. You sound happy."

She smiled a little. "I am. And tired, but no regrets. I think I did the right thing."

There was a pause, a pregnant one, where Laurel knew

he was trying to figure out what to say next. Or rather, how to say it. Her stomach tied up in little knots. For him to ask a favor and then have a hard time verbalizing it meant she probably wasn't going to like it.

"Dan, what's the call really about?"

"I might as well just say it: Ryan and me . . . we're getting married."

Her breath came out in a whoosh. God, she didn't know how to explain the strange feeling in her chest right now.

The fact that Dan had come out made things easier—and more difficult. On one hand, knowing the truth was almost a relief. The helplessness, the insecurity that came from watching her marriage slip through her fingers without knowing why and what *she* could do to bring them back, all of that was gone. But the cheating. No matter how often she told herself it wasn't a typical extramarital affair, it was about who he was on the inside, the fact remained that the man she'd vowed to love and honor until death hadn't felt the same. That instead of telling her, sharing himself with her, he'd lied. To them both. There was a small part of her that resented the upheaval in her life. She totally got that Dan's life had made a huge shift, but she'd had to make huge changes, too. It was hard work staying friends. Hell, most of the time she felt like Dan was being really insensitive, expecting her to be okay with it all. Sometimes she wished she'd just broken ties completely and moved on.

But she didn't, because no matter what happened, Dan had been her best friend and was important to her, and he said she was important to him, and she wanted to be supportive. That didn't mean it was easy. She'd loved him, thought she knew him, had envisioned a future with him. Kids. Trips. Grandbabies.

She'd have to sift through all those emotions later. Dan was still talking and she needed to focus.

"Laurel? You still there?"

"Sorry. I'm here. What were you saying?"

"We're planning on a June wedding."

Ah yes. The most popular wedding month of the year. Laurel was now glad that their anniversary fell in September. The symmetry might have been a tad too much.

"I'm happy for you," she said, trying to sound genuine. "But I don't know what this has to do with a favor."

"Well, it's where we want to get married. We drove down to Darling last weekend. I wanted to show Ryan the Kissing Bridge. And we were thinking it would be a great place to get married. The ceremony will be small, with the Justice of the Peace and a few guests."

She had to rewind to the beginning. "Wait, you were here? In Darling?"

"Just for a while. We were driving by the exit, and I thought of it, and . . . well, you know. I always did like the town."

Yes, he had. And part of her was offended he'd been here and hadn't stopped to say hello. Another part of her was relieved. And a small part of her resented that he'd intruded on her safe haven, the place that was supposed to be her second chance without him. She'd let him go, but there were times it really felt that he wasn't offering her the same courtesy.

She let out a slow, controlled breath. "And you wanted to make sure it was okay with me?"

"Well, yes. And . . ." Another big pause. "Laurel, we stayed friends, right? I mean, you still mean a lot to me."

They'd had this conversation a hundred times. The truth was, there was no actual falling out of love for Dan. In fact,

Dan had maintained throughout everything that he still loved her, just not in an in love, sexual kind of way. More like a best friend. Which explained why, particularly in the last months of their marriage, the sex had felt rather . . . dispassionate. Like something was off. The connection just wasn't there.

But she'd loved him. She'd meant her vows, heart and soul. She'd lain awake at night, wondering how to reach the husband who suddenly seemed distant. She'd tried to make their marriage work, and in the end he expected her to just accept that it had never been what she thought it was, and be perfectly okay with being friends.

Laurel liked to think she was a good person. A kind person. But that was perhaps expecting a bit much. It was only the history of their friendship that kept her from letting loose with all her feelings.

"You mean a lot to me, too," she murmured. "If you want me to be there, I'll be there."

She could somehow hear the relief in the brief silence. "Thank you, Laurel. I think somehow we both need your blessing."

Laurel closed her eyes. Well, bully for them. She thought of Aiden's shocked expression last night. She could just imagine what he'd say. *Fine time to be asking for approval, jackass.*

Why couldn't she just be completely happy for them, unfettered by any lingering feelings? The stupid thing was, she did wish them well. Any heaviness she felt right now was on her, not Dan. Her issues, not his. But goddammit, wasn't she entitled?

"I'm happy for you," she said earnestly. "I really am."

"So this is the part where I ask the favor," he said.

What? So the announcement and wanting her to go

wasn't it? Her eyes opened and her fingers tightened on the phone, pressing it to her ear.

"What do you want?"

"Well, we've checked with the town office and we can have the wedding in the park, by the bridge. The gardens in the park are lovely, or will be by the time everything blooms, but there's nothing really at the front of the bridge where we'd like to stand. So we were wondering if we could hire you to do some plant arrangements, to pretty it up a bit. Something that we could take back with us and use in the yard. Since you're familiar with both places . . . know what I mean?"

Damn. She let out a bitter laugh. "Oh God, Dan. Do you realize how inappropriate this is? That you're asking your ex-wife to help decorate your wedding site? You do realize that I'm your *ex-wife*, right?"

"You're not just my ex-wife, Laurel. You're more than that and you know it." His voice actually sounded hurt, and she pressed her fingers to the top of her nose. She was starting to get a headache.

"I know."

"Will you at least think about it? We're looking at the second Saturday in June."

She knew Dan. He'd persist until she said yes, and she would rather not have this conversation over and over again. "Fine. I'll think about it."

"Thank you, sweetheart. It means a lot to both of us."

Sweetheart. It was a meaningless endearment. And suddenly seemed to mean less than the soft, husky way Aiden had said her name last night.

"You're welcome."

"So," Dan asked, his voice lightening. "How's your love life?"

Her cheeks instantly burned. "Dan, you know the only thing more inappropriate than helping your ex plan their wedding?"

"What?"

"Talking about your respective sex lives."

"Ooooh. Does this mean you have one?"

They were supposed to be "friends." But not that kind of friend. Laurel would save those kinds of details for Willow, if at all. "No, I don't have one," she answered. One kiss after pizza and too much wine did not make a love life. "And if I did, it wouldn't be any of your business."

And calling it one kiss was the understatement of the century, but she'd ignore that little fact for a moment.

"Touchy," he replied, and she had the urge to reach through the phone to strangle him. "Don't sit on the shelf too long, sweetie. You're too good for that."

He was trying to be helpful and encouraging, but to Laurel he sounded smug. He'd landed on his feet. He was happy and moving on and she was still clawing her way up from the bottom. Worse, speaking to him brought out a side of her she didn't like very much.

Maybe she'd go home and till up another patch of the yard. So far it was the best form of therapy she'd found.

"Right, right. Well listen, I should go. Mom probably has dinner ready by now."

"Say hi to your parents. I miss them too."

"I will."

"Talk soon."

Laurel hung up and hugged her knees close. What the living hell? Moving home was supposed to make life simpler. Less complicated. Instead she was headfirst into running her own business, dealing with vandalism and robbery, kissing a man who she was supposed to hate, and suckered into supplying plants and flowers for her ex-husband's wedding.

"Laurel? You okay?"

Her mom was on the front step, hands on the railing.

"I'm fine. Just a phone call."

"Dinner's ready."

"Be right there."

And that was a little bit of normal she'd cling to. Her mother's mashed potatoes and apple pie. At least for the next thirty minutes, things might actually stay the same.

Aiden parked the cruiser along Main and got out, rolling his shoulders a bit to loosen the tension.

It was Tuesday. He hadn't seen Laurel since Saturday night. He deliberately hadn't called, hadn't stopped into the garden center because he had no idea what to say. He'd half hoped there'd be some news about her break-in, or the graffiti, just to give him an excuse. But there'd been nothing. The problem with the garden center was that it wasn't really near any other businesses, being just off the highway. No one had seen a thing.

Being back on shift was a relief. He was on until eleven tonight, and a meal at the Sugarbush Family Restaurant was just what he needed to fill the hole in his belly and pass the time.

And maybe stop thinking about Laurel. Kissing her had been awesome and a big mistake. She was barely divorced, for Pete's sake. It didn't take a genius to figure out that she was still a mess. He was still attracted to her, but her baggage was a big ol' red flag. Not just for him, but for her, too. She wasn't ready.

And Laurel Stone wasn't the kind of girl he could be

casual with. He'd be better off to just leave the situation alone.

Aiden went inside and sat at the lunch counter. He stayed away from the deep-fried food and went for the home cooking on the menu, ordering pork chops and applesauce with a plain baked potato and whatever the daily vegetable happened to be. When the food came his stomach growled in anticipation, and he dug in. A call could come at any moment, and he was starving. One of the things he loved about the Sugarbush was that cops got a twenty-five-percent discount on their bill. Some nights he packed a lunch and ate in the car. But now and then he liked stopping and getting something substantial, especially when he was working evenings.

The radio was blessedly quiet, so he finished his meal and fished out his wallet to pay the bill. He was just at the door to go outside when he saw George, off and to the left, sitting on the sidewalk and leaning up against a red maple that the town had planted between the road and the concrete walk.

He was still wearing the clothes Aiden had bought for him, and Aiden noticed the sneakers were holding up well. But George also looked tired, and he was counting through the bits of change he had in his palm.

Aiden made an about-face and went back to the counter.

"Hey, Julie." He greeted his waitress again. "Listen, you got anything done up quick in the kitchen I could take for takeout? Maybe not deep-fried?"

"You still hungry?" Julie was maybe thirty, cute as a button with blonde curls and generous curves, and a smile that lit up a room.

"I thought I'd pick up something for George."

Julie peered over his shoulder, glancing out the window. "Oh. Let me have a look in the kitchen, okay?"

"Something with some nutritional value," Aiden added, calling after her retreating figure.

She came back moments later, holding a takeout bag in her hands. "Here," she said, putting it on the counter. "Charlie had some turkey left from what he cooked this morning, and I put in a scoop of mashed potatoes and some of the daily vegetable. And a roll with butter and there's a piece of chocolate cake, too."

"You're a doll." Aiden reached toward his hip, and his wallet.

"Just take it, Aiden." Julie smiled but her eyes were soft with compassion. "The turkey was scraps and we'll never miss a few scoops of vegetables."

"You're sure?"

"I'm sure. It's a good thing you're doing."

"Thanks. Tell Charlie I said thanks too."

She leaned over the counter and winked. "Who said Charlie has to know?"

Aiden smiled. "You're a good woman, Julie."

"Go on. Give the man a meal."

He took the bag and left the restaurant.

George was still sitting under the tree, his ball hat on the ground beside him. He'd showered recently, Aiden realized. He must be staying at the shelter. But he'd lost more weight. Aiden went over and crouched down in front of him. "Hey, George."

George looked up. He'd shaved sometime in the last day or so, and Aiden was surprised to realize that George wasn't as old as he'd thought. The guy was mid-forties, if that. What on earth had happened to him to make this his life?

"Officer."

"Call me Aiden. I thought we went through that before."

George looked up. "I need to move, huh. Somebody complainin'?"

"No, you're okay for now. You going back to the shelter tonight?"

George nodded.

"I brought you some dinner. When's the last time you had a good meal, huh?"

George eyed the plastic bag. "It's hit and miss."

"You're sure you don't have any family around? Someone who could help you get on your feet?"

The look in George's eyes was haunted, and Aiden dropped the subject. He handed over the bag. "Lady inside says it's turkey and mashed potatoes and vegetables. And cake." He grinned, hoping to see the man smile, just a little.

"What kind of cake?"

"Chocolate."

"Damn," George said.

"Is there anything I can do for you?" Aiden said.

"Naw, this's good, brother. Thanks." George took the bag, then pulled in his ball cap, which held a few coins and nothing more. He took the money out of his hat and held it out to Aiden. "Here. For supper."

"You hold on to that," Aiden said, shaking his head, feeling his heart pang at the man's pride. "Tonight we're square."

George tucked the coins away. At the same moment, Aiden's radio crackled as dispatch sent out a call.

He listened for a moment and then turned back to George. "I gotta go. Enjoy your dinner and be safe, okay?"

George nodded. "Yes, sir."

Aiden walked back to his car. When he got there, he glanced over at where he'd left George sitting. George had opened his container and was already dipping into the potatoes and gravy.

An idea took hold, but he didn't have time to think about it much as he hopped in and started the engine. But somehow, he determined, he was going to get to the bottom of George's story. And then maybe he could help the guy get his life back.

CHAPTER 7

The May Chamber of Commerce breakfast was held at The Purple Pig. Laurel didn't dress up quite as fancy this time, opting for plain trousers and a comfortable, pretty shirt. Willow had put up a sign in the window, saying the café was closed for a private function from nine until eleven. Laurel stepped inside and was assaulted by the delectable scents of coffee, cinnamon, and chocolate.

Willow was putting out platters of croissants, scones, cinnamon rolls, and a big bowl of fruit salad. Still feeling slightly out of place, Laurel went over to lend a hand. She'd rather keep her hands busy.

"Hey, long time no see!" Willow shot her a grin. Today Willow's streaked hair was gathered up in a topknot and she wore one of her Purple Pig aprons.

"Hey." Laurel smiled back. "What can I do?"

"Go to the back and grab the tray of butter and jams for the scones," Willow said, putting a stack of plates on a long table.

For a few minutes Laurel helped out, marveling that her

friend ran this sort of business. The sourcing of ingredients alone had to be challenging. Everything was either locally sourced, organic, or both. A couple of her employees were already doing prep for the lunch crowd. Laurel figured Willow must have been up before dawn to have all this baking done.

"So what's new with you?" Willow took a moment to put her hands on her hips and stretch out her back. "Damn, I missed doing yoga this morning. It feels like my whole day's off if I don't do my practice before work."

Laurel couldn't imagine being up and doing a whole yoga practice before work, or even being zen before a second cup of coffee. She reached for a coffee cup and poured herself some of Willow's special Fair Trade blend. "Lots and lots of work. And we need to get together soon so I can fill your ears." She raised her eyebrows at Willow. "Now's not the time or place."

"Would it have anything to do with Aiden Gallagher and some lewd graffiti?"

Laurel choked on her coffee. "What?"

"I drove by the night of, thinking I'd stop in and give you a hand. I saw Aiden's truck and it looked like you two were painting together. Feud's over, huh?"

Oh Lord. Of course they'd been seen. "Sort of? Not really. I don't know." She had a hard time meeting Willow's gaze so she made a point of scanning the gathered business owners.

"Laurel?" Willow came closer. "What aren't you telling me?"

"Nothing. He stopped by and offered to help. We've buried the hatchet, I guess." They'd done a lot more than that, too, and Laurel's pelvic muscles contracted instinctively as she recalled how she'd locked her legs around his waist and let him grind against her. Oh Lord, she was in trouble.

"And you didn't bury it in his back? Wow. He must be some smooth talker, because you hated his guts." She frowned. "That night of the robbery, when he stopped by . . . there was tension between you."

"Yeah. It was kind of stupid to hold a grudge that long." She wasn't sure Aiden was a smooth talker, but he sure was a hell of a kisser. Not that she was going to say that to Willow. At least not right now. "And Dan has news, too. When are you free again?"

Willow laughed. "I own an eatery that's open seven days a week. How about you?"

Laurel sighed. "Same. Seriously, let's grab some dinner some night after we both close. I could use a wise ear."

"Me? Wise? Hah." Willow laughed lightly. "Hold that thought. The blueberry scones are nearly empty. Happens every time."

Laurel helped herself to a cinnamon roll and found a space to put her cup as she cut into the pastry with the side of her fork. Before long she was approached by Jack Sheridan, who ran a farm just outside of town and sold his produce at the Saturday Farmer's Market. When he asked if she was planning to stay open through the holidays, and she said yes, they worked out basic details for him to set up a Christmas tree lot at the Ladybug. That sparked a new idea, and Laurel made a point of touching base with Molly Flanagan, a local artisan. If Jack sold his trees at her place, then she should look at stocking more holiday items, like handcrafted ornaments and decorations.

The coffee hour was almost done when Oaklee Collier cornered her. Oaklee was young, with perfect skin and long blonde hair that curled around her shoulders like it was from a shampoo commercial. It didn't matter that Oaklee was sweet and nice. She was the kind of woman who made the person next to her feel dowdy and dumpy just because she was so damned attractive.

"Oaklee. What can I do for you?"

"Hi, Laurel. I just wanted to congratulate you on rejuvenating the old garden center. The Ladybug looks fabulous."

"Oh, well, thank you." Laurel smiled, aware that next to Oaklee, her trousers looked plain and her hair was a dull brown rather than the color of a thoroughbred.

Huh. Thoroughbred was the perfect way to describe her.

"I heard that you did the window boxes for the businesses along Main, from Birch to Sycamore. They look lovely."

"Everyone's been so supportive since the break-in, and put in orders for their planters and boxes. It's been a real boost for sure."

"I'm glad. But Darling's like that. We tend to support our own. I was sorry to hear about your divorce."

She sounded genuine, but Laurel bristled. Most people weren't so blunt about bringing it up, but she'd heard plenty of whispers at the meetings, and even in her store when no one thought she could hear. "Thank you," she replied, her tone significantly cooler than it had been before.

But Oaklee was undaunted. "Speaking of town support, are you on Twitter? Instagram? I'm the social media manager for the town and while I always put out information on what's going on in the community, I'd love to link to you and share. Instagram would be awesome for sure, because you could post pics of your products."

"We've got a Facebook page," Laurel said. Not that she'd been that great in posting often. "Honestly, I haven't had time to set up more than that." Her personal accounts had been neglected for months. The last time she'd logged in, the inspirational quotes alone made her want to throw her phone against the wall. Add to that all the DMs from old friends asking about the divorce, and she'd opted for a self-imposed cone of silence.

"Would it be okay if I stopped by sometime? I could help you set it up so that anything you post automatically goes to other platforms, saving you time. And if we add a town hashtag, I'll be sure to see it and can share."

Sure, Laurel thought. *I'll do all that in between all the other stuff I do all day, because I don't need sleep anyway.*

And yet Laurel knew Oaklee was right. The best way to reach a lot of her potential customers was online. "It's not a matter of knowing how. It's the time suck. Maybe I can hire a student to help me," she suggested. "You know, keep my website updated and stuff. Though that might not work if I wanted to post stuff more than once a week."

Oaklee waved a hand. "That's what scheduling posts is for. And if you're serious, there's probably a co-op student from the high school who'd be willing to take on a few hours a week, particularly over the summer."

"That's a great idea."

"I'll give you a call," Oaklee said. "Oh, and one more thing."

Maybe it was Oaklee's nonchalant tone that lured Laurel in. She really wasn't sure. But she answered, "How can I help?" and instantly regretted it when Oaklee's eyes lit up.

"You know we're rejuvenating the tourism campaign," Oaklee began, smiling brightly. "The picture of you and Aiden Gallagher is sweet, but it's over twenty years old. We'd like to revisit that."

"I told the mayor that I was fine with the old photo coming down," Laurel assured her.

"That's not exactly what we had in mind. We thought it would be really neat to re-create that moment." She frowned slightly. "Honestly, all this should have been done months ago. Anyway, the plan is to use the new campaign for at least a few years, so what we miss out on this summer, we can capitalize on next."

"I don't understand. Where do I come in?"

Oaklee put her hand on Laurel's arm. "We want the two of you to pose for a new, updated photo. I talked to Aiden already, and he's on board."

Laurel's mouth dropped open, and she struggled to close it again and compose herself. Bad enough they wanted her to pose for a new photo. But with Aiden! And he'd already agreed. When? Because he hadn't said anything to her about it.

"Oh? You spoke to Aiden?"

"Yes, a few weeks ago when we first came up with the concept. We're going with a whole new branding for the town, and we're going to put the pictures side by side. Didn't anyone mention it?"

Laurel's stomach turned. "No. This is the first I've heard of it. But surely someone else can model for it?" Even the word "model" felt strange in her mouth. She was so not model material.

Oaklee ignored her question. "We're hoping for the second week of July for the photo shoot. Unfortunately, the photographer we want to use is booked for a number of weddings and graduation events. But it does give us time to plan and do the rollout right."

Oaklee looked at her expectantly, and Laurel started to squirm. On the surface, it seemed like the obvious answer was yes. What would it hurt? But it was more complicated than that. "Do you mean just the two of us posing on the bridge?"

"Oh no," Oaklee replied, flipping her mane of hair over her shoulder. "Didn't I mention? The original has you in flower girl and ring bearer dress. We'd be putting you two in a tux and wedding dress for the occasion."

Oh God. Abso-freaking-lutely not. For one thing, her relationship with Aiden was complicated and weird and . . . undecided. For another, it would be awkward as hell, dressing up in a white gown for a photo shoot—she was no model. Or bride.

And then there was the plain fact that the idea of putting on a wedding dress made her just the slightest bit queasy. It felt so wrong and fraudulent. Maybe she'd handled herself well, at least she hoped she had. But her divorce had still left scars. Pretend pose or not, it was just too soon. She'd done enough pretending over the last year to last a lifetime.

"I'm sorry, Oaklee. I won't be able to help you. I'm sure you'll be able to find someone else."

Oaklee's face registered disappointment. "But the whole premise is based on the photo from the past and re-doing it for the present. It's a . . . a symmetry thing. It's not just the tourism board either. We're lining up press releases and the paper in Montpelier is doing a feature story. The bridge has always been a draw, but the new plan is to really put us on the map. The human interest part hinges on it being the same two people, don't you see? Even the branding alludes to it. *Kiss for a moment; love for a lifetime. Darling, Vermont.*"

Laurel hated saying no. She wasn't good at it. But she needed to learn sometime and now was as good a time as any. The idea of standing across from Aiden, dressed in a wedding gown . . . it would be uncomfortable. Humiliating. And then there was the fact that he'd kissed her senseless in her tiny foyer. Not that she had designs on marrying him, but there was still *context*. The original photo had the two of them kissing, an innocent preschool kind of kiss, but lip-to-lip just the same. Would they be expected to recreate that, too?

"I'm just too busy. My business is quite seasonal, as you know, and it's taking up so much of my time. Besides, you'll do far better with an actual model. Someone who knows what they're doing in front of a camera."

Oaklee's happy expression had fled and her face flattened with clear disappointment. "Well, darn. We thought since Aiden had already agreed . . ."

Laurel pondered Oaklee's age. If Laurel was twenty-eight, then Oaklee had to be twenty-four or twenty-five. Maybe she'd been too young to remember when the whole kerfluffle with Aiden had erupted. She certainly didn't seem to fathom that Laurel and Aiden weren't friends.

Or at least they weren't then. Now . . . she wasn't so sure where things stood. Not *not* friends, not something more, either. It didn't help that he hadn't even called since their steamy kiss.

"Sorry," Laurel repeated, and tried very hard to sound sincere. "Good luck though. It's a great concept."

Before Oaklee could say anything more to try to change her mind, Laurel excused herself and snuck out the door. She walked all the way back to her house and stalked inside, unbuttoning her floral blouse and shrugging it off on the way to the bedroom.

Jeans, sneakers, her Ladybug golf shirt, and a tidy and efficient ponytail. That was her usual uniform. Maybe if

Oaklee had seen her dressed like that, she would have abandoned any idea of having Laurel appear in the picture.

It was a stupid idea. Laurel laughed out loud at the very suggestion that she put on a wedding dress and stand across from Aiden. And when did Aiden ever wear a tuxedo?

Then again, he did look rather sexy, all buttoned up in his uniform. Aiden in a tuxedo would be hard to resist.

And why the heck was she even giving it a second thought?

She stopped in front of her mirror, stared at the figure there dressed in nothing but a bra and panties. She was nothing spectacular. Just . . . plain. She'd always been plain. The one time she'd really gone all out and been done up was when she'd married Dan in the big church with the tall spire and huge windows. That hadn't been her. She hadn't wanted such a big, elaborate production. Instead she'd become someone she'd wanted to be, pretended to be. Who she thought she should be.

She couldn't do that again. Dan wasn't the only one who'd lied that day. She had, too.

She couldn't do it. She couldn't put on a wedding dress and pretend to be someone else again.

Willow lived in an apartment above The Purple Pig. Or something like an apartment. It was all one big open concept, mostly dominated by gleaming maple hardwood floors.

Laurel closed the door behind her, inhaling deeply. Something smelled delicious, and her stomach rumbled. She really needed to start eating more regular meals.

"Heya," Willow called out. She was standing in front of the stove, stirring something in a pan, her hair tied back in some sort of scarf. "I need to keep on top of this, but come on in."

Laurel took off her sandals and left them by the door. There was something so sunny and open about Willow's place. Maybe it was that she kept the window blinds up, letting in all the natural light. Or maybe it was the utter simplicity of the décor. There was a futon and a few comfortable papasan chairs on either side. Her kitchen table was small and only had two chairs, and there was another small occasional table beside the futon that held a charging dock and right now, a small laptop. Those two items formed the sum total of technology. The rest of the room was Willow's yoga room. There was a Buddha, a stone fountain that trickled water, which Laurel couldn't hear right now because of the sizzling in the pan, and a row of mats, blocks, bolsters and straps, all precisely organized. The walls were painted a creamy white, but the solid wall in the yoga area was a pale green. In the center was a large white lotus flower. It was airy and serene—just like Willow.

"Have I ever told you how much I love your place?" Laurel asked, taking her cloth bag to the small counter space in the kitchen area.

Willow shrugged. "It's simple. Not much to love."

"That's just it. It's so peaceful. There's no clutter. No fuss. I come in here and it's as if my stress just melts away."

Willow smiled. "Well, that's the general idea." She took the bag, took out the bottle of wine, and stuck it in the fridge. "Go sit in the chair. I know you want to. There's another five minutes before dinner is ready."

They'd finally made time for dinner and a good gab. The more time that had passed, the more Laurel was sure she was making a lot out of nothing where Aiden was concerned. Either way, she could really use the downtime. Particularly with Willow, who practically exuded calm and rationality.

Besides, she had *the chair.*

Laurel grinned and headed right to the corner of the room, past the Buddha and the fountain. The chair was actually a freestanding hammock chair, and it faced the big, long windows along the back of the building. There wasn't much to see out the back, and that was perfect. Laurel could see the roofs of the houses on Liberty Street, one block off of Main, but the trees were mature and kept the view private. Laurel slipped into the chair and relaxed, and stared out at the new leaves on the trees, a pair of chickadees dipping and darting, and a squirrel racing up the trunk of a huge spruce.

She nudged the floor with her toe, sending the chair in the smallest motion, and let out a breath.

She really needed to get one of these.

There was a *pop* from the kitchen; Willow had opened the bottle of Riesling that Laurel had brought along. "Food's ready," Willow called, and Laurel stopped the swing with a little regret. Not too much, though. Today had been so busy that she'd forgotten to eat lunch. Maybe that was good for her waistline, but not so much for her mood.

"What'd you make?" she asked. She looked at the plate in Willow's hands and honestly couldn't quite tell. It looked like there was something green and ribbon-y, and chicken, and sauce that smelled spicy and Asian.

"Spicy chicken and zucchini ribbons," Willow replied. "Free range chicken, tomato, zucchini, chili, and tamari. But I add more vegetables than the recipe says. There are onions, peppers, and some choy in there."

"Wow. This kind of beats my takeout offer."

"This is better for you," Willow informed her, putting the plates down on the table. "And it hardly took any work at all."

As Laurel sat, Willow poured the wine. "Cheers. To finally having a whole evening for dinner and . . ." She smiled wickedly. "Whatever else we might get up to."

Laurel laughed and touched the rim of her glass to Willow's. "I'm too old for that shit." She took a drink of the wine and put down the glass. "And we were such goody-two-shoes in school. I think we missed our window of opportunity."

"Seems like a lifetime ago, doesn't it?" Willow put down her glass, too, and picked up her fork.

"You got that right," Laurel muttered, and tasted a bit of the chicken. It was scrumptious.

They chatted and ate for a few minutes, talking about nothing of major consequence until Willow asked, "Have you heard anything about the robbery? Did they ever find who did it?"

It was a source of frustration for Laurel that whoever had damaged her store and stole her money was still out there, scot-free. "No. Apparently no one saw anything, and I don't have cameras, so it's just a dead end." She sighed. "Same thing for the graffiti. Several spots got tagged that night, not just the store. Did you know they even painted the memorial fountain in the park?"

"I'd heard."

"I bet the town will be installing more cameras." Laurel frowned. "It's a real shame. One of the things I liked about Darling was that it didn't seem to need all that, not like other places. But I guess I was wrong."

"Maybe we've seen the end of the trouble," Willow said hopefully. She swiped a zucchini ribbon through the sauce on her plate. "Of course, something's got to keep guys like Aiden Gallagher in a job."

Laurel had anticipated comments about Aiden. But even expecting it, hearing his name sent a rush of heat through her.

Willow didn't stop, either. "Though I hear he could have a promising future as a painter."

Laurel adopted an innocent look. "This was yummy. I'm betting there's dessert?"

"Lemon pound cake from the café. And don't change the subject."

"There was a subject?" Grinning, Laurel stood and took the dirty plates to the sink.

"Oh, girlfriend," Willow said significantly. "Something happened, didn't it?"

"I don't know what you're getting at." She did, but she wasn't going to give it up this easily. Not when she could string Willow along a bit longer.

Willow's tinkling laugh echoed as she went to the cupboard and took out a square container. "You pretty much spilled it at the meeting the other day, so you might as well tell me the details. I know you're just trying to make me wait." She turned to Laurel. "Tea, or more wine?"

"What do you think?"

Willow grinned. "Wine it is."

They took their cake and wine over to the futon, which was made up like a sofa with an abundance of throw pillows. Laurel put her glass down on the little table and cut into her cake, while Willow managed to gracefully sit cross-legged, balancing the plate with the cake on the hollow where her ankles met, and keeping her wineglass in her hand.

Laurel had the thought that maybe she should give yoga

a try. If she could manage a tenth of Willow's serenity and grace, it might be worth it. Instead she rather suspected she was getting man-arms from all the lifting at work.

"Okay," she said, letting Willow off the hook. "So after Aiden stopped by and helped me paint over the very crudely drawn genitalia, he grabbed a pizza and brought it over. Neither of us had had dinner. And sadly, I don't have your skills in the kitchen."

"I'll sift through that sentence and say 'Aiden helped me paint blah blah and brought over pizza, blah blah.' Don't try to distract me with extraneous information."

Crumbs of cake caught in Laurel's mouth as she tried not to laugh. "God. Sometimes I forget that you've got the capability to be ruthless. You would have made a good lawyer, Wil."

"Funny. The law is not for me. I would want to strangle people within five minutes. Hence the yoga. People are far nicer when I've done yoga. And that was a distraction too. Tell me what happened. Did you do it? Knock boots? Do the nasty?" She waggled her eyebrows.

Those descriptions were so unlike Willow that Laurel burst out laughing. "Oh, it must have hurt you just to say that," she gasped, reaching for her wine. "And no. We didn't do the nasty." Though come to think of it, she could imagine it well enough. And the room suddenly felt just a little bit hotter.

"Well, something happened. Come on, Laurel. I don't have a love life. I have to live vicariously."

Laurel wondered why. Willow was a little quirky, sure. But she was gorgeous, and talented, and sweet. And yet there had never been any man around or even mentioned. Not a past boyfriend or current interest.

"We talked, that's all. Cleared the air and had pizza and

I had some wine." She looked ruefully at her glass. "I seem to be doing that a lot lately."

"And . . ."

"And he kissed me before he left, that's all. No biggie. I haven't even talked to him since."

And wasn't that just driving her crazy? As much as she'd like to say it wasn't, couldn't he have at least called to say hey? Or stopped at the store when she was working, which was always?

She plopped a large bite of cake into her mouth.

"But what kind of kiss? A good-night-thanks-for-pizza kiss or an OMG-I-want-to-eat-your-face kiss?" Willow asked.

"First of all, eew. That is the grossest description of a kiss I've ever heard." Sadly, it was also quite accurate.

"Okay, let's try another. Was it a curl-your-toes-and-want-to-have-breakfast-the-next-morning kiss?"

Laurel swallowed. "Bingo," she whispered. "Aw, shit."

Willow gaped, then put her empty plate down on the floor. "Really? It was that good? I was just kidding, but wow."

"I didn't even expect it," Laurel admitted. "One moment we were saying good-bye at the door, and the next he was coming back inside and he took me in his arms and . . ." She stopped. She couldn't give a play-by-play. It was too embarrassing.

But she didn't need to. Willow clued in right away. "Oh, that's swoony," she said, falling back against the cushions, cradling her glass. "And then what happened?"

"Well, it lasted a while. I mean, he didn't really hurry. And then he just left. Said he didn't want to say anything to ruin it, and boom. Out the door. And that's the last I've seen of him."

Willow's eyes were wide. "Did he leave a glass slipper on the steps?"

That made Laurel giggle like a schoolgirl, and she grabbed one of the throw pillows and threw it at Willow. "Shut up."

They laughed for a bit, but then Willow asked the question Laurel had been asking herself for days.

"So, do you want to see him again?"

"I don't know." That was the answer she kept coming up with, time and time again. "It's not really the high school thing. He apologized for that, and I know people grow up. Honestly, I think I was so angry at him because it saved me being embarrassed about my own part in it. I could have handled it differently. Better."

Willow shook her head. "Naw. Aiden got exactly what he deserved that day. Though it was a waste of a perfectly good vanilla milkshake."

They smiled again, but the mood had gone slightly serious.

"It's more . . . I'm not sure I'm ready to date anyone. The part that sticks with what happened with Dan is that it was a lie. What I thought was a real thing turned out to be anything but. And you know the old saying, fool me once . . ." She frowned, studied the pale liquid in her glass. "Dan's not a bad guy, deep down. But once again I found myself in a position where what I thought was reality was so far from it . . . I don't know how to trust people anymore. I don't know how to believe that they mean what they say. Does that make any sense?"

Willow's eyes had softened during Laurel's confession. "It makes a ton of sense," she replied softly. "Because it's not just about trusting other people, it's about trusting yourself, too, isn't it?"

SOMEBODY LIKE YOU   101

Laurel nodded. "It really is. My judgment hasn't been so shit-hot in the past."

"Preach it, sister." Willow smiled half-heartedly.

"About Dan . . . there's more." Laurel felt the need for more fortification so she went to the kitchen and topped up her glass. "He called last Sunday. He and Ryan are going to tie the knot, right at our very own Kissing Bridge." She headed back to the sofa, and gave Willow a mock toast with her glass.

"You're joking. Herc?"

"Yep."

"That's kind of . . ."

"Insensitive, to my mind," Laurel said. She contemplated her glass again. "Oh look. Truth juice."

"It's kind of rubbing your nose in it, isn't it?"

But it wasn't. "There's not a vindictive bone in Dan's body. He's just happy. And he doesn't understand how much damage he's done, maybe because I've tried to be supportive. Granted, I freaked out when I first found out the truth. And I shed my share of tears and threw a few things and . . . well, I was pretty angry. I mean, this was a life-altering revelation, you know? I . . ." Her throat started to close up. "That night when he said we needed to talk, I got so excited. I thought he was going to say it was time we could think about starting our family."

"Oh, honey."

Laurel cleared her throat. "He's happy, and I'm happy for him. I truly am, deep down. But that doesn't mean that it's easy or that I need ringside seats." She sighed. "Some days I really wish I were a better person."

Willow straightened her shoulders. "You are a good person. Don't ever think you're not. Most people wouldn't even speak to their ex after that. I've seen plenty of divorced couples who hate each other just as passionately as they loved each other and it's ugly."

The rim of the glass was getting fuzzy, and Laurel figured she'd better call it a day where the wine was concerned. "That's just it, Wil. I don't hate him passionately. And that makes me think I didn't love him passionately, either. And I don't know if that makes it better or worse."

"Maybe it just means you're a grown-up. That you're more forgiving than you realize."

Laurel looked over at her friend. She could always count on Willow to make her feel better. "I love you, Wil."

Willow's eyes softened. "I love you too, dork."

They sat in silence for a while.

"So you're going to the wedding?" Willow finally asked.

"Better than that. I'm helping with the decorating. They want plants and shrubs and baskets and stuff. The idea is that they can take them home after and add them to the yard."

"Oh God. So it's a case of help us have a pretty wedding and then fancy up our perfect home?"

"The home that was my home. It's awkward. And I think it's a lot to ask."

"But you'll do it anyway. Because that's who you are."

She shrugged.

"Do you ever say no to anything?" Willow drained the last of her wine and put the glass down on her floor.

"I said no to the photo project the town has planned. It's bad enough they have a picture of me when I was five. They don't need one of me twenty-odd years later."

"You really did say no? To Oaklee? Because she's persistent."

"I'm not putting on a wedding dress and pretending to

gaze lovingly into Aiden Gallagher's eyes. Not after . . . well, everything. Oaklee's probably nice enough, but I don't owe her anything."

"True enough." Willow got up from the futon and went to a small cabinet. She took out a DVD and came back, holding it out to Laurel. "Here. You're in desperate need of yoga. Try a few of these practices. I'll loan you a mat."

"Willow . . ."

But Willow had flitted over to the kitchen and was scribbling on a slip of paper. "And this is the YouTube channel of my favorite meditations. Go look it up. You need some peace and serenity. If I didn't already know you'd refuse, I'd ask you to come with me next weekend and get your chakras balanced."

Laurel rolled her eyes.

"Hey," Willow insisted. "Don't knock it until you try it. That kind of woo-woo stuff saved my life."

Laurel looked at her friend, more closely than she had in the past. Willow was serious, and Laurel felt a pang in her heart knowing that somewhere along the line Wil had been hurt. This was the most Willow had shared with her, so she didn't press. Laurel got the sense that Willow would tell her on her own time.

"I'll look it up and try onc," she promised.

"Good. Wanna watch a movie or something?"

"That sounds nice," Laurel agreed. She should go home and start planning Dan's arrangements, but it could wait for another day.

Tonight she was going to hang out with her best friend and do absolutely nothing. And it felt wonderful.

CHAPTER 8

Memorial Day weekend was always a big deal in Darling. There was a monument in the park in honor of those who'd served, and a garden with a fountain that remembered the victims and first responders of 9/11. There was a parade, local churches had special services, the fire and police departments sponsored open houses and other events, and families all over town had their first big backyard barbecue of the season.

Aiden had volunteered to go to the Ladybug Garden Center on behalf of the force, to purchase a hanging basket to raffle off in support of their scholarship fund. He hadn't seen Laurel in a few weeks, and his sister Hannah had heard from Oaklee that Laurel had turned down the photo proposition. She seemed to be over the whole "never speaking to you again" thing, and he was surprised she'd been able to say no. Oaklee was known for getting her way.

Truth be told, he'd thought the picture might be fun for a laugh. There was, after all, a certain irony in it. But maybe she didn't agree. Maybe it had something to do with their kiss, and the fact that he hadn't called. And the longer time went on, the more difficult it became.

He searched for a parking spot in the already nearly-full lot. They were sure doing a brisk business, he noted, watching someone wheel out a cart holding several baskets and flats of plants. With the weather forecast for the long weekend being sunny and warm, he supposed a lot of people would be in their gardens. His mom included. Maybe he should pick up something for her, too. Butter her up a bit. He hadn't been around much and she was constantly lamenting her sons' absence. Rory showed up slightly more often than Aiden, but that was just because Aiden often worked over the dinner hour.

When he entered the store, Laurel looked up from behind the cash register and their eyes met. He felt the jolt right to his toes and suppressed a frown. Granted, it had been one hell of a kiss they'd shared, but this whole chemistry thing was a bit much. And it kept happening.

It had shaken him more than he'd planned. And he'd been a coward ever since—so much for not repeating past history. At least the raffle baskets gave him a good excuse to see her, and he could test the waters. See if she was really angry. He really wasn't sure he would ever figure women out, or know the right thing to say or do.

Baskets hung from the rafters, big and small, various colors and different flowers he couldn't identify. Tables were lined with six-packs of blooms, little pots of individual plants, grasses, vegetables ready to go into a garden. He wondered if Laurel had finished planting her garden in her backyard, and what vegetables she was growing.

The end of the greenhouse area housed gallon pots of shrubs, some leafy green, some blossoming. Half a dozen lilacs were in a corner and the sweet perfume of them re-minded him of home.

But as far as what he should get for the raffle? He was completely clueless.

"Shopping for something in particular?"

Her voice. Soft, yet with an underlying steel that sug-gested he wasn't quite off the hook. Damn, he liked that about her. She challenged him. When they were toe to toe, he forgot to second-guess everything he said and did. Laurel was a top-notch distraction from his faults—except for when she was pointing them out. Right now, just the hint of ice in her tone reminded him of what a coward he was when it came to talking about emotions. He really should have called her.

When he turned around, she was watching him with an utterly professional expression on her face. He had visions of pressing her against the wall, her legs wrapped tightly around him, her dark hair falling against her cheek, and he momentarily forgot what he was going to say.

"Aiden? It's busy. If there's something you need help with . . ."

"Right. Sorry." *Yeah, sorry I was thinking about running my hands over your skin. Kissing that mouth that's drawn up tight.* "I'm here on behalf of the station. We have this scholarship fund. This weekend, during our open house, we want to raffle off some baskets or some-thing to raise money for it."

"Who benefits from the scholarship?" she asked, shift-ing her weight onto her hip.

"Generally it's a high school student going into some type of post-secondary program who has a parent either in emergency services or the military."

"Nice." She offered a small smile then. "So what are you looking for? Planters or hanging baskets?"

He shrugged. "I was going to ask you what you thought. You're the professional." He tried a smile.

"How much are tickets?"

"Five dollars. Three for ten."

She led him down an aisle to a group of arranged urns. "These are quite large. We've got . . ." She looked at him and smiled again. "Okay, so I'll leave off the actual plant names, since you don't really care about that. They've got spiky stuff in the middle, then blooming flowers, and some ivy and other stuff that cascades over the side. See?"

They were beautiful, he couldn't argue that. But somehow they didn't seem quite right.

Apparently Laurel could tell he wasn't that keen because she moved further down the line. "What about a pair of hanging baskets, then? I did these up for Memorial Day and they might suit your particular needs well."

She looked up. He followed the path of her gaze, and agreed with her assessment one hundred percent.

The baskets were large, in wire-and-moss pots that for whatever reason looked more natural—and expensive—than the ones in plastic. A profusion of blossoms filled each to overflowing in red, white, and blue.

"Wow," he said.

"I know. I put in a special order. I'm really happy with them. And they're not going to last long around here. I've sold twenty already this morning. It's red begonias surrounded by white million bells and blue lobelia. Not a lot of deadheading required, mostly just for the begonias. I've got ones for shade, too, a bit smaller, but with red and white impatiens." She pointed to the next row over. They were pretty, but not as stunning as the ones directly above them. "They're better in shade. Impatiens don't like the sun."

"I like these ones," he admitted. "And you're right. The red, white, and blue is perfect."

"I'll get them down for you."

He watched as she grabbed a hook and deftly removed the baskets from the wire and placed them on the floor. "That's pretty slick."

"When you've done it a zillion times, you get fast at it."

Again with the businesslike smile. It was driving him slightly crazy. They stepped aside as a couple of customers went by, and then Aiden picked up both baskets. They were heavier than he expected, and his biceps flexed. To his gratification, Laurel seemed to notice. Her gaze strayed to his arms and her lips parted just a little bit. Good. Maybe she wasn't quite as immune to him as she let on.

"Do you want help taking them to your truck?"

"I think I can manage. I'll need to get my wallet out at the cash register though. Unless you want to reach into my pocket to get it?" He waggled his eyebrows.

She snorted. "Nice try. Besides, they're on me."

"Sorry?"

"The baskets. There's no charge."

He hadn't been expecting that. "Laurel, we budgeted for this. Don't worry."

"I'm not worried. Consider it my donation to the fund, since I won't be buying tickets. Winning hanging baskets would be kind of pointless for me."

"It's too much." He'd seen the price tags on the baskets. They weren't cheap. "At least let me buy them at cost."

"Seriously, I'll write them off." She reached over and took one from his hand. "It's a couple of baskets, Aiden. Not my firstborn."

They reached his truck and he opened the tailgate. "Well, thanks," he said, putting his basket inside and then taking the other one too. He shut the tailgate with a solid thump. "On behalf of the police department, that is."

"You're most welcome. The police department, that is." She mimicked him and he couldn't stop the crooked smile from touching his lips. Maybe he was forgiven. At least a bit.

She looked over her shoulder, as if anxious to return. There were two people working besides her, at least that Aiden could see. One was dealing with the lineup at the cash register, and the other was bustling about, helping customers. "I heard you turned down the town about the photo," he finally said.

"I did. I just . . . well, it's a busy time of year."

"Is that all? I wondered if it was because it was me. I know I didn't call after we . . ." He paused. Looked at her. "After we got pizza."

"No, you didn't. Which was fine. I think what happened was a bit unexpected for both of us."

Damn, she made it sound so bland. Like she hadn't been as turned on as he had. "I wasn't sure what to say. I thought you were probably pissed at me."

"Did I look mad?" she asked.

"I don't know. I left before you had a chance." He laughed a little, but the truth was she hadn't looked mad at all. She'd looked . . . glorious. Rumpled and dazed and two steps from going to bed with him.

"I'm not very good at talking about feelings. You might have gathered that from my past actions."

"I just assumed you figured it was a mistake."

He hesitated, then decided he should at least try to say what had been on his mind ever since leaving her house.

"I was pretty sure that if I opened my mouth, I'd ruin what had been a perfect moment. I have a habit of doing that."

God, had he just said the words "perfect moment"? Gah, wasn't he getting sappy?

Apparently, though, it had been the right thing to say because Laurel's rather severe expression mellowed. "I wasn't mad at you for kissing me," she said quietly. "Surprised, but not mad. Unless, of course, you had a pool going on at the station or something."

"Of course not!" he bristled at the insinuation, but then looked at her face. Her eyes were sparkling at him and her lips curved up at the corners, just a little bit.

"Touché," he muttered.

"I had other reasons for saying no to the photo, though the thought did cross my mind that it might be awkward as well."

"What kind of reasons?" He was curious now. "I mean, I'm not crazy about dressing up in a tux, but when Oaklee explained the idea of the rebrand to me, it made sense."

"I've got to get back, Aiden. It's crazy busy today, in case you haven't noticed."

"And you're avoiding the question."

"Maybe just a little," she admitted.

"So explain it to me later. Go to dinner with me."

Where the hell had that come from? He hadn't planned on asking her out—he'd just hoped she wouldn't rip his head off for being a jerk again. Now he wanted to make it up to her. This Dan guy had made her feel bad enough. It was time for Aiden to man up and simply ask for what he wanted. And what he wanted was to spend more time with her.

"Aiden. If we go to dinner, someone will see us. And if

people see us, they'll start talking and I am so not up to that. I don't want the gossip and I don't want the questions. And not because it's you, okay? I just don't."

She looked rather desperate at the idea.

"Have people been gossiping?"

She nodded, but looked away. "About me, about Dan, about seeing you helping me paint that night. Darling does have a tendency to be a bit claustrophobic."

He could see her point. All that well-intentioned neighborliness was almost an armchair sport. "Well, what about the Memorial Day picnic at my folks' place? We grill some steaks, have a few beers, take our lives in our hands with old-fashioned lawn darts and tackle Frisbee. No public appearances required."

"Dinner out versus a family get-together? Honestly, I'm not sure which is scarier."

"Don't be scared," he insisted. "It's really very low key. Plus you know everyone already. What time do you close on Monday?"

She hesitated, and he wondered if she was considering not telling the truth. Instead she admitted, "I'm actually closed all day. It's a holiday and I haven't had a day off in close to three months."

"Perfect. I'll come by your house to get you around three." When he sensed she was going to backtrack, he pushed on. "Don't even think of saying no. I'm going to show up at your door regardless. Look at it this way. On your day off you don't have to cook. You don't have to do anything. Just come and have a good time and let go of some of that weight on your shoulders."

"So it isn't a date?"

He hesitated. The truth was, he kept telling himself he

didn't want anything romantic with Laurel but then he continually found himself seeking her out and prolonging their time together. He liked her. And this chemistry thing . . . it knocked him for a loop but he couldn't very well ignore it, could he? He did want something. Maybe he always had.

"If you don't want it to be a date, it's not a date," he assured her, and wondered if he should cross his fingers behind his back.

"Okay, then," she agreed. "Because I don't think you're going to let me alone if I refuse."

"You know me so well."

They were smiling at each other when Jordan yelled across the lot. "Hey, Laurel, can you give me a hand for a sec?"

"I've gotta go," she said, and he was gratified that she actually looked a little disappointed.

"Thanks for the baskets."

She turned and got about five steps away before spinning back to face him. "Does this mean we're becoming friends, do you think?"

"There's a good chance," he replied.

She turned and walked away, into the greenhouse and the problem that awaited her.

Aiden hopped back into his truck and started the engine. There was a very good chance that they were friends. And if he had his way, more than friends. But slowly. There was no need to rush anything. They had all the time in the world. Neither of them was going anywhere.

He was whistling as he stopped at the main road and waited for a few cars to pass before pulling into traffic. Once he got the baskets back to the station, he'd have to call his mom and let her know he was bringing a friend to the party. Maybe he'd be on the "good child" list for once.

Laurel saw right away that Memorial Day at the Gallaghers' place was a big deal.

Swoops of red, white, and blue garland were draped over the deck railings, and paper flags stuck out of flowerpots, including the impatiens ones from the shop. Cars were already in the yard and as Laurel and Aiden drove in, two little boys came racing around the corner of the house with a man in hot pursuit.

Rory. She remembered because he was the only one in the family with dark hair instead of the coppery tones of the rest of the kids.

"You okay?" Aiden looked over at her.

"Sure, why not?" She smiled, but inside her stomach was churning. Friends, he'd said. And he'd done nothing to make it seem more than that. But it did. Driving into his family home for a picnic felt very much like a date.

It hadn't helped that she'd gone to the parade today, she mused, as Aiden parked the truck and sent her a reassuring smile. He'd been there in his uniform, his shoes spit-shined and his eyes shadowed by his cap as he'd walked the route next to his fellow officers. Why was she such a sucker for a man in uniform, anyway?

Except maybe it wasn't just any uniform. Or any man. Because she'd recognized his brother Ethan, too, as he'd marched as part of the fire department. There hadn't been any of that toe-curling, heart-racing reaction stuff then.

Damn.

She hopped out of the truck and shouldered her handbag. Well, she was here now, and she might as well make the best of it.

Aiden led the way straight to the backyard, and Laurel followed. The Gallaghers had a great spot: a cozy-looking colonial on a couple of acres, with rolling lawns and mature trees. She knew John Gallagher had built it himself; he was a local contractor and when she'd been in high school, he'd worked with a developer on the new subdivision on the north side of town. He'd made the family home big enough to house all of his kids—and there were six— and she was a bit in awe of the sprawling structure.

She was even more surprised when she turned the corner of the house and saw the backyard.

Interlocking blocks led from the deck to a fenced-in pool area. The pool had a solar cover on it now, but Laurel could just imagine the commotion in the summer when Ethan's little boys got splashing around and rushing down the slide. Next to the pool were two tables with umbrellas and chairs, perfect for enjoying a summer day. To take away the utilitarian look of the chain-link fence, Aiden's mom had planted hostas around the bottom.

The green grass was lush and full, and there was a volleyball net set up off to one side where the yard was perfectly level. Ethan and John were playing bocce ball in a rather large, open space, and Rory came zooming back, chasing Ethan's boys again.

So far Laurel was the only woman in attendance. She wasn't sure if that was a good or a bad thing. She felt rather conspicuous and out of place, but at the same time, the women in the family would be more likely to presume and speculate and ask potentially uncomfortable questions.

"Hey, bro," Rory called, lifting his hand as he ran by.

"It's monkey tag. Want to give me a break and chase these two around for a while?"

"Maybe later," Aiden answered, laughing.

"Hey, Laurel," Rory called back, and he was off again. Moments later there was a squeal, and then the silliest impression of a monkey she'd ever heard.

"You want something to drink? There'll be sodas and lemonade and coolers inside. If Hannah's here, there's a good chance there'll be margaritas."

"Um . . . you're not going to have anything?"

"I brought the truck."

"Right." And she remembered his zero tolerance policy. "If you wanted to, I could drive back to town. If you don't mind me driving your truck."

"It's up to you. You're the guest today. If you want to have a few wobbly pops, you should."

She laughed a little. Honestly, she was nervous enough that she wasn't sure adding alcohol to the mix was smart. She'd be apt to say something stupid or embarrassing. Besides, Aiden was here with his brothers. She imagined he'd like to kick back with a few beers.

"I'll drive," she decided. "Lemonade works for me."

A swooshing noise came from above and they both looked up. The sliding doors to the above patio had just opened and Aiden's mother came out onto the deck. She grinned down at them. "Were you going to come in and say hello?"

"Just getting to it," Aiden replied. He threw a smile at Laurel, as if to say, *here we go*, and led the way to the stairs.

Once inside, Laurel suddenly realized why she hadn't seen any of the Gallagher women in the yard. They were all in the huge kitchen, laughing and bustling their way around each other, dirtying dishes, dragging out ingredients, stirring things together. It was chaos, and Laurel was both shocked and amused. She tried to imagine this much bedlam in her mom's kitchen and simply couldn't. Everything at the Stones' place was always neat and orderly and the motto was "tidy as you go."

"Welcome to the circus, Laurel." That came from Hannah, who grinned and then pressed a button on the food processor, cutting out all hopes of a reply. Moira was shaking something onto a platter of burgers, and the two youngest daughters were cutting up vegetables and putting them on a platter.

"What would you like to drink?" Hannah turned from the processor and grinned. "I can make margaritas. Or there are some berry coolers in the fridge that the twins brought." From the sound of it, Hannah wasn't enamored of the coolers. "There's beer, and wine, and sodas, and lemonade."

"More selection than I get at Suds and Spuds." Laurel grinned. The town watering hole specialized in beer and over two dozen varieties of fries and chips. It also focused its resources on the food and not the ambiance.

Aiden chuckled. "Hey, at least the beer's cold and their chili fries are to die for." He looked at Hannah. "I'll have a Coke."

"Coming up. Laurel?"

"Maybe lemonade? It sounds delicious."

The pitcher that appeared proved to be full of pink lemonade. As Hannah poured, she said, "Not too sweet, not to sour, just too, ah . . . pink." She said it in exactly the same tone as Uncle Max in *The Sound of Music*, and Laurel burst out laughing.

"Oh my God. You just made a *Sound of Music* joke." It wasn't unheard of. The von Trapps were famous in this part of Vermont, particularly since Darling wasn't all that far from Stowe.

"I know. So lame. If I've heard one at the real estate office, I've heard them all," Hannah replied, pouring lemonade in a glass. "Bottoms up."

Aiden touched Laurel's elbow. "I'm going to go see if I can take on the bocce winner. You okay in here?"

"She's fine," Moira replied for her, shooing Aiden away. "Go on. We're going to put her to work."

Moira's announcement made Laurel feel far more comfortable. She didn't really want to be a guest, sitting around and being waited on. She looked over at Aiden's older sister, Hannah. She'd been through high school when Laurel had been a freshman. Now that they were older, they seemed closer in age.

"What are you making?" she asked, looking at the bowl of the processor.

"Homemade hummus to go with the vegetables."

One of the twins went past Hannah to get to the fridge and delivered a hip check on the way by. "Hannah's all health freaky. She's a runner."

The tone of voice was slightly mocking, and Hannah hip-checked right back. "Shut up, brat."

"What sort of running?" Laurel asked.

"I did my first marathon last year," Hannah admitted. "But I'm thinking of trying for a triathlon either this fall or in the spring."

"Wow." Laurel suddenly felt slightly soft and out of shape, which she hadn't before. She generally thought the physical labor of running the business kept her trim, but it seemed Hannah was hard core. Laurel looked at her differently now, and could see how her muscles were lean and defined.

"Here," Moira said, handing her a bunch of tomatoes on the vine. "You can chop these, if you like. I'm making a bruschetta dip."

Happy to have something to do, Laurel stood up to the counter and took the knife and cutting board that Moira offered. As she sliced and chopped, she asked Hannah about her training and eating habits.

"Do you go to The Purple Pig?" she asked. "Willow's stuff is all very natural and clean."

"I love it there!" Hannah beamed. My office is right at the end of the same building. Willow's great. Her bean salad is to die for."

Caitlyn and Claire made identical gagging noises.

"You two could use some bean salad," Hannah advised. "Rather than the pizza and hot dogs you keep stuffing yourselves with. It's going to catch up with you. Right in your ass."

Laurel laughed.

"So, you and Aiden," Caitlyn said. "When did that happen?"

"Oh, it's not like that," Laurel insisted, focusing on the tomatoes and hoping she wasn't blushing. "He came in to the store to get some baskets for the department, and invited me since I have the day off."

But Claire joined in, making Laurel glad she didn't have little sisters. "He said he helped you paint over the graffiti on your sign. But Rory said it was well past dark when he got home."

The sentence hung, heavy with suggestion. Laurel suppressed a sigh. "Oh," she said casually, "neither of us had eaten. Aiden grabbed a . . ." She looked up at Hannah and grinned. "A pizza. I suspect it went right to my ass."

That started Hannah on the topic of the evils of pizza

crust, salty meats, and too much cheese and how pizza should be the way real Italians made it, and Laurel was saved from the interrogation.

But not for long. As she scooped the tomatoes into a bowl, she caught a glimpse of Aiden in the backyard, helping Ethan's oldest toss a red bocce ball toward the white marker, their red heads close together.

When she looked back, Moira was watching her with a shrewd expression on her face. But she said nothing.

And Laurel knew she didn't have to. Chances were Moira had seen the longing that Laurel felt. And there was no sense protesting it.

CHAPTER 9

Aiden looked up at the deck as the sound of laughter echoed through the yard. The sliding door opened and closed again, and his sisters came outside with dessert. And Laurel was there, too, carrying plates in her hands, laughing at something the twins had said.

Lord, she was pretty.

He looked over at Hannah. There was no question that Hannah was gorgeous with her dramatic red hair and flawless skin. Even as her brother, he could appreciate the fact that Hannah had "it." Laurel wasn't like that. She wasn't flashy or attention-grabbing, but instead had that indefinable "girl next door" quality that reached in and grabbed a man in a subtler, but no less real, way. There was something in her quiet, easy smile that put people at ease. She'd put her hair up in some sort of clip this afternoon, and the style emphasized the long column of her neck. And she did have extraordinary eyes and a perfect mouth—not too wide, lips just the right fullness. He itched to touch her again as he watched her come down the deck steps, using care since she was holding the plates and forks. She was soft where a woman needed to be soft, and firm where she should be. His hands remembered.

"What's for dessert, Mom?" Rory called out.

"Strawberry shortcake," Moira replied. "And I made extra whipped cream because you're a pig."

Aiden laughed. He loved his family. They were nosy and annoying but also fun and loving.

They all settled around the patio tables once more. There'd been a break between the main meal and dessert. Mainly to make room for dessert, but they'd taken the opportunity to clean up, too. The guys had chipped in, carrying dirty plates and bowls inside and loading the dishwasher while his mom made her to-die-for biscuits for the shortcake. When he'd been washing up the bowl from potato salad, he'd looked out and watched Laurel, sipping a cup of coffee while sitting with his sisters and chatting.

He liked having her here. He just hoped that no one told her the thing they were all thinking. He hadn't brought a girl home for dinner since he'd broken it off with Erica. If they told her that, she'd surely go running for the hills.

The days were stretching longer and longer now. His father lit a fire in the fire pit to help keep the bugs away, and second helpings of shortcake were served to nearly everyone but Hannah, who was keeping to just berries with the smallest dollop of whipped cream. The little boys got tired and Ethan took them inside for a bath and bed, and then came back out with a cold beer and let out a sigh. Aiden knew he'd have a few drinks and stay here tonight rather than at his house. Holidays were hard for Ethan since his wife, Lisa, had died.

The girls got into their coolers, and even Hannah and Moira sparked up the margarita maker again. "You want something, Aiden?" John grabbed a beer from the cooler and popped the top.

"Naw, I'm going to drive Laurel home later. I'm good."

"I said I'd drive," she murmured. "If you want to."

He looked over at her. "I'm fine. Really." He wanted to be the one to drive her to her door, to drop her off and maybe kiss her good night. Maybe he was old-fashioned that way. Wouldn't his siblings get a kick out of that?

"You're all welcome to stay," Moira said. "We've got lots of room. You too, Laurel. I'm pretty sure we have a spare toothbrush somewhere."

"Oh, that's kind of you. But I have to open the store to-morrow morning."

"All work and no play, this one," Aiden teased.

"I took today off, didn't I?"

Their gazes met. "Yes, you did. Are you glad?"

She nodded. "I am. I've had a wonderful day." She smiled at the family in general. "I think Aiden's partly right. I've been working so much I almost forgot what it's like to kick back and have fun."

"You're welcome any time," Moira offered, looking meaningfully at Aiden.

"Thanks."

That was all Laurel said, and Aiden could tell she was a little embarrassed, so he decided to ask her a question. "Speaking of, do you want to go to the fireworks? They fire them off on the beach, and they don't start for another forty-five minutes."

"Um . . . I guess so. If you want to."

"Sure. Then I can drop you off after and you can still get a good night's sleep."

He tried not to cringe. That sounded almost scripted, didn't it? Was it so wrong that he wanted a little time alone with her? Maybe away from eyes that continually assessed and speculated? Not that it hadn't been a good day—it had. But he was ready for something more.

He really was. And the idea that the something more he wanted was with Laurel took him by surprise.

Everyone chatted for a few more minutes, but then Aiden checked his watch. "Are you ready? If we leave now, we can get a good spot for viewing."

"Oh, sure." She smiled up at him. "Let me get my purse. I think I left it inside."

She excused herself and disappeared into the house. Aiden gathered up some empties in an attempt to help tidy a bit, and took them up to the deck to the recycling can. Hannah followed him up the stairs, her empty glass and a couple of cooler bottles in her hands.

"Aiden, are you sure you know what you're doing?"

He held the lid of the can open for her and she put the bottles in. "I'm tidying up. Pretty sure I know what that's all about."

"Don't be obtuse. I mean with Laurel."

"Frankly, that's none of your business, Hannah." His voice hardened and his annoyance grew. The twins teased. Rory teased. Ethan generally silently approved or disapproved. But Hannah . . . she stuck her nose in. It was a well-meaning nose, but it went in just the same.

"Don't get all defensive, now. We all know you've dated over the past few years, but this is the first time you've brought anyone around. And it's Laurel. You guys have history. I remember you crushing so hard on her in high school."

"You know, I wish everyone would forget about that," he muttered, closing the lid.

"In this town? Not a chance." Hannah chuckled. "You

screwed that up big-time. No one's forgotten that it's the two of you in that photo, you know. So spending time with her now . . ."

"What? What real difference does it make?"

Hannah frowned. "She could hurt you again, Aiden. I mean, she just got divorced and her husband is *gay*." She hushed her voice, like the whole world would hear about the scandal. Aiden's temper started to flare.

"Ex-husband," he started to say, but he heard a sound come from behind him. He and Hannah both looked over and saw Laurel standing there, a false smile on her lips but a coolness in her eyes that wasn't there before.

"I'm ready," she said lightly. He'd heard that tone before, like fine lace over steel. He had no doubt that she'd heard Hannah's last words.

"Me, too," he said firmly, sending Hannah a glare. "Nice work," he muttered.

They went down the steps and paused at the bottom to say their good-byes. She was good and mad, Aiden figured, when her shorter legs outpaced him on the brief walk to the truck.

"Hold up," he called quietly, jogging to catch up with her, trying to take the keys out of his pocket at the same time.

He'd locked the doors. She tried the handle and then had to stand and wait while he hit the button to release the lock. "Sorry. Occupational hazard," he offered, and held her door while she hopped up into the cab.

The air inside was icy cold. And not from any air-conditioning. Laurel looked out the window and treated him to stony silence.

He waited until they had pulled away from the house

before speaking. "Hey," he said, trying a soothing tone. "I'm sorry for what Hannah said."

"Why?" Laurel spared him a glance. "I *am* newly divorced and Dan *is* gay. She didn't lie." She sighed. "You know what? It was awkward as ass in the office once the news broke, and I thought coming home would get me away from that. I guess running never solved anything, huh? Maybe I should have gone somewhere I didn't know anyone."

"That sounds lonely," Aiden offered.

She shrugged. "Better than always being reminded."

"I agree with you."

She looked at him funny.

"I do," he insisted. "It's no one's damned business. Is that the kind of thing you've had to listen to?"

"Yes."

"If he'd left you for another woman there'd be talk, too, you know."

"I know." She blew out a breath. "I'm sorry, Aiden. Sometimes I just feel like my life is a tabloid story. It's stupid."

"You ever try telling people to mind their own business?" He turned onto the main road, smiling as he turned the wheel.

"I have a business to run. Alienating potential customers isn't a great way to build goodwill."

He shrugged again. "Maybe they'll respect you more for it. Maybe they think you're hiding from it, and that adds to the mystery."

She laughed a little. "They won't think that much longer. Where are we going?"

He wasn't heading to the middle of town, where most

of the residents would watch the firework display. He looked over at her. "The golf course."

"The golf course."

"Yep. Apparently you get a perfect view from the seventh tee."

She rolled her eyes, making him want to laugh. "And you know this how?"

"Ethan. He told me a few years ago."

"Really."

"He took his wife here on July 4th one time. That was the night he proposed. But don't worry. I'm not planning anything like that. I just thought it might be nice for some privacy."

"Aiden, if I gave the wrong impression . . ."

"I thought you might not want to give the entire town the wrong impression," he interrupted her. And she was quiet for a few minutes, as he turned off the road and started down a slightly narrower lane.

The gate to the course was closed at night, and it was far enough off the road that most people didn't bother venturing through after dark. Aiden parked far over on the shoulder, grabbed an old blanket from the back and threw it over his arm. "You might want to get out my side," he cautioned. "You're pretty close to the ditch on the passenger side."

She took his advice and he held out his hand to help her down. She ignored it and hopped down herself, and he grinned a little. She wasn't easy, and she was independent and he liked those traits in her now, appreciated them more than he had when they were kids.

Stars began popping out through the indigo sky, little pinpoints of light appearing out of nowhere. It was a clear night, mild but without a lot of humidity, and cool enough Laurel was probably going to wish she'd brought a sweater. Quietly they walked the course, following the path past the clubhouse, the first and second tees, around the pond hazard, past the third tee, over a little stone bridge that had been constructed to mimic the Kissing Bridge. He didn't stop, though he considered it. They went past the fourth that led to a narrow fairway with trees on both sides, then the fifth that bordered the lake, around the backside of the hole to the sixth, and up a hill to the seventh.

Ethan had been right. The incline meant the lake glittered below them, the surface shining and shifting with moon and starlight. He paused and Laurel stopped beside him. The staging area was a good distance away, a mile or so by his guess. They couldn't hear anything that was happening, not even on the clear, crisp air. But he saw little figures of people moving about, saw a truck with four-way flashers on, and a firetruck back from the scene, lights flashing, monitoring the situation. On the opposite bank, a crowd was already gathering for front-row seats to the spectacle.

"See? Isn't this nicer than being in a crowd?"

"Hm." Laurel looked up at him. "I know I shouldn't exactly trust you, but yeah, this is nice."

He spread out the blanket and sat down, stretching out his legs. "Come on down. I won't bite. I'll be on my best behavior."

"Hah," she replied, but she sat down and drew her knees into her chest. She looked so young that way, so fresh and, well, sweet. He pondered that for a minute. Yes, Laurel had always been sweet. Not a pushover, but kind. Nice.

He liked nice girls. Problem was, they didn't often like him.

"Penny for your thoughts," she said, tilting her chin to the sky, looking up at the stars.

He snorted. "I was just thinking what a nice girl you are."

She burst out laughing. "Oh hell. With one sentence you managed to make me feel old *and* super-boring." With a sigh, she flopped back onto the blanket. "I guess I'll just go home after this and get out my knitting and sit in my rocker."

He laughed, too. "That's not what I meant. I just . . . I don't know."

Quiet settled around them. "There are a lot of stars out tonight," she said quietly.

"Mmm-hmm," he agreed.

For a few minutes, they didn't speak. For Aiden, it was a unique and pleasant moment in time where he didn't feel he had to make conversation. In the silence, he felt closer to Laurel than he'd felt to anyone in a long, long time.

He didn't want to be the first one to break the quiet. Instead, he waited, his breath shallow in the darkness, until they heard the first pop of the fireworks starting. A few seconds later the sky was filled with a cascade of blue and purple stars.

The show went on, and it was a good one by Darling standards. Multiple colors and types of cascading fireworks lit the sky, drowning out the twinkle of stars with something far more garish and impressive. "Which are your favorite?" he asked quietly, not looking away from the display. Not wanting to break the tenuous connection they had right now, tethered together by the pyrotechnics before them.

"Those ones. No, those." She pointed at the sky. "I don't know what they're called, but when they fall like that, all cascading and stuff, it's so pretty."

"Willow," he supplied. He knew because he'd helped in the past, and because Ethan usually worked one of the displays each year as part of the fire department. "The other one you pointed at is called the Chrysanthemum."

"And it does look like the flower. What's your favorite?" she asked in return.

"Kamuro. They'll have those soon, and I'll show you."

"How do you know this stuff?"

"From Ethan."

They paused to oooh and aaah at a particularly nice sequence. "So, what does Kamuro mean?"

He laughed. "Ethan told me it has something to do with some hairstyle or something. I don't know if it's true." There was a break in the display for squiggly bursts and horsetails, and then as the program moved to the last half, bigger, bolder bursts. "There," he said, pointing. There were three in a row: blue, then white, then red. They piled on top of each other before disintegrating as they fell. "That's the Kamuro."

"It's beautiful."

More silence, but there was something different now. The air had changed between them. There was a tension, a delicious little acknowledgement that there was something here, something pulling them together.

Her fingers crept along the blanket and tangled with his, and he closed his eyes briefly. *Sweet*, he thought, and the idea made his heart ache a little bit. He knew in school he'd played the jock. The goofball. No one saw this quieter, more serious side of him, and he found it frustrating sometimes.

And yet he knew it was his own fault. No one saw it because he didn't let them see it. He laughed things off. Acted as if he didn't have a care in the world.

The truth was he was hurt more easily than he'd ever let on. And growing up he'd never shown it. He hadn't wanted to be any trouble. A burden.

So he held her hand and said nothing more. They just watched the end of the show, the big finale with colors and loud bangs and screams that ended with cheering and clapping from the lake shores, the sound tinny and thin as it reached them up on the golf course and the seventh tee where they were utterly and completely alone.

Laurel closed her eyes as the pops and bangs faded away. She wanted to absorb this minute and hold on to it as long as she could. In the distance were cheers and clapping of appreciation, but up here, where they were surrounded by trees and manicured grass, there was just her, and Aiden, and the feel of her smaller hand tucked securely into his warm one.

"Laurel?"

She didn't know if it was the lack of background noise, or the darkness, or the fragility of the moment, but Aiden's voice sounded deeper and softer when he said her name. It sent ripples of awareness fluttering over her skin, and she shivered.

"Yes?"

"You're cold."

"I'm fine."

He shook his head. "Here." He sat up, then shimmied closer on the blanket so she could lean back into his arms. It was intimate and cozy and both scary and exciting, being in the circle of his arms. Even though he hadn't tried

a single thing that was sexual, he didn't have to. The proximity was plenty.

"Is that better?" he asked.

It was. His arms were strong and warm and she resisted
the urge to snuggle down even more. "It is, thanks."

"I was going to ask. . . . Before, when you said something like the town had no idea . . . what did you mean?"

She should have known that slip wouldn't escape his
notice. Aiden remembered everything. Maybe it was a by-
product of his occupation or maybe he was just sharp.
Either way, she knew she had to answer him. Because the
other trait she knew he possessed was the one that didn't
give up until he had answers.

"I don't suppose it's big news, now." She tried to down-
play the importance. "It's just that Dan's getting married."

"Oh." And then a few seconds later, "Ohhh."

"Yeah." She took a deep breath, let it out. It really did
feel lovely, being held like this. Maybe more than it had
when he'd been kissing her. "And I agreed to help with the
wedding."

She felt him shift, looked sideways and caught him staring at her. "You did?"

She shrugged. "He wanted help with plants and flowers and stuff for around the bridge. How could I say no? It
would make me seem so small and petty."

Aiden cursed softly. "Setting boundaries isn't being
small and petty. It's a big thing he's asked of you."

"I know."

"How do you feel about it?"

She shrugged again, realized she'd been doing that a lot
lately to avoid what had really been on her mind. "I'm
okay. I'm glad he's going to be happy."

Aiden was quiet for a moment and then he gave her

arms as squeeze as he tightened his embrace. "No," he said softly, "I didn't ask you for the office press response. I mean, how do you really feel about it?"

Her throat seemed to tighten all of a sudden. Leave it to Aiden to not be content with face value. Her parents had told her she was crazy, and Willow had been great, but they'd accepted her words as truth when really she was far more upset about it than she let on.

"I'm . . . I'm mad as hell," she admitted. The impact of her confession took the wind right out of her lungs and she gulped in some air. "Oh, I feel awful saying that. I shouldn't be mad. And I am happy for him, but God. There's 'let's stay friends' and then there's over-involvement, you know? And I think this is Dan's way of trying to apologize and maybe even make himself feel better because he hasn't left me out in the cold. Some days I just wish he would. Get on with his life and stop trying so hard."

"Why don't you tell him that?"

Good question. "I don't know. Maybe because he's a good guy underneath it all, and he's had to deal with a lot lately. Maybe after the wedding he'll just focus on his life and realize he doesn't have to be a part of mine. I don't need him to ease away gently."

It was true, she realized. It would have been easier if they'd just made a polite but clean break. This insistence on remaining friends was difficult. Even with Willow, she'd put a happy face on it. But tonight was the first time she'd ever come right out and said that she wished Dan would make a permanent exit from her life.

She lowered her voice. "Trouble is, Aiden, I think he has to be the one to do it. I meant it when I said he's been through a lot. I don't want to be one more person who craps all over him, you know? Not everyone's been supportive. I just want to move on."

Aiden chuckled a little, the sound warm as his chest vibrated against her ribs. "You didn't worry so much about my feelings way back when. Maybe Dan needs a milk-shake treatment."

Laurel knew she should laugh, but couldn't bring her-self to. "I am sorry about that. I truly am. We were young and stupid and . . . hot-headed." She sighed. "Our prob-lems back then were so huge at the time. Now I look back and wish I hadn't been so narrow-sighted."

"I hurt you. I get it. And embarrassed you. You picked the perfect response. I just wish I could have apologized better at the time."

"Hey, growing up is all about learning and growing. I'll let you off the hook, once and for all, and maybe you can forgive me for losing my temper." She sighed. "God, at seventeen we were all so dramatic."

He did laugh then, and more goose bumps erupted on her body.

"This feels like a real truce," he said. "Not just lip ser-vice."

"Maybe it is. Maybe I'm starting to realize that life is too short."

"Too short for what?"

"To hang on to stuff that doesn't make you happy." She decided something then. After the wedding she was going to talk to Dan. They could be civil, but this pretense of friendship was too much. Too awkward. And it was keep-ing her from moving forward with her life.

Just making the decision lifted a weight off her shoulders and she relaxed into Aiden's embrace. Despite Hannah's rather blunt observations, Laurel had had a really great day. This was a perfect way to end it, too. They were all alone, under the stars, listening to the wind in the maples and birches lining the golf course. A pale moon shone down on them, lighting some corners and casting shadows in others.

Awareness shimmered between them. Neither said anything, and Laurel didn't want to be the first to break the tenuous spell wrapping around them. Instead she offered the tiniest invitation: she moved her head, just the smallest bit, lifting her chin so that her temple rubbed against his jaw.

He moved his right hand, sliding it up along her arm in slow, grazing motions.

I'm interested, her nudge said.

I'll go slow, his fingers responded.

She leaned back more, so that her head rested against his broad shoulder, and in response his hand slid off her arm and over her ribs, then up to her breast; an easy, feather-light touch.

More, the open angle of her neck invited.

More, he agreed, cupping her breast in his hand.

Her breath caught in her chest as a dart of desire shot straight to her core. When she tried to inhale, her breath was shaky.

"Mmm," he murmured against her ear, and the warm vibration had her shuddering in his hands.

"Mmm," she agreed, and turned her head so that her lips touched the warm, taut skin of his neck. She kissed the hollow of his throat, felt his pulse there, tasted the slight saltiness of his skin.

"Laurel," he whispered.

"You wanted privacy, didn't you?" she asked, feeling rather bold. Glad he'd chosen the golf course instead of watching the fireworks with the throngs of people below. No one needed to know they were here. No one needed to speculate or ponder or comment. It was just her, and him, and this lovely soft blanket beneath them, and the scent of new grass and fresh earth.

He didn't answer her question, but he shifted his weight so that she was suddenly the one with her back closest to the blanket and he was above her, holding her with one strong arm. She lifted her hand and placed it on his chest, then deliberately reached back to remove her hair band and shake her hair free, tipping her head back in silent invitation.

He pressed his weight against her, cushioning her with his hand as he lay her down on the blanket. Then and only then did he kiss her, small, nibbling bites that fueled her desire and made her long for more. He kissed her lips and cheeks and eyelids and jaw, trailed his mouth over the sensitive hollow of her neck.

"Oh," she gasped, and she arched against him in response.

He rested on his side, his hip bearing most of his weight, and he captured her lips in a more consuming kiss this time, a dance of tongues and intentions while his hand resumed fondling her breast, rubbing his thumb over the hard tip. She twined her leg around his, holding him close against her body, giving her leverage as she pressed her pelvis against him.

"Laurel," he whispered in the darkness. "God, Laurel."

"Don't stop," she whispered back. "Touch me again, Aiden." She wanted this so much. Wanted the contact.

Wanted . . . oh God. Wanted to be with someone who really wanted her. She hadn't realized how much doubt she'd been left with after the divorce. "Touch me and tell me it's real."

"It's real." He pushed up her shirt, tugged at it until he got it over her head, and she was in her bra on the blanket. His gaze blazed into hers and she knew he had to be telling her the truth. Between that and the evidence pressed against her outer thigh, she knew he was right there with her in the turned-on department.

"It's so real." To her surprise, he reached behind his head and grabbed the neck of his shirt, pulling it off in one efficient movement.

He was magnificent. That night at her house it had been too quick, and all clothing had stayed on. And when he'd changed his shirt, he'd been over by his truck. This time though . . . Oh. His skin was pale and lightly freckled. Muscles rippled along his shoulders, down his arms, across his wide chest and tapered to lean, toned abs. "I want to touch you, too," she whispered, lifting her hand and running her fingers over the skin of his stomach.

His eyes slammed closed and he took a sharp breath. Encouraged, she let her hands trail over his chest, stopping to graze the tiny, hard nipples, running the backs of her fingers down his pecs and ribs to his abs. "You're hard. And soft. And awesome," she murmured.

He opened his eyes and met her gaze. Then he reached behind her back and undid the clasp of her bra with one hand.

He peeled the fabric back and Laurel felt the cool air on her breasts. It was a strangely erotic feeling, something she'd never felt before. Her sex life had been rather vanilla, without much of a sense of adventure. This felt risky, and different, and exciting. It was even better when he bent his head and laved his tongue over her nipple.

She couldn't help the reaction. She arched her back, pressing herself even more fully against his mouth.

It was suddenly just *more*. More frantic, more demanding, more everything. Laurel closed her eyes, shutting out the moon and stars and letting herself simply feel the glorious sensations of Aiden's mouth and hands. He made sounds of pleasure against her skin; she gasped for breath as arousal pounded through her veins. He slid his tongue up her body, leaving a wet trail that cooled in the evening breeze, before pressing his hot mouth to hers. And then he slid his hand down, down, cupping her through her shorts, then flicking open the button at her waist and slipping his hand inside. Inside her shorts. Inside her panties.

She was hot and ready, and she cried out a little when he hit his target.

This was where they'd been all those years ago when they'd been parking in his car and she'd begged him to stop. She'd been in leggings and a sweater and the windows were steamed up and his hand had been down her pants into territory she'd never been in before.

She wasn't that green girl any longer, and she had needs and wants and experience. Laurel stopped thinking and focused on simply feeling. And right now she felt wonderful and deliciously taut with growing arousal.

"Touch me," Aiden demanded, and she pressed her hand against the zipper of his jeans. It became very clear where they both wanted this evening to go. His hips jerked against her fingers as they fit around his form through the denim.

Breath, hot and labored. Gasping into the air, breathing against her skin, his tongue was hot, his fingers strong and talented. Sensations began to build deep in her abdomen.

"Hey! Hey you down there!"

A flashlight beam cut through the darkness.

CHAPTER 10

"Fuck." Aiden swore succinctly as they froze.

"Hey! This is private property!"

"Don't move," Aiden cautioned. "Hang on." He reached a few feet away for her shirt, slid it over her chest to at least cover her breasts from view.

"Hey, can you cut the light for a second?" Aiden called out into the darkness.

"Gallagher, is that you?"

Aiden repeated his earlier word. Three times. "Yeah. So how about some privacy, huh?"

The beam shifted to the left and Laurel heard laughter echoing through the air. Her cheeks flamed with embarrassment. "Did you . . . I mean, did you know? That there was security?"

"Of course not." Aiden reached for his shirt and pulled it on over his head. "Believe me, the last thing I wanted just now was to be interrupted."

He wasn't the only one. Her body still pulsed, longing for release.

"Block me so they can't see me, okay?" she asked, shifting on the blanket. Aiden moved, shielding her from view while she pulled on her shirt. "Hand me my bra?" She figured getting her shirt on first was the biggest priority. As quickly as she could, she fastened the clasp and pulled up the shoulder straps.

"Okay," she said. "I'm good now."

"Stay here. I'll handle this."

"Hey, Gallagher? You 'bout done?"

"Will you shut up, please? Just go. We'll leave, promise."

"Can't do that, buddy. Gotta make sure you're off the premises." Whoever it was sounded like they were enjoying things just a little too much.

Aiden sighed, looked back at Laurel. "They're gonna stick it to me, Laurel. I'm so sorry."

"It's fine." It wasn't, really. The whole purpose of being up here was privacy and she'd let herself go because she'd thought they were completely alone. Now she'd been caught, literally with her pants down, with the very guy everyone thought she hated.

"I'll try to get rid of them."

She watched him stride away. What had she been thinking? Only moments ago she'd been coming apart in his arms and now. . . . It was like hot and cold. Light and dark. Reality and unreality. She got up, adjusted her clothing, and started folding the blanket. After this, a quick exit was probably the best plan.

"Hey, Laurel," came the congenial shout, and she sighed. So much for going unrecognized. Or maybe Aiden had given up her name.

She sighed. "Hey," she called back, and the folding of the blanket got more precise.

"Come on, man. Give me a break." Laurel heard Aiden's voice plead with the other man, who she now understood by the shape of his cap was an officer and coworker.

"Dude, you parked your truck right next to the gate. And you know it's trespassing."

"It's the golf course, for God's sake. It's not like we were tearing it up on the greens or anything."

"Yes, but after the latest vandalism issues, cameras were installed."

Laurel was nearly to the group when the cop spoke the last line, and she blanched. "Cameras?" she asked weakly.

Aiden shook his head. "Not there. Right, Kyle?"

"No, not there. Just at the gates and clubhouse." Kyle's face softened a little when he looked over at Laurel. "Hey, I love to stick it to this guy, but don't worry, Miss Stone. There's nothing, uh . . . compromising. On camera."

"You're sure?" Aiden asked.

"That much security costs too much money. Don't worry. Entrances and exits only."

"Any chance you'll keep this from the guys?" Aiden asked.

"None. You can't bribe me, either. This kind of leverage doesn't come along every day."

Laurel's head began to ache. It had been an up and down day, but now it was too similar to their previous history. Guys and their belt notches, she thought angrily. This wasn't a joke. Or leverage. It was private. Maybe this wasn't the baseball team, but it seemed cops had their own brotherhood and code. Maybe boys didn't really grow up after all.

"Kyle," Aiden warned in a low voice.

Kyle looked over at Laurel. "You have to understand.

Straight and narrow Gallagher here just got caught in the act. But I can promise you this. I'll keep your name out of it, if you want."

Straight and narrow Gallagher? Since when? she wondered. "I'd definitely like my name kept out of it," she replied, holding the blanket close. She looked up at Aiden. "Can we go now, please?"

"Yeah, we can."

He put his hand under her elbow, but she shifted away from his touch.

"See ya, Kyle," Aiden called out.

"Keep it out of the wilderness, brother," Kyle called back. "And don't forget to do a tick check."

Laurel grimaced. Seriously, ticks? The idea of going home now and having to check her armpits and other . . . crevasses for the disgusting things was just the cherry on top today.

Kyle was right behind them as they walked to Aiden's truck and got inside. Laurel threw the blanket into the back and stayed to her side of the cab, so uncomfortable that she wished she could snap her fingers and be back at home again. It took several minutes to exit the long lane and then head into town, then to Laurel's street. Porch lights were on. One house had a line of cars parked along the curb, presumably a Memorial Day barbecue going long into the evening. Aiden hadn't said anything to her the whole drive home.

He parked in her driveway and killed the engine.

"I'm really sorry how things ended," he said quietly.

"Remind you of anything?" She couldn't resist.

"I thought we called a truce."

"We did," she admitted. "But oh my God, Aiden. We got busted making out on the golf course. Do you know how humiliating that is?"

She looked over at him. The dashboard lights were off, and his face was only illuminated by the circle of the carriage lights on the front of the garage. His jaw was tight, and his nostrils flared. He wasn't just sorry. He was angry. At her? What had she done?

"Which part exactly was humiliating? Getting caught? Or the fact that you were with me?"

She opened her mouth and then shut it again. She really didn't know how to answer. "Maybe both," she finally replied, her voice tight. "It's bad enough to get caught like a couple of horny teenagers, but worse when it's the same horny teenager you got caught with the last time." She put her hand out to touch his arm and then pulled back. "Even if we call a truce, other people remember."

"I guess you'd say no if I asked you out to dinner, then," he commented. The words were casually spoken, but he stared straight out the windshield.

"To . . . dinner?"

"Yeah. Like on a real date. But if you don't want to be seen with me . . . that finishes that."

She realized how very much she'd goofed. "Aiden, I didn't mean . . ."

But he cut her off. "No, no, it's fine. It's no less than I expected, really."

"Don't do that. Oh, I've messed this up because I'm upset and embarrassed. I wish I didn't care so much what people think."

"But you do. Because you're tying yourself up in knots trying to figure out how to keep tonight's details quiet."

"Because I was caught nearly naked on a blanket in public! Not because I was with you, you idiot!"

There was a stunned pause, and she was glad she'd

blurted it out. Aiden had been on her mind far too much lately.

"Is that the truth?" he demanded.

Was it? Did she really not care if it was Aiden? It was surprising to realize that she was telling the truth. "If I really didn't want anyone to see us together, why would I have gone to your family's thing today? Rory and Ethan won't say much, but Hannah will. And the twins . . . they might or might not. But I knew that when I said yes." She put her hand to her head. "Lord, Aiden. There's a huge difference between showing up with someone at a picnic and being sprawled out on a blanket on the seventh tee."

He chuckled then, and his shoulders relaxed. "Good," he said. "Good. Because I like you, Laurel."

"I could tell." And she smiled a little bit.

"Dinner, then? Where we may or may not be in public?"

She nodded. "Dinner I can do, but we'll have to find a night where you're off and I can take some time off from the garden center."

"Leave that to me," he said.

"And Aiden?"

"Yeah?"

She turned on the seat so she was facing him. "Despite appearances to the contrary, I'm a slow mover. I'm not ready for . . . for something too heavy. Know what I'm saying? I just don't want you to get expectations and then get frustrated and stuff."

"Why, Miss Stone. How very romantic of you." He raised an eyebrow. "Okay, so let me know if I've got this straight. No moving too fast." He ticked off a finger. "No to PDAs." He ticked off another finger. "Any other rules I should be aware of?"

"I'll let you know if I think of any. Oh! No shellfish. I can't stand it."

"Noted. Now I have one question."

"Okay."

"Can I kiss you good night?"

She met his gaze. He was earnest, and on the verge of smiling though his lips weren't quite curved up in what she could call a smile. "You actually want to kiss me after what happened? The world's biggest cock block?"

He did laugh then. "Technically, I'm thinking being caught by your mother would be the world's biggest, but it was a good one, wasn't it? And yes, I want to kiss you. I'd rather end tonight on a high note. If it doesn't violate your PDA rule."

She looked around. The lights in the truck were off, and she didn't see anyone around. "I think we're safe. Even Mrs. Ford's lights are off." She grinned. "One good-night kiss. That's all."

"That's enough," he replied, and he leaned over to kiss her, softly, sweetly.

He pulled back first, and then hopped out of the truck to jog around and open her door.

He left her at her door and went back to the truck, lifted a hand to wave at her as he backed out the driveway.

She stood there watching him leave and touched her fingers to her lips. Aiden was wrong. It wasn't enough.

And she was starting to think it would never be enough. Not with him.

"Excuse me, Miss. I'd like to buy two of your geranium planters."

Laurel spun around and grinned as Willow stood before her, hands on hips, a teasing smile on her lips. She must have had her hair done recently, because the pink and purple streaks seemed more vivid today. "Of course, ma'am," she replied, smiling back. "Just let me get those for you and ring you up at the register."

"Where've you been?" Willow asked. "Since the night we had dinner I haven't seen you at all. You wouldn't be avoiding me, would you?"

Laurel knew the truth was "sort of," but she wasn't about to admit it. She'd been worried that she'd be tempted to tell Willow about Memorial Day and she was keeping that information close to her chest. She wasn't quite sure why, except that things were still tenuous between her and Aiden. Better to keep things quiet for now.

"I've just been busy. Crazy time of year, you know. It'll settle down soon, once people have finished their spring plantings and stuff. Plus it's prom and wedding season."

"You're not a florist, Laurel. Prom and wedding can't be that big for you."

"You'd be surprised at some of the requests I get. Some people seem to think I'm a landscaper, too." She leaned closer to her friend as she hefted a square planter. "One woman came in asking if I could install an arch with climbing roses for a June wedding. I assured her I could, but the roses wouldn't have climbed all that far in two weeks." She shook her head as if to say, *some people*.

"Backyard events are getting to be a bigger thing," Willow said. "I get catering requests, too. Enough that I seriously consider opening a catering side. But with the café taking up so much of my time . . ."

"I know. Heck, the sheer number of graduation parties and baby or bridal showers . . . I don't ever remember things being such a big deal when we graduated, do you?"

Willow's face fell, and Laurel wished she could take back the words. She'd forgotten how Willow's home life had been different from her own. There'd never been a grad party or prom pictures.

"It's like people have a 'my backyard is prettier than your backyard' contest or something," Willow agreed, and the look disappeared, replaced by her normal, cheerful self again.

"That's sixty-two-fifty," Laurel said. "Anything else you need?"

"Not right now. My thyme isn't looking great, though. I might need a few next week if I can't nurse them along." She handed over a credit card. "And I thought those were forty dollars apiece."

Laurel smiled. "I gave you the best-friend discount."

"You're not going to make a lot of money if you give everyone discounts."

"I'll get by. Besides, you give me coffee for free."

Willow shrugged. "So. Any plans for, I don't know, tonight or anything?"

Laurel shook her head. "I'm planning on leaving at six and letting the staff close. It'll give me a chance to do some laundry and maybe vacuum the floors."

"You're sure? Nothing on the docket?"

"Why? Do you know something I don't?" Laurel stared at Willow, slightly confused. Did she suspect that Laurel had hung out with Aiden on the long weekend? Were people talking? She wasn't about to ask, even though it was driving her a bit crazy.

"No, no reason. Can you carry one of these to my car?"

"Of course."

She was putting one of the planters on the floor of the

backseat when Willow piped up, "Did you hear that the elementary school got vandalized last night?"

"Again? I mean, not the school, but what is it with this stuff?"

"It wasn't just spray paint this time. They broke over a dozen windows, too, and lit a fire in the dumpster."

"I wish they'd figure out who was doing it," Laurel said. "I sure don't want to get hit again. And it's costing a lot of money to fix the damages."

"Well, make sure you lock up. A lot of business owners on Main Street are talking about chipping in on corner cameras so we can keep an eye on our businesses. We took it to Brent, but the Mayor's Office says there's no room in the budget for it this year. If we do it, it's on us."

Laurel shut the back door of the car. "Watch the turns so the pots don't tip over, okay? We'll have to catch up soon. Maybe I'll sneak in to the Pig for a bite later. I miss you."

"When's the big wedding?"

Laurel sighed. "Just under three weeks. Actually, maybe you can help me out. You've always been artistic, and I can't quite decide how I want the layout around the bridge to go, and I need to make sure I pick things that will suit their backyard, too."

"I'll help you on one condition," Willow said. "You come to my place some morning and do a yoga practice with me before work. You're tense and stressed, sweetie. You need to stretch and breathe and let some of that go."

Laurel was afraid of what a yoga session with Willow would entail. She wasn't really keen about turning herself into a pretzel, but she figured it was a good idea anyway. "Deal. I'll call you and pick a morning when I don't have a delivery coming in."

"Perfect. Have a good day, okay?" The little smile was back, and Laurel felt once again like perhaps Willow knew something she didn't. But that was silly, so she gave her friend a quick hug and sent her on her way.

It turned out it wasn't so silly after all.

CHAPTER 11

At five minutes to six, Laurel looked up from the schedule and saw Aiden's truck pulling into the yard. Her stomach did a quick flutter, which she knew she should ignore but secretly enjoyed. She honestly couldn't remember the last time she'd felt the delicious sort of anticipation she was feeling right now, just from the mere appearance of someone. The fluttering intensified as he hopped out of his truck.

"Someone to see you?" Jordan asked, a knowing tone in her voice. Laurel looked over. The college student was barely twenty and her pretty eyes twinkled at Laurel. "He's pretty hot, you know."

"Shhh," Laurel said, her face heating. "He'll hear you."

Jordan laughed. "Like he doesn't already know it. Dude's got swagger."

He did indeed. As he got closer, Laurel knew he'd just showered because his hair was a few shades darker than normal. He wore clean jeans and a button-down shirt in a deep blue, which she knew would bring out the gray in his eyes. Their gazes caught and he smiled, a little sideways grin that she knew was just for her.

I am in so much trouble, she thought. The fluttering was infused with a little bit of panic. *I'm not ready for this.*

"Did I manage to get you at quitting time?" he asked.

"Hmm. Just. What a coincidence." She raised an eyebrow.

"Isn't it? Hello, Jordan. Mind if I steal your boss away?"

"She's all yours." Jordan smiled sweetly. "Don't worry, Laurel. Tim and I will lock up."

She was being ganged up on and she should mind, but somehow she didn't. Even so, she couldn't resist adding, "We're getting low on Bone Meal and some of the fertilizers. If you could stock before you go home and add anything we need to the reorder list, that'd be great."

"No problem."

Laurel looked up at Aiden. "Say, you didn't see Willow today, did you?"

He made a silly face, as if he had to really think about the answer. "You know, I might have."

"I'm sure." Laurel resisted a smile and reached under the counter for her handbag. "All right. What's up?"

"I'm here to collect on that dinner you promised me."

Oh Lord. She was in jeans and a golf shirt that she was sure must have a smudge of dirt on it somewhere. Her very basic "presentable for work" makeup had probably long since worn off, and her hair was shoved in that blunt ponytail she usually wore, topped with a ball cap. "Aiden, I can't go to dinner. Not without going home and showering and . . . I wish you had asked me and we could have planned something."

"Not everything needs to be planned." He was walking

toward his truck and she was following like a silly lamb. "Besides, you're fine just the way you are."

Either he was incredibly blind, or he was planning on taking her out of Darling and through the nearest McDonald's drive-thru.

"I'm gross."

He laughed. "Not for what I have planned. Come on. I'll bring you back for your car later."

They drove out of Darling and to the highway. "Hey," she said, frowning a little. "Where the heck are we going? Seriously, Aiden, I'm not dressed for going anywhere."

He grinned and just kept on driving. "We're getting out of Darling. This way there's no gossip, no speculation, no well-meaning people stopping by our table to make small talk. There's just us."

The last time it was just them, they'd been caught making out on the golf course. Laurel wasn't sure she trusted his version of "just us."

"Unless it's fast food . . ." She looked down at her jeans. Sure enough, there was a dirty spot on her knee where she must have knelt down earlier. She brushed at it with her hand.

Aiden spared her a glance. "I promise it's not fast food and I promise you're not underdressed. Trust me, Laurel."

Trust him. She knew he meant about dinner but for some reason it felt deeper than that. Trust him . . . to do what? He was a good guy. She knew that now, and it hadn't taken her that long to figure it out. But trust was a tricky thing. It wasn't just about the other person; it was about her and far more complicated.

She let out a breath and tried to relax as the minutes went by. Even when she realized they were close to Burlington, she still didn't know their final destination. But when Aiden turned the truck on to Queen City Park Road, she knew, and a smile spread across her face.

"The park. We're going to the park."

He nodded. "I thought about the waterfront in Darling, but again . . . no privacy. And then I thought of coming here. There's no parking inside the gates for another few weeks, but I don't mind walking in if you don't."

"Of course not. I haven't been here in ages. I always thought it was the perfect place to walk a dog and just forget that I lived in a city."

He slowed as they neared the entrance gates. Other cars were parked along the side, and he pulled in behind a small SUV.

"So what happened to the dog?"

"What?"

"You said it was the perfect place to walk the dog. Did it become a casualty of the divorce?"

She shook her head and then sighed. "I said 'a' dog, not 'the.' We didn't have a dog. Dan's allergic. But I thought it would be nice just the same."

"Why don't you get one now?" he asked, shutting off the engine.

"With my hours? It'd hardly be fair to leave a dog at home for twelve or more hours a day. I've thought about a cat, but I'm thinking I'll wait until later in the fall, when the business has slowed a bit and I have more time."

"That makes sense."

"How about you? Any dogs? Cats? Hamsters?"

He laughed and got out of the truck. She hopped out, too, and brushed her hands down her jeans. It was only six thirty, and the sun was still warm and lazy. "It rotates at our place. With Rory working at the clinic downstairs, the apartment is generally pet-free. Unless he has one that needs watching through the night. Last night it was a pair of sick puppies in a basket in his room. How he sleeps through all those puppy noises beats me."

Aiden reached behind his seat and took out a pack. "Hope you don't mind dinner to go."

A picnic. He'd packed a picnic. She couldn't help it, she was charmed. She couldn't imagine a better date than a picnic, particularly one in a park like Red Rocks. It was big enough that there was privacy and peace and quiet; Lake Champlain was right here and there were walking trails throughout. If she remembered right, one path led straight from the parking area down to a picnic spot.

"It depends," she said, teasing a little. "Did you do the cooking?"

He chuckled. "No way. I'll confess, I did see Willow today. This morning, actually. I sent her on a little recon mission."

"And she helped you. That Judas."

"She's only a Judas if you have regrets. Do you?"

She looked over at him as they walked. "No. I know I'm outside a lot of the day, but it's still a limited environment. Getting out like this is perfect. And if she's responsible for what's in your pack, that's even better."

He nodded. "She even loaned me the bag. You should see this thing. It's totally tricked out."

She laughed. And as they walked down the path toward the lake, he reached over and took her hand. She let him. It felt good, her hand inside his. It felt right, and exciting. She'd always thought that when she got to be a certain age—she was on the downhill slide to thirty now—she'd be beyond those sorts of breathless moments from something as simple as holding hands. She wasn't and it felt amazing.

As her fingers twined with his, she had the urge to stop right there in the middle of the path and kiss him. To be with him, to make that statement of togetherness. Goodness knows she felt it on the inside; that sense of belonging and accepting of each other. It was fear that held her back. Fear of seeming foolish, of making more of their relationship than it was, of moving way too fast emotionally than she was ready for.

"You're quiet," he observed, squeezing her fingers.

"I'm just thinking. This is really nice, Aiden. The grass and the trees and the lake, and I swear I let out a big breath and my stress just melts away."

"That's the general idea." They reached the picnic spot and picked a table. There were other people around, but no one else at the picnic area at the moment, and Aiden slid the pack off his shoulders. She noticed now that two straps along the front held a blanket. He unbuckled the fastenings and shook it out, then put it on the table as a tablecloth. "Unless you prefer the ground," he said.

"The table's fine." Her stomach rumbled at the idea of food. "So what have you got in there, anyway?"

"I thought you'd never ask."

He started unpacking. There was a bottle of something sparkly and lemon-looking, as well as two plastic stem glasses. Plates, knives, forks, and napkins came out of little compartments in the front section of the pack. The food was in the main part, and Willow, being the person that she was, had packed everything in reusable containers.

There were pita triangles, fresh hummus, herbed cheese, a dish of Willow's famous bean salad, another dish of a salad that appeared to be made of tomatoes, cucumbers, and roasted corn, and a last one containing sliced turkey breast. Aiden put it down with the others. "Willow made a point of letting me know this is free range turkey and that the herbs are from her own garden."

"She's something, isn't she?"

"I wanted something nicer than takeout from the Sugarbush."

"It's gorgeous. And I'm starving. What's in the bottle?"

"Lemon Italian soda."

"God, that sounds good."

They sat on opposite sides of the table and dug in, helping themselves to portions of Willow's delectable cooking. While they ate, they chatted about work and little happenings around town. Nothing heavy, nothing serious. A couple of joggers passed by on the path; an older couple walked by with their two spaniels who seemed particularly interested in a chattering squirrel in a nearby tree. The soda was slightly sweet and tart, and once Laurel's plate was empty, she rested her elbows on the table and relaxed. "That was so good."

"I slaved all day," Aiden joked, and they laughed. "Seriously, though, there's dessert. Do you want it now or save it for later?"

"We could always go for a walk first. Maybe stop and get a coffee or something on the way back to Darling and have it then."

"Sounds good to me."

They packed up the picnic together, and Laurel folded the cloth while Aiden zipped up the compartments. The sun was still well in the sky but the air had cooled a bit, and they walked the pedestrian path down toward the lake.

It was a popular spot, though the size of the park lent a certain privacy as they only occasionally met other walkers, many with dogs on-leash. The early summer weather meant the trees were in full leaf, creating a sibilant canopy above their heads as they strolled. On their left, the lake glittered, gray-blue and immense.

"I always find it crazy how many people still jump from the cliffs into the lake," Laurel said. "I'm scared of heights, so that wouldn't be me anyway, but so many people have been hurt. You just don't know what's down there, under the water."

Aiden thought for a minute. "You know," he replied, "I think there's something about the unknown, about the risk, that lures people. Especially younger people who think they're invincible."

"Like you were?"

"Maybe." He smiled over at her. "I first thought about being a cop because it seemed exciting to me. If I'd only known . . ." He laughed. "Most days my job is boring as dirt. But I have to always be on my guard because it's also unpredictable."

"Traffic stops and loitering?"

"Don't forget shoplifting. And graffiti."

"I guess in all the latest with the vandalism, I kind of forgot that Darling isn't really a place for violent crime, is it?"

"Occasionally, but not often. It has the same problems as anywhere else. Mom thinks I'm itching to go be a city detective or something, but I'm not. I just want to make a difference. Writing a ticket for illegal parking or telling some kid to stop skateboarding on private property . . . sometimes it feels futile."

Laurel looked over at him for a long time. Where was the cocky, self-absorbed boy she'd known? "You grew up into a good man, Aiden."

"I don't know about that."

"I do. I mean, I actually *wanted* to hate you. And I don't."

"I'm really glad to hear that."

Their steps shuffled over the path as they slowed to an ambling pace. "So," she asked, "tell me how you want to make a difference."

He didn't even pause. "You know the vagrant in town? George?"

"Yeah."

"I·try to help him when I can. He won't talk about himself, and I don't pry. Everyone has a right to their own story, you know? But I've taken him shopping for clothes at the goodwill. I'll buy him a meal now and again. Make sure he gets to the shelter for the night. I wish I could help him get his life back, but he doesn't seem really interested in that. So I just do what I can."

What a softie he was turning out to be. She could tell by the affection in his voice that he really had a tender spot for this George guy. "You are helping him. You look out for him. You can't make people do something they don't want to do."

"I know. It's just . . . when I get a call from one of the businesses, saying he's hanging around, I want to tell them to find some compassion, you know?"

She put her hand on his arm. "Know what? I think the number one thing a cop is supposed to do is be there to help people. Sometimes the smallest things have the biggest ripple effects. Don't sell yourself short, okay?" She slid her fingers off his arm, more words sitting on her tongue. She was too embarrassed to speak them, though. The truth was, hearing Aiden talk like this made her want to be a better person . . . and up until now she'd been pretty squared away with herself. But maybe she had a long way to go.

Maybe, just maybe, she'd been thinking about herself and her problems and her life a little too often.

She was still pondering it when a distinct cry came from above them, a loud, laughing call. Both of them looked up immediately. "There," Aiden said, pointing at a rather dead spruce tree about fifty yards away. "Halfway up. Look."

She squinted and searched for a few seconds, but then a motion caught her eye. A large bird hopped around the trunk of the tree, his scarlet crown announcing his presence. "That's the biggest woodpecker I've ever seen."

He laughed quietly. "It's a pileated woodpecker. I had one go over my head once and I thought I was being dive-bombed by an eagle or something. They're huge."

The woodpecker drummed at the tree, his beak pounding out a rhythm that was far deeper and more resonant than the usual woodpeckers she heard. "And beautiful. Oh wow."

She must have said it too loudly, because he launched himself off the tree and flew away, his wings making whooshing sounds.

"Shoot," she whispered, disappointed.

They walked on, looping through the park. They saw squirrels and chipmunks, a couple of chickadees darting from place to place, and at a small inlet they found a pool of ducks, diving and bobbing. Aiden pointed out toward more open water and she watched as a loon disappeared beneath the surface completely, coming up again several seconds later and several feet away from where he'd gone under. They stood for a long time and watched, Aiden behind her with his arms around her. His body kept her bare arms warm in the cooling evening, and when the loons sent up their plaintive, beautiful call, she let out a contented sigh.

She'd needed this. More than a picnic with his family or fireworks. She'd needed a walk in nature, a simple meal, and easy company. She'd needed him, she realized, and it scared her to death. She didn't want to need anyone. And yet how could something that felt so good for her be a bad thing?

"You want to head back now? I've got some sort of brownie thing in this pack that's in desperate need of a hot chocolate to go with it."

"I guess." She leaned into his embrace. "In a minute. This is so perfect." The waves lapped rhythmically on the shore.

"I always liked it here. We can stay as long as you like. I thought you might be getting cold. Or tired."

"Both," she admitted. "But a little longer. I like watching the ducks."

They stayed until the shadows lengthened and Laurel started to shiver in the cooling air. Then they turned away from the lake and walked the remainder of the trail back to the parking area, then out to the gates.

"So," he said, starting the truck. "Good time?"

"A very good time. Best date I've had in . . . well, I don't remember when. I haven't really dated since the divorce."

He grinned at her. "And here I thought I couldn't top Memorial Day."

"That was pretty good, except for the embarrassing ending." She raised one eyebrow. "Did you catch much grief about it at work?"

He nodded, then focused on making a U-turn. "A fair bit."

"Do they really think you're straight and narrow?"

"Don't you?"

"Not exactly. But I wouldn't want you to be too good. That's a bit boring."

"I can be bad when I want to be."

That swirl of attraction was happening again. His words, paired with the memory of the other night, added a tension to the atmosphere of the truck. "Don't I know it," she murmured.

He turned his face to her briefly. There was an intensity in his gaze that sent little flames of desire licking all over her. "You do realize," he said huskily, "that there's nothing I want to do more right now than pull the truck over and show you."

Her mouth went dry. "But you won't."

"No, I won't."

There was relief that rushed through her, but at the same time the tension remained. She wanted him. She longed for him, and he was over there and she was in her seat with her seatbelt on like a good girl, and why on earth did this drive seem to take so long?

"When I start something with you," he said, "I intend to finish it. Alone. Without interruptions."

Melt. Puddle. Right then and there.

"Aiden," she whispered. "Don't . . ."

The exit to Darling appeared on the right and he slowed, precisely to the speed limit posted on the sign for the ramp, so controlled. Until she looked at his hands, clenching the wheel. It wasn't just her. He was feeling the same urgency, and it only added to the fragile excitement. Fragile because this was all new . . .

"Rory's probably home at my place," he said, stopping at a stop sign.

"I don't have a roommate," she replied, breathless. The invitation was clear.

Were they going to do this? And what was "this"? She didn't want to think about it too much. Didn't want to analyze it or worry about it. She just wanted to focus on the moment. He looked over at her once more and it was like a jolt of electricity passed between them.

She remembered feeling like this once before, with him. They'd been in his car and it had been dark and they'd looked at each other in that moment before he first kissed her. She'd felt like she might burst out of her skin, wanting him to finally like her "that" way. And when they'd kissed, when he'd touched her, it hadn't mattered that they were seventeen. He'd been the first boy she'd let go that far. The first boy she'd wanted so much that she'd nearly thrown caution to the wind, caught up in the intensity of the moment.

They were grown-ups now. Smarter, hopefully wiser. As a high school senior, it had felt risky, daring. As an adult, it simply felt . . .

Inevitable.

Neither of them had said a word for the last few minutes. Aiden pulled up in front of her house and shut off the engine. There was no question of him dropping her off and driving away; he got out at the same time she did, and he grabbed the pack from the backseat before following her to the door, their footsteps beating a fast tattoo on the stones.

Her fingers trembled as she fumbled, trying to put the key in the lock.

"Relax," he said from behind her, his voice a sexy, low rumble that turned her on even further.

"My hands are shaking," she admitted, and he put his fingers over hers.

"We've got all night." He guided the key home and turned the lock.

Laurel could barely breathe as they stepped into her little foyer. The last time they'd stood here he'd pushed her against the wall and kissed her silly. This time, though, she turned around and he'd put down the pack. And instead of coming to her, he stood there and waited.

"Your call," he said. "You know what I want, Laurel. So come take what you want."

She was no good at this kind of thing; she didn't know what to do. As if he read her mind, Aiden spoke again in that hypnotic timbre that turned her all hot and liquid.

"Do what you feel like doing and stop overthinking. There's no wrong move, here." He paused, then added, "Just touch me."

Touch me.

She pushed off her shoes so that she was in her sock feet, and took the three steps necessary to be directly in front of him. And then she did what she really, really wanted to do. She reached for the button on his shirt, the one right at the hollow at his throat. She slipped it from the buttonhole and released the next one, and the next, and the next . . . until she pulled the tails out of his jeans and finished with all the buttons and his shirt gaped open.

Then she finally touched him.

His chest rose and fell quickly with a sharp intake of breath. Laurel ran her fingers down his pecs, over his taut abs, which he sucked in at her feathered touch. She pushed the light shirt off his shoulders and it dropped to the floor behind them, and she was sure that there was never a sexier picture than Aiden Gallagher standing shirtless and in jeans. He was taller than her by several inches, which put her lips just about even with his chest. She took advantage of the height, rubbing her lips over the warm skin, using her tongue to flick at the tiny nipple while her hands ran over his shoulders, touching, tasting.

"You're so hard," she murmured against his skin.

"You've got no idea," he replied hoarsely.

And because she was feeling brave, she slid one hand down to the zipper of his jeans, pressed it against his very obvious erection. "Oh, I think I do," she answered.

"Laurel."

"Yes?" She was licking his chest again, and his breath shook. She loved that she might actually have the power to shake his hold on his control.

"We didn't have dessert yet. And that's what *I'd* really like."

She lifted her head. "Dessert? Are you serious?"

"Very." His gaze burned into hers. He reached down into the pack and took out two containers. "Come to the kitchen with me."

She followed him, watching the rear view with new appreciation. His strong shoulders tapered down to a narrow waist and hips. The other night she hadn't been able to see the flex and form of his muscles, but she could now and marveled at them. The last thing she cared about was dessert, but she was afraid to speak up. Aiden seemed so much more sure of himself than she did. She could follow his lead.

He put one dish in the microwave and turned it on, then opened the other to reveal two perfectly square, chocolate brownies.

"Forks?"

Her body was still humming and he was asking for

forks? She went to a drawer and took out two. "Just one, I think. And a spoon," he amended.

The microwave dinged. He took out the dish and she realized it was fudge sauce. He poured half the bowl over the brownies. Then he dipped in his fork, cut a small corner, and offered it to her.

She tasted it. It was moist, sinful heaven.

"You got a bit of sauce right here," he said, and before she could react, he kissed the side of her mouth, licking away the chocolate at the corner.

This wasn't dessert, she realized with a shock. It was foreplay. It was . . . sweet seduction. And she had the sneaky suspicion she might just be in over her head.

He reached for her hand, guided it to the dish and swiped one of her fingers in the warm fudge. Then he moved her finger to his mouth, where he sucked it all off, rolling his tongue over her fingertip. Arousal slammed into her, tightening her muscles between her legs so completely that she ached.

"Aiden," she breathed.

"I'm really afraid that you'll get brownie all over your work shirt," he said, adopting a worried tone. "Here. Let me help." A moment later her cotton golf shirt was on the floor and she stood before him in her black lace bra.

"Mmm," he approved, pausing to pull her close for a thorough kiss. His hand molded her breast, the lace rubbing against her sensitive skin.

She broke away and cut a piece of the brownie, then put it between her teeth. Then she stood on tiptoe and put her hand on the back of his neck, pulling his head down to meet hers, giving him the bite of brownie and a hot swipe of her tongue.

"You're catching on."

Things got more heated after that. Kisses led to Aiden picking her up and sitting her on the table, so their hips were pressed against each other. Brownie bites were shared and drips of sauce licked away, until Aiden flicked the clasp on her bra and lay her back on the table. Laurel could hardly breathe as he trickled warm chocolate over her breasts and in the valley just below, between her ribs. At the first touch of his tongue on her breast, her hips jerked upward. Never, ever had her body been this turned on, needy, demanding. And Aiden didn't bother being delicate. He was very deliberate in his attentions, licking and sucking away the chocolate while Laurel tried not to moan with delight.

"You are a beautiful mess," he murmured. "Better than any dessert. Better than anything." He carelessly tossed the nearly empty container in the sink and came back to the table. She looked down. Her pale skin was streaked with little bits of chocolate, her nipples hard and pointed. She held out her hand and Aiden took it, pulling her up, and she wrapped her legs around him as their skin pressed together and they kissed, long, deeply, completely.

She wanted to take the lead. Wanted to be sexually confident in a way she'd never been before. When their bodies parted, they stuck a bit, sticky from the sauce, and she grinned, coming up with the perfect solution.

"Oh dear. I appear to have gotten you all sticky."

"I don't mind." He started to move in again, but she put a hand on his chest.

"Oh, but I do. And I really, really need a shower." When his face fell a bit she laughed. "I was thinking a shower for two. Unless you're not into that."

"Oh, I'm into it. If it's with you."

She loved that he'd added that last part. He didn't need

to know that her only carnal experience was with her ex. It would surely make her look naïve and, well, not very worldly. He seemed far more comfortable with the little games they were playing, but she wouldn't let the disparity of experience dampen her new sense of adventure.

"Oh, it's with me." They'd started something that they'd finish tonight. "It's all with me, if you want it."

"I want it," he confirmed. "I want all of you."

She took his hand and led him to the shower.

CHAPTER 12

Aiden stepped into the shower, aroused beyond reason and scared beyond measure. There were only two things he knew for sure tonight. He wanted Laurel more than he'd ever wanted a woman before. And the fact that he was going to have her scared him right to the soles of his size eleven feet.

She was in the shower already, completely naked, and his chest cramped as he caught his breath. God, she was beautiful. The hot water had already washed the streaks of chocolate off her breasts and diaphragm, and her skin looked warm and wet and perfect.

Laurel took some liquid soap between her hands, rubbed them together, and then smoothed her fingers over his chest and abs. But instead of scrubbing, she pressed herself against him and lifted her head for a kiss. It was no innocent, sweet thing. It was as hot and steamy as the spray they stood under, and the way her body moved against his lathered the soap.

"Mmm," she hummed, running her soapy hands over

his back, down over his butt. He pressed against her, throbbing with need, but she was taking her time. He loved it and hated it all at once. He didn't want to rush, but his body had other ideas.

Her hand slid down between them and his eyes nearly rolled back in his head. "Easy," he murmured. "I'm a bit of a hair trigger tonight."

She smiled against his mouth. Saucy wench.

But he let her take control because he sensed she needed it. Each time he'd kissed her before tonight, he'd had to make the move and she'd been totally reactive. But not tonight. She was right there with him, giving as good as she took, and it was incredibly arousing.

He lathered his hands and rubbed them all over her, trailing his fingers over sensitive spots, kissing her neck and collarbone. When the soap was gone, he did what he'd nearly done at the golf course. He slipped his hand between her legs where it was hot and wet; instead of resistance she surprised him by lifting her foot and putting it on the little seat in the back corner, giving him better access.

And the spray cascaded over them as her moans and cries echoed through the bathroom, her muscles contracting around his fingers.

Urgency took over and he shut off the shower, opened the door and grabbed the towels she'd hastily thrown on the floor. The drying job was cursory and incomplete at best, but Aiden was done with play. He lifted her in his arms and carried her out of the bathroom to the adjoining bedroom and laid her on the bed.

And for the first time, he thought about protection.

"Laurel . . . do you have . . . shit. I don't have a condom."

"I've been on the pill for years. It's okay."

He met her gaze. "Are you sure?"

"Don't you want to do this?" she asked, and her eyes looked uncertain for a moment.

"Look at me," he said. "Hell yes, I want to do this." He reached out and touched her, trailing his fingers from her collarbone to her core. "I want this more than anything. I'm dying for this. But . . ."

"But safety first." Her gaze softened, and he wasn't sure he was comfortable with what he saw there. It looked almost like . . . affection. Like . . .

No. Not love. That would be foolish. And definitely premature.

"I'm sure," she whispered. "Please, Aiden. Please."

There wasn't begging in her voice, but there was longing. Yearning. And he responded by slipping into her, surely, completely, deeply.

And then forgot about everything else but her.

Laurel woke before the alarm. A quick check told her it was only five-thirty. But then, she'd slept like the dead. The long day, plus the fresh air, the walk, and then the sexual workout had completely worn her out.

She rolled carefully to her side. Aiden was still there, his back to her, sleeping soundly. She heard his deep breathing and smiled as she looked at the light freckles on his back. God, that had been amazing. Had she really been stretched out on her table, had she really had an orgasm in the shower?

And all that was before the sex. The mind-numbing, crazy-cakes sex that had turned her world upside down. He'd taken care to be gentle, but in the end it had been wild and demanding and . . . dare she think it . . . damn near primal.

She blushed thinking about it. And wanted it again. Wanted to hear him grind out her name, feel the force of his body against hers. To possess and be possessed.

But it was daylight and they had thinking to do. Never mind the fact that he'd stayed the night and his truck was right outside. It was a small town. People knew vehicles. And a lot of people figured it was their duty to inform other people of the goings on of the neighbors.

So much for keeping this discreet.

She wasn't sure if he sensed she was awake or it was just his natural way of waking, but he lengthened and stretched. She watched the play of muscles in his back and shoulders, wanted to touch.

"Good morning," she said quietly.

He rolled over, rubbed his eyes, and smiled. "Good morning to you, too."

They were quiet for a minute, and it was slightly awkward. Then he smiled his cheeky smile. "Know what?"

"What?"

"We're naked under here."

Her lips twitched a little. "Know what else?"

"What?" They were both smiling now.

"Your truck's been parked outside all night."

His eyes shadowed. "Does that bother you?"

"Maybe a little. But I need to get over it. I should stop caring so much what other people think."

"That's easier said than done." He reached out and tucked a piece of hair behind her ear. "Do you want me to go before all the neighbors are up?"

Right now she was just loving the feel of his fingers along her temple. "Honestly? I don't know. I've . . . I've never been in this situation before."

His smile was slow and sweet. "I'm glad."

He ran his fingers over her shoulder and they lay there, simply looking at each other for several seconds. "What time do you have to be to work?" she asked.

"I'm off today."

She suddenly wished she was, too. Oh, to have the sublime luxury of spending a day in bed—with company. But she couldn't. It was Friday. A truck would be arriving before noon with a load of bedding plants, not to mention bags of mulch and soil that would need unloading with the forklift.

"I take it from your expression, you're not," he said, his fingers still stroking back and forth.

"Unfortunately not."

He slid his hand down her arm, then slipped it beneath the sheets, where he found her breast and fondled it lightly. She sighed, wondering where the new sexual appetite came from. Last night should have left her satisfied, but she wanted more. His hand moved downward and she opened for him, welcoming his touch.

"Jesus, Laurel. You're . . ."

She arched into his hand. "I'm what?"

"So much more than I expected."

"Aiden, I'm more than *I* expected." She smiled, feeling slightly smug and very turned on. "Lie back."

His eyes widened as she shifted her leg and straddled him. And then he closed his eyes and she drew a long breath from him as she started to move.

It ended up being after seven when Aiden finally left her house. He left the pack with her to return to Willow, and didn't waste any time getting in the truck and driving away. The less fuss, the better. Laurel was right about small towns. The guys at the station had been quiet about the golf course incident, but they probably wouldn't be forever. Especially if other talk started going around.

He didn't mind so much. People hooked up; so what? But he knew Laurel cared, and he didn't blame her. There was lots of gossip going around about her as it was.

Rory was up when he arrived home, stirring some scrambled eggs on the stove, dressed in sleep pants and no shirt. "Hey. Early morning or late night?"

Aiden threw his keys on the counter. "Maybe a little of both."

Rory grinned. "You want eggs?"

"I ate already."

"I just bet you did."

Rory's sideways grin was teasing and Aiden couldn't help but grin back. "Screw off, brother."

"What'd I do? I was home in my own bed like a good little boy. You're the one who stayed out all night." He dished the eggs onto a plate. "So Laurel, huh? Funny."

"Don't go spreading it around. Laurel likes her private life to be private."

"She probably made a mistake moving back to Darling, then." Rory frowned. "Hey, have you seen the raspberry jam?"

"Back of the fridge, second shelf, left-hand side." He'd put it there deliberately, just to get on Rory's nerves. Rory kept all the jam and spreads on the right-hand side, on the short shelf. It was one of the perks of being Rory's roommate. Someday he'd have to get over his neat-freak stuff. The way Aiden figured it, eventually Rory would stop dating here and there and actually settle down with someone. That girl would appreciate how much hard work Aiden had put in, trying to loosen his brother up a bit.

Rory grabbed the jam, two slices of toast from the

toaster, and sat down at the table. "So, are you in love with her or what?" He spread jam on his toast and looked up at Aiden.

Aiden poured himself a cup of coffee and sat down at the table. "Hell, I don't know. I like spending time with her. She's . . . easy." At Rory's mischievous expression, Aiden sighed. "Not like that, you idiot. She's just . . . low maintenance. Last night we went to Red Rocks for a picnic and a walk. Doesn't get more simple than that."

"And then back to her place."

"I didn't want the screaming to keep you up."

Rory balled up his napkin and threw it at Aiden, while both of them laughed. "Ew."

"You started it." He took a drink of coffee and grimaced. He wished his brother made better brew. He'd have to make a stop at the café later.

"So, what next?"

"I don't know. One day at a time, I think. She's cautious and rightly so."

Rory's teasing grin faded. "And what about you? Are you cautious?"

Aiden cradled his cup in his hands and stared down into the dark brew. "I wish I could say no, but I am. I mean, I try not to be. It shouldn't be a big deal . . ."

"But it is."

"Yeah."

"Because it's Laurel, and she means something."

"Now is not the time to get all wise, bro," Aiden warned.

Rory sat back in his chair. "Dude, I know being with Erica messed you up. You haven't had a serious girlfriend since."

"That's different. Erica wanted to get serious. She wanted to start talking about ring shopping and mortgages and . . ." He stopped, scowled. "Babies. I was barely twenty-one. All I could see were the walls closing in around me. I wasn't ready to be a husband and father."

"You didn't handle it the best."

"And I paid for it." He looked up at Rory and the crooked grin was back. "Anyway, no rush. It's new, you know? We can just enjoy that for a while. She's in no hurry and neither am I."

"Just be careful. I can tell she means a lot to you. You don't want to go screwing that up."

Rory pushed back from the table and took his plate to the dishwasher. Aiden remained at the table, staring into his bitter coffee. He wasn't exactly comfortable examining the level of his feelings for Laurel, but he reminded himself of what he'd just told his brother.

They were both cautious. No sense putting the cart before the horse. They could definitely take it one day at a time.

CHAPTER 13

Laurel took her lunch break and decided to pop into The Purple Pig for a coffee and to return the picnic pack. She'd washed everything and put it back precisely, and when she walked into the café, Willow's beaming face greeted her.

"So? How was it?"

Laurel felt a blush creep up her cheeks. "It was delicious. Particularly the brownies."

"Did you like the fudge sauce? It's definitely not low fat, but it's from all-natural ingredients."

Laurel coughed a little. "It was . . . scrumptious." Her face was so hot now she knew she had to be bright pink. She handed over the pack. "Thanks for the use of the bag. It's really neat."

"Oh, there's more to the story than that. Let's grab a drink."

Laurel accepted a mug of steaming coffee while Willow brewed herself a cup of mint tea. They sat in a back corner at an empty table.

"Laurel," Willow said, leaning forward and looking right into Laurel's eyes. "You've got morning-after glow."

"Hush." Laurel looked over her shoulder, hoping no one had heard. "We just went for a picnic, that's all."

Willow laughed. "Oh, I call bullshit."

Laurel kicked her under the table. "I mean it."

"Sweetheart, it's plain as the nose on your face that you're smitten with Aiden Gallagher. It was true ten years ago and it's true now. And this time I'm guessing he didn't take you out on a bet."

"Thanks for the summary and reminder." Laurel scowled. The coffee suddenly wasn't quite as appetizing. She had been sweet on him then. Really sweet. It was actually kind of embarrassing.

"He's smitten with you, too. You should have seen him yesterday, asking if I knew what time you were done work, what he should take on a picnic. It was adorbs."

This time Laurel rolled her eyes. "No one says 'adorbs.'"

Willow shrugged. "Tell that to the teenage girls who came in last night. They thought it was very cool to have all-natural, vegan, free trade, ecologically responsible food. So cool that they posted all sorts of pictures of it on their phones while wearing clothes that were probably produced in some Bangladesh sweatshop."

Willow's annoyance was so genuine that Laurel burst out laughing. "Well. Someone's spooled up this morning."

"Right. Back to you. Did he stay over?"

"What did you hear?" Laurel responded quickly, her eyes narrowing.

"Nothing. But that response told me all I needed to know. Good for you. It's about time, I say."

Laurel took a sip of her coffee. "Promise me you won't say a word to anyone. Promise, Wil."

"Of course I promise. I don't gossip. You see? I went straight to the source." Willow blew on her tea. "So . . . is this the real thing or just bumping uglies?"

"Oh my God! You really are full of it today."

"Just answer the question. Best-friend privilege."

"What if I say it's neither?" Laurel met Willow's gaze. "I really like him. I think he's a good guy and there's this crazy chemistry thing happening. He didn't even seem to mind that I had my hair in my ratty ponytail and dirt on my work shirt."

She recalled walking through the woods with him last night, simply chatting. "I like spending time with him, but it's too early to say anything more."

Willow smiled softly. "There, was that so difficult?" When Laurel would have answered her, Willow held up her hand. "Seriously, I just want you to be happy. Today you look happy, so whatever you're doing, hang on to it. You deserve it, sweetie. Don't let anyone tell you otherwise."

Laurel lowered her gaze, touched by Willow's little speech. She didn't know if Willow had guessed or was just saying the right things, but lots of times over the past few months, Laurel had wondered if she was the kind of person someone could really love. More often, she felt like the consolation prize. Funny how that term came to mind. Aiden had used it regarding her return and she'd denied it. She frowned. Why was that? Didn't she believe she deserved to be first in her own life?

"I'm not ready for serious," she admitted. "But I'll admit I'm open to . . . exploration." She couldn't help how her lips curved up as she said it. Maybe Willow was right. Maybe she did have morning-after glow. She certainly felt more relaxed.

"Oh, my giddy aunt." Willow's smile widened. "That's not a conversation for public, is it?"

"It really, really isn't," Laurel admitted, and laughed a little bit. "Wil, you have *no* idea."

"Good for you." Willow looked over toward the counter and Laurel followed her gaze. The shop was getting busy again, and she'd taken up enough of her friend's time.

"I'll let you get back to work. Thanks for the coffee and the help yesterday."

"Of course. And you still owe me a yoga day."

"Right."

Willow got up and dropped a little kiss on Laurel's cheek. "Be good," she whispered. "But not too good. You've got to be bad for the both of us."

Laurel choked on her laugh and watched as Willow walked away, her hips swaying gently. Willow stopped and re-tied her apron before stepping up to the counter and helping a customer.

Laurel leaned back and finished her coffee. Yes, she was feeling particularly blessed today. For the first time in months, she really got the feeling that Life Was Good.

She left The Purple Pig and turned right, toward where she'd parked her car. There, sitting on a bench not ten feet from her parking space was the man she knew must be George. She'd seen him around before and after listening to Aiden talk about him last night, she knew it had to be the same guy.

She did an about-face and went back into the café and ordered a sandwich. When she went back outside into the sun, she took a moment to pause and look around.

No one made eye contact with George. No one spoke. People adjusted their path to go behind the bench rather than in front of it. And yet Aiden had said he made a point of stopping. Speaking to him and offering help. And it wasn't because he was a police officer, she realized. It was because that was the kind of person he was.

"George?" she asked softly, approaching the bench.

He turned his head. He had a few days of beard growth on his face and a ratty ball cap on his head. Laurel ignored the dirt stains on his clothes and instead looked into his eyes. They looked tired . . . and wary.

"George, my name's Laurel. I'm a friend of Aiden Gallagher's."

When he didn't answer, she added, "The police officer."

"Hi," he said. And that was it.

It was an incredibly awkward moment, but Laurel pressed on. "I thought you might like a sandwich. My friend Willow has the café here. Her sandwiches are delicious. Are you hungry?"

He looked up at her again. "Okay."

She smiled, went closer, and perched on the edge of the bench, not wanting to overwhelm him. She handed over the paper-wrapped sandwich. "Here. It's turkey and cheese."

He took the sandwich from her hand, opened the paper. She watched as he took a few bites, then used the brown paper napkin to wipe his mouth.

It was a move that surprised her. Whatever the circumstances, he hadn't forgotten manners. And when she looked past his rough appearance, she realized that he was actually quite good looking. There was a tattoo on his right arm and he wore a simple black bracelet on his wrist. Where had he come from and why had he ended up on the streets?

He finished the sandwich, folded the paper neatly. "Thank you," he said quietly.

"George," she said, "what did you do before . . . before you came to Darling?"

His face closed off, shutting her out.

"Oh, well, I'm sorry I pried. Forget I asked." She tried a smile, remembering how Aiden had spoken of taking George to get clothing or getting him a meal. Maybe she would be able to get through to him a little better. Aiden had to be very big and officious looking in his uniform. She couldn't imagine that she was very intimidating. "I was wondering, are you interested in a job?"

His gaze met hers. "What kind of job?"

"I own the Ladybug Garden Center. It's really busy. I could use someone to come in for a few hours each day and do some general things around the place. Sweep the greenhouse floors, water the plants, that sort of thing."

She got the feeling he was interested, but didn't want her to know it. "Would I have to talk to people?"

Her heart melted a little bit. "Not really. If a customer were to come up to you, you could send them to one of the other staff. I know it's not much, but I'm willing to try it if you are."

"Why?" he asked.

"Why what?"

"Why are you asking me?" His words were slow, not from lack of intelligence, but from what she thought might be an awkward sort of caution. Her heart softened further.

"Because I want to help. I don't need to know your story, or any of your business. Aiden believes in you and that's enough for me."

Something lit in the other man's eyes. "He's a good guy," he said.

"I know. Are you interested? I can take you back to the garden center and show you around. I see you have good sneakers. You'll have to wear one of our golf shirts, of course. I should have some in your size in my office."

George turned away. "I don't know. You just feel sorry for me."

She put her hand on his arm. He startled, but she left it there, firm but gentle. "Yes, I do. That doesn't mean I shouldn't help. And believe me, there's work for you. You'll stay busy enough."

He looked back at her. "You're a nice lady, Miss . . ."

"Stone. Laurel Stone."

"Not . . . not this afternoon. But I could come by tomorrow morning."

Disappointment weighed on her. She knew what that meant. If he didn't go with her now, chances were he wouldn't show up at all. Not without someone prodding him. She'd tried. And maybe it wasn't her fault, or anyone's fault. Aiden had said that George was very private and single-minded.

"That would be fine," she replied, encouraging anyway. "I'm there at eight. We don't open until nine, so I could show you the ropes and stuff."

"Okay."

"Okay?"

He nodded. "Yuh."

She smiled. Maybe he meant it, maybe he didn't. At the very worst, he'd had something decent to eat today. All she could do was make the offer. The rest was up to him.

Laurel got up from the bench and held out her hand. "I'll see you tomorrow, then," she said, and waited.

Hesitantly, he reached out with his hand and shook hers. His hand was strong and rough, the knuckles scarred and a little dirt beneath his nails, but the connection felt good.

Right. She smiled at him and let go, gave him a brief nod. "Very good. Until tomorrow, George. Eight o'clock."

"Miss Stone?" She was half a dozen steps away when he called out to her.

She turned back briefly, wondering if he had another question. "Yes?"

"Thank you," he said.

"You're most welcome."

She went back to work, unsure of what the next day would bring but glad she'd stopped, glad she'd made the offer. It had just taken Aiden to make her see that she'd been entirely too focused on herself lately.

Laurel was at work by seven-thirty the next morning. Aiden had sent a quick text saying he'd been called into work but would she like to get together the next evening for dinner? She'd texted back yes, feeling those lovely little butterflies again. She took a duster and began cleaning the shelves of the small interior store, which had been neglected a bit during the last few crazy days.

She was really, really hoping that George showed up for work, and she also had wanted to be here in case he did.

Eight o'clock came and went and no George. Disappointed, she finished dusting and fronting the shelves and then went outside to uncoil the hose to start the watering. She'd start with the hanging baskets, then move on to the tables and tables of bedding plants and vegetable transplants and then trees and shrubs. The other staff would be in at nine. She really shouldn't have gotten her hopes up.

At eight-twenty she was watering the last row of hanging baskets when a voice called her name. "Miss Stone?"

She looked down from her perch.

It was George. At least, it had to be. He had the same blue eyes, the same cheekbones and chin. But there was such a difference from yesterday that she couldn't stop her mouth from dropping open a little.

"You made it." She smiled, determined to not make a big deal over his improved appearance. He'd had his hair cut, she realized. And he'd shaved. And had on clean, well-fitting clothes.

It was silly, she supposed, because she hardly knew him. But she felt so proud of him right now.

"I'm sorry I'm late. I misjudged how long it would take me to get here."

She looked behind him and felt a sudden jolt of embarrassment. Why had she not considered transportation to work? It had to be a good three miles from the shelter on the other side of town, and the town was too small for any transit service.

"Oh, that's okay." She smiled, shut off the hose and got down from the small step ladder. "I'll open the gate and show you around."

She was dying to ask him questions now but would not. Instead she showed him the greenhouses first, then the inside of the store, the storage room, and the shed. At each spot he was attentive, and appeared to be taking mental notes as he nodded or asked quiet questions. At eight-forty-five she handed over a red golf shirt in size large, shooed him to the bathroom to change, and then put him to work finishing the watering while she prepared the cashes to open.

When staff arrived, she simply introduced him as George and said that he'd be working a few hours, helping out with the greenhouse work.

By noon, everything was watered and swept and she'd

shown him how to properly dead head the blossoms on the various plants. Laurel paid him out of the till and asked him if he'd like a lift back into town. He declined, and she let it go. She understood that he probably wanted to remain as independent as possible. She wasn't even sure he'd be back the next morning, but she smiled and sent him off and said she'd see him tomorrow.

The next day he arrived at five minutes to eight, ready to work. A shipment of soil and mulch arrived, and to Laurel's delight, George offered to man the forklift and unloaded and moved it all in half the time that it would have taken her. He even smiled at Jordan once, and offered a shy hello to a few people before withdrawing back into his duties.

Four hours a day wasn't a lot of time and definitely not enough to make a huge financial difference, but Laurel rather hoped that it would be the start of something for him. Like her relationship with Aiden, she figured "one day at a time" was as good a motto as any.

On Sunday, Laurel locked up at four and rushed home to hit the shower. She hadn't seen Aiden since Friday morning, and she was nervous and excited. Would things be different between them now? Better? Awkward? He'd texted again to say to dress up a bit for dinner, so she could only assume that tonight's date wasn't going to be a picnic in the park.

She scoured her closet for something suitable. Gosh, she'd been in jeans and cotton shirts for so long now it felt strange to see her remaining old work clothes hanging up, unused. And they weren't right either. They were too . . . professional. Pressed and plain. She wanted something a little more relaxed. Something that . . .

She smiled to herself. Something that reflected the

person she was now. The real Laurel. After all, she was doing what she wanted, and living life on her own terms. There was no one influencing her as far as friends or clothes or what to eat . . . the freedom that had been incredibly lonely for weeks and months now felt a bit more like a gift.

In the end she chose a simple sheath-style ivory dress dotted with little pink flowers. Her hair was still a little damp, too damp to curl, so she pulled a bit back from each side of her face and tacked it in place with hidden bobby pins. A little makeup, a pair of ivory heels, and she was satisfied. She hoped Aiden would be, too. This was their first fancy date where plans were made in advance. There was something momentous about that.

He took her to the Foxborough Inn, a sprawling, massive colonial with white pillars and black shutters and which the locals simply referred to as "The Inn" because there was none other like it nearby. The Inn boasted twenty impeccably decorated rooms, all with antique furniture and rich fabrics, a stunning parlor decorated in wine-and-gold draperies and upholstery, and a dining room that seated around fifty.

And he'd worn a suit.

A suit.

She'd seen him in his uniform, so a suit shouldn't have seemed like such a stretch. But it was. Aiden had such a rough-and-ready look about him that to see him in a starchy white shirt, red striped tie, and navy trousers and jacket made him seem a bit like a sexy stranger. He'd opened her door for her when leaving her house, when they reached the inn, and then again when they went inside. She was very glad that she'd worn the dress, which suited the occasion perfectly. Their table wasn't quite ready, so the hostess led them to the parlor, where they were offered drinks while they waited.

Aiden asked for ginger ale. Laurel selected a Pinot Grigio and they sat on a tufted settee together to drink.

"Wow. When you said dress up, you meant it."

"Have you ever eaten here?" he asked, taking a drink of his soda.

"Not in years. We did once, for Mother's Day, I think. There was some special brunch on and Dad got reservations really early."

"We came for Dad's birthday last year. I thought this might be nicer than the other spots in town. For, you know. A real date."

She smiled at him, her heart doing a little flutter. "For what it's worth, I consider our picnic and walk a real date. But this is lovely, Aiden. Really special."

"Cheers to that," he replied, and they touched their glasses together.

She couldn't look away from him. Not when she lifted her glass to drink the smooth wine, not when the outside door opened and closed again. She was getting rather lost, she thought. But why not? Didn't she deserve a little bit of romance? A thought bubbled up and made her smile to herself. Wasn't it appropriate that it was Aiden giving it to her? Maybe he was a few years late, but he sure knew how to make up for past transgressions.

There'd be time enough later to let reality set in. Right now she was determined to enjoy the evening, and to let it be special and wonderful.

"Mr. Gallagher? Your table's ready, if you'll follow me."

The hostess led them into the dining room, and to a front corner which held a table for two and was next to a window overlooking a green expanse of lawn. It was still light out, but it was mellowing as evening approached, and the hostess lit a trio of little candles in the middle of their table. "Your waiter will be right with you," she said, handing them each a leather-bound menu. "Enjoy your evening."

Could it have been more perfect?

They began with appetizers: pancetta wrapped scallops for Aiden and an arugula salad for Laurel, which had an orangey-vinaigrette that was light and made the flavors pop. Just that much had felt extravagant, but then their main course came and Laurel hesitated. It looked like a work of art.

"Something wrong?" Aiden leaned forward.

"Oh, no, of course not. It's just . . . wow. It looks so good."

He laughed. "Hopefully it tastes as good as it looks."

He'd opted for the pork chop which had come with sweet potatoes and roasted Brussels sprouts, the colors contrasting on the white china. Her meal was just as delightfully presented, from the golden chicken breast to the polenta, roasted tomato, and kale.

Her first bite melted in her mouth.

"So it lives up to the hype?"

She blotted her mouth with her napkin. "Oh, more than." As she arranged the linen on her lap again, the waiter returned to refill Laurel's wineglass.

"Aiden, this is . . . goodness. I don't know what to say."

"It's good to treat yourself once in a while, I think." He sliced into his delicately done chop. "There's not much occasion around here. And I wanted to do this for you. You've been working incredibly hard."

It meant a lot that he realized it. "Owning my own business is a heck of a lot of work," she admitted. "It's not just the store. It's payroll and administration and advertising and the like. I'm good at those things. I've got an accounting degree. But it does make for long hours this time of year."

"Maybe you should hire more help."

The words sat on her tongue. She wanted to tell him about George so badly. But she wasn't sure it was her place to tell, and she didn't want Aiden to think she'd done it to, well, impress him. Maybe his mention of George had started the ball rolling, but Laurel was becoming genuinely fond of her new employee and wanted to respect his privacy. "I've definitely been considering it," she hedged, focusing on cutting into her tomato.

"That's good. All work and no play . . ."

She laughed a little and looked up at him from beneath her lashes.

"Look at you," he said softly. "Your eyes are sparkly and your cheeks are pink. What are you thinking?"

"I've had the better part of two glasses of wine," she answered. She really did have a crappy poker face.

"Wine," he parroted, raising one eyebrow.

"Well, that and the company I'm in." She held his gaze for a prolonged moment. "Oh listen, that reminds me. Can you come by the store tomorrow morning? I've put a few things aside for your mother and I thought perhaps you could run them out to her."

"My mother?"

"Just some tomato plants and a few peppers she mentioned wanting when I was over before. If you can't, it's no biggie. I can run them out after work."

"I work tomorrow afternoon, so it'll be between nine and ten, I suppose."

"That'd be great." She licked her lips, sudden nerves jumbling around in her stomach. "Or . . . oh, never mind. That wouldn't work." Her shoulders slumped a little.

"What wouldn't work?"

She didn't answer so he nudged his foot against her leg. "Laurel?"

"I was going to say . . . you could just go in the morning . . . with me. If you, uh, wanted to stay over."

The air between them seemed to crackle. All it had taken was the awkward invitation and the tension ramped up. "Stay with you."

"Yeah. It's okay if you would rather not. Especially if you have to work . . ." Damn, why had she asked him in the middle of the restaurant? The table next to them was empty, but the dining room certainly wasn't.

"Oh, I want to," he answered, and his voice was low and enticing. "I just didn't think you'd ask."

"I never thought about your suit, though," she said, disappointed. Picking up garden items in an expensive suit was silly.

Not to mention the Walk of Shame he'd be doing in the morning. Now that idea made her perk up a bit. That cliché was usually reserved for women in heels and little black dresses with last night's hairdo askew.

A rumpled Aiden in a wrinkled suit was much more alluring.

"Remember the night we painted? What did I tell you?"

She thought back, but couldn't quite remember.

"I always keep a change of clothes in the truck," he reminded her.

Right. Her face heated. This meant that when dinner was over, the night wasn't.

"Laurel?"

The waiter picked that exact moment to return. "Is everything okay here? Will you be wanting to see a dessert menu this evening?"

No! Laurel wanted to scream. What she wanted—quite irrationally—was to pay the bill and get out of there right now. To drive back to her place and slide that tie out of its knot, get Aiden out of his clothes and . . .

God, she was turning into some sort of sex maniac. That was a new development.

But Aiden looked up at the waiter and smiled. "Yes, I think we would. We're in no rush."

When the waiter disappeared, Laurel lifted her gaze to his.

"We've got all night," he said, holding her gaze steadily.

It was sweet torture, sitting through a shared serving of lemon cream tart, then lingering over Irish coffee. When they finally rose to leave, Aiden's palm was warm against the hollow of her back. Having decided, and then put off leaving for over half an hour, had all her senses on alert, and even the smallest touch was magnified.

The drive home was quiet, but not awkward. Instead it was fueled by anticipation and a strange sort of certainty that felt good. Right. At home, he followed her inside, shutting and locking the door behind him. Laurel's heels clicked on the hardwood floor as she took him by the hand and led him straight to the bedroom.

When they got there, he stopped and took both her hands in his. "Laurel. Are you sure this is what you want? Really sure?"

She lifted her chin. If she were being honest with herself, she couldn't remember a time when she wanted anything more. This wasn't a spur-of-the-moment, heat-of-passion decision. They'd done that already. This was planned, verbalized, and at the point of being put into action and she had no reservations. Maybe she should, but she didn't.

Instead she felt strong, confident, and hungry. This sort of sexual hunger had been a stranger for so long, and now she gloried in the feeling.

"I want you," she said, emphasizing the last syllable.

He reached for the tie on her dress.

CHAPTER 14

Aiden watched as Laurel pulled a clean work shirt over her head. The red golf shirt was practical, but the shapeless fit hid the curves he'd now memorized.

The memorizing he'd done with his hands—a few times during the night.

He slipped on his jeans and buttoned them, the scent of her shower gel clinging to his skin. She was taking socks out of her drawer when he put his arms around her from behind. "I think you need to seriously redesign your work shirts."

"You do? What's wrong with them?"

Her damp hair pressed against his shoulder. "You need girl shirts. You know, ones that . . ." He opened his hands and made an hourglass motion in front of her.

"Wow. Sexist." But he could tell she wasn't offended and was teasing. She had that sideways grin happening.

"The twins have both waitressed from time to time. They swear their tips double on days they wear lower cut shirts."

"Aiden!" She spun around. But that put her up against his bare chest and he found he didn't mind. At all.

"Not too low," he said, "because then three big brothers would have had a major issue. But it's true. Imagine how many perennials you could sell."

"Oh my God. Are you serious?"

She started to pull away but he roped her back in, nuzzling at her neck. "Listen, Tiger," he said, trying hard not to laugh. "What I'm saying is . . . you've got a hot body. Not sure why you hide it most of the time."

She looked up at him. "I never really thought about it. I guess . . . I never really felt that pretty. And Dan's family was pretty conservative, and then at the accounting firm . . ."

"Right. Buttoned to the neck, skirts to the knee?"

She laughed. "Not quite that bad. But yeah. I guess I just thought . . . practical. My wardrobe has always been practical."

He lifted his hand and cradled her jaw. "Last night you didn't look practical. You looked beautiful. You have nothing to hide from, okay? I know coming home has had its challenges. You shouldn't have to hide like you've done something wrong."

She put her arms around his middle and held him close. "Thanks for that."

"Anytime." He drank in the scent of her hair. "Anyway, after living with lots of women in the house for many, many years, I'm smart enough to know that you should wear what makes you feel pretty and confident and comfortable and not to please anyone else. If you like the shirts, keep 'em."

"You have wise sisters."

"I do. But if you say that to them I'll deny it to my dying breath."

She laughed.

"What time do you have to be to work? It's quarter to eight."

"It is?" A look of alarm passed over her face. "I should be there already. And you haven't eaten breakfast or anything. Shit." She pulled out of his embrace and grabbed a hair band from the dresser, working frantically to pull her hair back and anchor it in her customary ponytail. He liked her hair better down, kissing her shoulders.

"Tell you what. You go to work and I'll come along behind with some breakfast sandwiches and coffee."

"Oh, that'd be awesome!" She looked so grateful he nearly laughed. "Can you grab an extra sandwich, do you think? Something lunch-ish?"

"I don't see why not."

"Thanks, Aiden."

"You go. I'll lock up and be right behind you."

"You're a lifesaver!" She plopped a quick kiss on his cheek and dashed out of the bedroom. A few moments later she shouted out a good-bye and slammed the door.

He'd spent the night. He was locking up her place and going to pick up breakfast. This was damned domesticated, especially for him. The crazy thing was he liked it. He liked her. A lot. Last night when she'd said she wanted him . . .

But no "L" word had been spoken or even alluded to. He was smart enough to know that this was a lust period. It was just handy that they also seemed to like each other. Considering the withering looks she'd given him only a month ago, it was major progress.

Besides, despite her self-assuredness last night, he sensed a fragility in her that he had to be careful with. She wasn't as confident in bed as she let on. It was in her tentative touches, her questioning looks. Almost as if to ask, "Is this okay?" or "Do you like this?"

Her past experience had to cast a lot of doubts her way.

Aiden went to the closet and grabbed a hanger, then hung his trousers, shirt, and jacket on it. He locked the door behind him, hung the suit on the hook in the backseat of his truck, and headed for the highway and the coffee shop drive-thru. By the time he bought sandwiches, coffee, and her extra sandwich she'd requested, it was past eight-thirty. Perfect time to stop by the garden center. Employees would be there but they wouldn't be open for customers yet. Maybe they could actually sit and eat together.

Laurel's car was parked next to another that he recognized as Jordan's. The gate to the greenhouse area was still pulled closed, but unlocked, and the closed sign hadn't yet been turned over. He pulled in beside her sedan and grabbed the paper bag of sandwiches and the tray holding coffee. He'd bought extra, thinking her employees might be around.

She'd seen him pull in, apparently, because she appeared at the gate and opened it a bit for him to enter. After he slid through, she closed it again. "That smells delicious," she said. "I'm starving."

"I bet you are," he replied, looking down at her and speaking in a low, intimate voice. Her cheeks colored.

"You brought coffee for everyone?"

"I wasn't sure who'd be here. There are cream and sugars in the bag."

Her eyes twinkled up at him and she looked oddly excited about something as simple as a sandwich and coffee. "What?"

She shrugged. "Oh, nothing."

Nothing his big toe. He watched as she took paper cups out of the drink tray, wondering what she was up to.

"Hey guys, come get a coffee!" she called out.

Jordan was over in seconds flat, looking for sugar and cream both and thanking Aiden for the beverage. A second employee he didn't recognize hung back, looking uncertain. "Come on, there's one for you too," Aiden said, smiling. "You must be new. I'm Aiden."

The guy came closer, and to Aiden he looked familiar. Where had he seen him before?

"George." The guy held out his hand.

Aiden's jaw dropped. He was aware of Laurel standing beside him, smiling, but he simply stared at the man in plain jeans, sneakers, and one of Laurel's Ladybug golf shirts. His hat was gone and his hair was clean and freshly cut. And if Aiden didn't know better, he'd say George was standing taller than he remembered.

"George," Aiden said, and then clasped the offered hand. "Well, I'll be damned. When . . . how . . ." He looked over at Laurel for a moment, then back at George.

"It's been so busy that I hired George to work mornings, doing the watering and sweeping up and stuff. He's been a huge help with deliveries, too. I'm happy to hand off most of the forklift work."

George nodded. "I like being outside. And the flowers are . . ." He seemed to swallow thickly. "Nice."

"Do you take cream and sugar, George?" Laurel asked, taking the lid off the fourth coffee cup."

"Just cream, Ms. Stone."

"You ever going to call me Laurel?"

"No, ma'am."

She added cream to the coffee, gave it a stir with a stir

stick, and handed it over. "Go ahead, take five or ten minutes to enjoy it. The lilacs can wait."

He took the cup, nodded at Aiden, and went back to the shrubs and trees.

Laurel sighed. "He's very quiet and shy. There's a bench back there. He'll sit there and have his coffee by himself. But I made him a deal that he doesn't have to work with customers. I don't want him to be overwhelmed, you know? And he's loosening up bit by bit. I think he likes the plants and flowers."

"Jesus, Laurel." Aiden looked down at her, feeling like he'd been hit by a truck. "Why didn't you tell me?"

"I thought about it. I wanted to. But then George is so private that I held off. When you mentioned new staff last night . . . it was so hard not to say he was here. But it's also early days. He's still easing his way in. I don't know." She shrugged. "He's not a sideshow. He's been through something, I can tell. And he's so reliant on other people. I thought maybe he should own this one thing."

In that moment, Aiden knew he was in real danger of falling for her. Like *really* falling, headfirst, no life preserver, all-in, in a go-big-or-go-home sort of way. She reached over and touched his hand. "Without you I wouldn't have given him a second thought. After hearing you talk about him, I wanted to help, that's all." She took a sip of coffee as if it was no big deal. But it was a big deal to him. Huge.

"He always shut down when I talked about work or helping him find a job," Aiden replied, still trying to reconcile the homeless, hopeless man with the one sipping coffee in a work uniform. The change was remarkable.

"No offense, Aiden, but I'm a girl." This time her smile was wide and cheeky.

"You are? I hadn't noticed."

"Liar." Her laugh filled the air. "Come on, let's grab a couple of chairs and enjoy this before it gets cold and customers start arriving."

They got folding chairs out of her office and sat in a corner of the greenhouse, surrounded by geraniums, begonias, and gerbera daisies. Aiden unwrapped his sandwich and took a huge bite. It had cooled on the drive but was still warm enough to enjoy, and they didn't waste any time scarfing them down.

Laurel shoved her crumpled wrapper into the bag, then sat back and sighed. "That was good. Thanks."

"Anytime." Scary how much he meant that literally.

"So, the George thing. Maybe it was just easier coming from a woman, you know? Is there a man-code or something? Or some weird pride thing that gets in the way? You'd talked about him, I saw him in town, and I just thought maybe I could help."

"He's really working out okay?"

She nodded. "More than okay. He walks from the shelter each morning. I've offered to drive him home a couple of times, but he won't accept it. Maybe it's a pride thing again, or not wanting to be too reliant. Anyway, I know they feed him breakfast before he comes. And I always pay him before he leaves. It's not much, and certainly not enough for him to be independent. I know that. But maybe . . . I dunno. Maybe it's a start is all."

"Everyone has to start somewhere." He put his hand over hers and met her gaze. "Thank you," he said simply. "I love that you did this."

"The extra sandwich today is for him. I'll give it to him before he leaves for lunch."

Aiden wasn't one for getting sentimental or overly

emotional. But the woman beside him had such a good heart. Right now, as he shared a simple breakfast with her, he felt his heart expand and fill with a strange emotion. It wasn't just happiness, or attraction, like last night. It was . . . fulfillment.

"You make me want to be a better person," he murmured, twining his fingers with hers.

She smiled, a sweet, sweet smile that reached into his chest and wouldn't let go. "Funny," she replied, "I was going to say the same thing about you."

"Maybe we bring out the best in each other."

"Isn't that a lovely thought?"

He hesitated. "Laurel, we're really starting something here, aren't we?"

She bit down on her lip. "I think so. And I'll admit it scares me a little."

"Because you don't want to move too fast."

She nodded.

"Me, either." The last thing he wanted to do was scare her away, and it was crazy as hell that he was the one with all the feelings here and she was the one who needed . . . what, convincing? He was pretty sure she hadn't even considered the word "love."

And now he'd thought it. He'd actually let that "L" word loose in his brain and he couldn't tuck it away again. His stomach slid to his feet while his heart felt lighter than it had in a long, long time. If this was what love felt like, holy hell. It wasn't much wonder people got confused.

"I'm glad," she was saying, and he wondered if he'd missed any of her words. "No commitments, no labels. We can just enjoy each other's company, right?"

"Sure," he agreed. *Liar,* said his brain.

She laughed a bit. "Okay, so I know I just said no labels, blah blah . . . but I do have a favor to ask."

Anything, he wanted to say, but instead he asked, "What is it?"

"Dan's wedding is next weekend. I'm setting up the morning of, and then the ceremony is at two. I can go by myself, but it's . . . well, dammit. I'm honest enough to admit that when your ex gets remarried, it's nice if you can at least have a date. I don't want to look pathetic." She sighed and dropped her head into her hands. "Oh, and that just made me pathetic, didn't it?"

He smiled softly. He was actually glad to see she had a little pride where her marriage was concerned. Laurel tended to do what everyone asked but not necessarily what she wanted to do. He was pretty sure she wouldn't have offered to help with the wedding if Dan hadn't asked. If she wanted someone on her arm for the wedding, he'd make it happen.

"You want some arm candy." He tried a teasing tone.

"Don't make it sound like that! But yes." Her cheeks were bright pink now. "That makes me so superficial, doesn't it?"

"Hardly. Does anyone ever want to go to a wedding alone? Let alone their ex's? Besides, I'm totally okay with you parading me around like your studmuffin for the day."

She elbowed him and he started laughing. "Stop it," she commanded. But he could see she was trying not to grin. "Not that you're not studly. You are. But there will be no parading."

"Laurel, would you like a date for the wedding?" He cut through the joking around and asked the simple question.

"I would. Yes."

"Consider it done. I'll pick you up on Saturday at, say, one-fifteen?"

"That'd be perfect."

"Okay." He checked his watch. "And it's nine-oh-five and you're not opened yet. I should blast off and let you get to work."

"You're a terrible influence. I'm late for the second time today."

He took her empty coffee cup and stacked it inside of his. "I would apologize, but I'm not really sorry."

"Wanna know a secret?"

"What?"

She leaned over close to him. "I'm not sorry, either." She looked around for a second and then stood up on tiptoe and pressed her lips to his. They were sweet, soft, and alluring as hell.

"Thanks for dinner last night," she whispered, giving him one last, lingering kiss.

"You're welcome."

"And for breakfast."

He smiled against her lips. "That too."

"You'd better get going." Little nibbles on his lips. His body hardened.

"You've got to stop kissing me, then," he advised.

"Damn. You're right."

She stepped back. Her eyes glowed at him, and he wished they could just blow off work for the day and spend it together. But all indications said that this was an adult relationship and they both had adult responsibilities. He led the way back down the concrete aisle to the entrance.

"Call you later this week?" he asked, wanting to see her, not wanting to appear needy. This relationship that was kind of a free-flow thing was damned hard to navigate.

"I hope so."

They stopped by the gate, and Laurel lifted it out of the way and swung it back, opening the store for business.

Aiden saw George about fifteen feet away. He lifted a hand in farewell and smiled, and George waved and smiled back.

"Thank you for that," he said softly. He doubted she really knew how much it meant to him, and he didn't want to get all sentimental. Not when they were keeping things "light." But George was special for some reason. When Aiden got frustrated with some of the banal nature of being a cop in a quiet, little town, it was the idea of helping people like George that made it worth it.

Laurel caught herself humming as she worked around the shop. With a laugh, she realized neither of them had remembered the items for his mom. Aiden was pleased that she'd hired George, and she suspected equally pleased that George had accepted.

When noon rolled around, George was finishing up for the day. Laurel grabbed the sandwich from the fridge, stopped at the cash register and took out George's pay, and went to the far corner, where he was rolling up the hose. "Hey, George. Good job today."

"Thanks, Ms. Stone."

"Are you ever going to call me Laurel?"

He treated her to a rare grin. "Probably not." This was getting to be a routine with them, and she liked it.

She smiled back. "Listen, I've got your day's pay here." She'd hesitated giving him a check, since she hadn't wanted to pry about the logistics of a bank account or not having a fixed address. "And Aiden brought an extra sandwich this morning." She held out the wrapped package. "You might as well have it."

George's gaze met hers. "Ms. Stone, I didn't take this job for charity."

She'd offended him. She'd bought him a meal before and he'd said nothing. He'd relied on other people's goodwill. But perhaps she was guilty of not putting herself in his shoes. "I'm not trying to hit you in the pride, George. It's a sandwich. Not a new car." She tried an encouraging smile, but it wasn't returned.

"I'll take the money because I earned it. But not . . . I can go buy myself some lunch. I don't . . ." his words faded, and to Laurel's chagrin, she saw tears in his eyes.

"I'm sorry," she said gently.

"This is the first time I've had anything to feel proud about in a long time," he admitted, his words a little disjointed as he struggled to contain his emotions. "I need to learn how to do things on my own."

She reached out with her free hand and put it on his arm. "And sometimes we need to learn that it's okay to ask for help. There's strength in that, George."

"You don't know."

"I know I don't. I have a better idea." She carefully peeled back the paper on the sandwich, which was cut in two halves. "We share. You take half, and I'll take half, and we can be friends." She smiled encouragingly.

"Ms. Stone," he said with a sigh.

"Someday you're going to be standing where I am right now, George. And you're going to pay it forward. So let's bond over bacon and whatever else is in here and call it a day, okay?"

He shook his head. "You're one stubborn lady."

"The sooner you realize that, the better."

He laughed then. A rusty, wheezy kind of laugh that sounded like he was out of practice. And then he took the half sandwich and took a big bite.

"So, you and the cop. You're a thing, huh?" He said it through the bite of crusty bread.

Holy Hannah, George was making small talk. Laurel tried to affect a nonchalant expression and shrugged. "Yeah, I guess we are."

"He's a good guy." George swallowed. "Always looked at me rather than around me, like most people, you know?"

She did. She'd seen it that day she'd offered him the job. Up until that moment, she'd been one of those "most people."

"I've known him a long time," Laurel admitted. "George, if I'm prying, don't answer, but why Darling? Are you from here, or nearby or something?"

His chewing slowed and the wary, guarded look masked his face again. "Never mind," she hurried to say. "I don't want to upset you."

"I'd better get going," he said, wrapping up the rest of the sandwich.

"Do you want a drive today? I can run you into town."

"No, ma'am. Thank you."

Dammit. "George, I'm sorry. I keep putting my foot in my mouth. Forget I said anything. I'm an idiot."

That, at least, garnered a small smile from him. "You're not an idiot. I just can't, that's all. Not now. Maybe not ever."

She felt like she'd made a mess of everything, until he went to pass by her. Then he reached out and patted her arm a couple of times.

It was as close to forgiveness as she was going to get, she figured.

CHAPTER 15

Laurel really hadn't known what to wear to Dan's wedding. What did you wear when your ex-husband was getting married? She looked at the dress on the hanger and fretted. Was it too much?

She'd had to call in reinforcements and Willow had taken her shopping at a little vintage store she knew. They'd come out with this minty-green chiffon concoction that was more girly than anything Laurel had ever worn before. But she'd liked it and enjoyed how it felt swishing against her legs when she moved. Then Willow had taken her to get her hair cut. The blunt ends were gone, and now she sported a sleek bob that ended at the bottom of her collar. Her hairstyle today was simple. Willow, with all her handiwork, had fashioned a headband from matching green silk with an aqua-silk reverse side. The aqua was the precise shade of the underskirt of the dress. The little pop of color was both surprising and pretty. The ensemble was completed with a cute pair of aqua-blue shoes with ankle straps and faux buttons up the top of the feet.

She pressed her hand to her stomach. It was already twelve thirty. Aiden would be here at one fifteen. She still had to fuss with her hair and put on makeup.

First things first, though. She unzipped the dress and put it on. The wrap-style bodice was comfortable and hid any perceived sins, and the V-neckline accentuated her breasts. The full skirt was fun, though frothier than she was used to, but when she looked in her mirror she liked how it made her waist look small. Aiden had been right about her hiding away behind her work shirts and jeans. Not today. Today she wasn't going to hide. She was going to feel pretty, dammit. If it killed her.

The makeup wasn't difficult, since she didn't usually wear much. She just went a little heavier than normal and actually put on lipstick. It was the hair giving her fits. The hairdresser had thinned it out, but it still wanted to flip up on a few of the ends. She spent twenty precious minutes with a big-barrel curling iron, trying to smooth out the bottom so it curled under just right. Then another seven fiddling with the headband. When she got it as close to perfect as she could manage, she sprayed the hell out of it with hairspray.

How had she actually done this every day when she'd worked at the firm?

The preparations had kept her mind off the logistics of the afternoon, but now that she was ready, it all came back and hit her right in the nerves. The plants, urns, and flower arrangements were all set up by the bridge, and in less than an hour Dan would be standing there with Ryan and she'd be sitting in a rented white folding chair watching them make the same promises she and Dan had made to each other.

And she was expected to smile throughout the whole thing.

The knock at the door shook her out of her thoughts, and she let out a big breath. When she opened the door, she expected to see Aiden in the navy suit she remembered. Instead, he looked very summery and handsome in sand-colored trousers, a white shirt, and a tie that was more of a champagne color.

"Wow," she said, looking into his eyes. The light colors seemed to emphasize his gray-blue irises and suited his dark ginger hair perfectly.

"I was going to say the same thing." He smiled, leaned down, and kissed her cheek. "I don't want to mess up your lipstick."

"Appreciated. Though maybe we can revisit that later."

"Mmm. That sounds like a plan. How late do we have to stay at this thing?"

She stepped outside and closed the door behind her. "Well, there's the ceremony. And pictures. And the reception is a summer tea under white tents."

"God."

She laughed and they made their way down the walk. "Do you want to take my car?"

"Would you mind? The truck feels kind of . . . I don't know, rednecky." He grinned. "And you're looking way too fine to be sitting up in the cab of a half-ton truck."

"Flatterer."

They stopped by her car and he opened the door, but stood in the way of her getting in. "You look very pretty today, Laurel. I like the dress. And the hair." He lifted his hand and rubbed a few strands through his fingers. "You've always had the prettiest hair."

The compliment went straight to her heart. "Willow helped."

"Willow is a very nice friend." He smiled and then

stood back from the car so she could slide into the passenger seat. She handed him the keys and watched him go around the hood to the driver's side.

The small parking lot next to the park was already full when they arrived. Laurel felt a little sick to her stomach, thinking about facing the people waiting. There'd be Dan's family—her former in-laws. Her former coworkers, too. Aiden crept down the street, searching for a spot and parked across from the memorial statue. "Are you okay?" He shut off the car and looked over at her, his hand resting on the steering wheel.

"I will be. I just realized that I'm going to see my in-laws, and the people from the office. I haven't seen them since I moved. They're going to be looking at me, Aiden. Trying to guess at my feelings. Assessing."

"You don't have to do this," he said. "We can turn around and go home and not worry about a single soul."

"I can't do that. I said I'd be here. It's his wedding day."

He made a weird nose in the back of his throat, and she knew he disapproved. "What?" she asked.

"Nothing," he replied, letting out a small sigh. He met her gaze. "Look, I said I'd be here for moral support and I will. So it's whatever you want to do. I just . . . well, if you wanted to back out, I'll back you up. That's all."

And she was glad of it. It was nice to know he was there in her corner. "I'm fine, really. Just stay close, okay? I think I'll feel better facing everyone if you're there with me."

"Of course." He took her hand briefly. "Besides, it's not like I know anyone else, really. I'll be sticking close to you, too."

"What a couple of weenies we are." She laughed lightly. Nervous as she was, it was good to know they had each other. And she did want to do this. Not just for Dan, but

for herself. She could show everyone that she was okay.
More than okay. She had a new life now and was happy.

She squeezed Aiden's fingers. She was happy. What a
lovely revelation.

"Let's do it," she said.

"I'll get your door. Sit tight."

Aiden went around and opened her door, even offered
her his hand to help her out of the car. She took it and
smiled, then reached back for her clutch purse. "Ready?"
he asked, holding out his arm.

Gallantry. She hadn't expected that from him, but
she nodded and put her arm through his elbow. "Ready,"
she replied.

Her heels sank into the grass as they walked across the
lawn toward the bridge. Laurel could see a small crowd
already gathered by the chairs, though no one was seated
yet. The ceremony was set up to be on a forty-five-degree
angle to the bridge, so that the stone arch formed part of
the background. They'd rented some sort of platform for
the officiant, only about eight inches high but enough to
give the impression of an altar. On either side were Laurel's planter arrangements. She'd put white lilacs at the
back, the large plastic pots encased in far more decorative
pottery for the occasion. Their sweet fragrance wafted
through the air, mingling with the nearby roses which had
just started to bloom. She knew Dan's yard and that he
liked a variety of color, so around the base of the lilacs
she'd added azaleas of different shades: fuchsia, creamy
orange, lemony yellow. There was a spiky lavender in rich
purple on either side, and she'd finished it all off with low,
tumbling planters full of multi-colored giant impatiens, ivy,
and trailing lobelia. They sat at the front and the trailing
flowers helped camouflage the pots. It did look rather

pretty, she realized, and was delighted when a few butterflies flitted around happily.

It was a perfect wedding day.

"Laurel! Oh my, it's good to see you."

Her delight was tempered when she recognized
Dan's mother's voice. She'd always liked her mother-in-
law, and when she and Dan had first split, Denise had been
shocked and dismayed. Clearly they'd come around and
accepted Dan and Ryan's relationship, but it had been tense
for a few months for sure.

"Denise. Hi." She put on her best smile. "Gorgeous day
for it, isn't it?"

Denise nodded. "Tony, look, it's Laurel."

Tony enfolded her in a quick hug. "Hello, sweetheart."

She'd missed her in-laws, she realized. When you
divorced, you divorced a whole family, it seemed.

"Hi, Tony," she responded, and hugged him back. "I
should introduce you guys. This is Aiden, a friend of mine.
Aiden, these are Dan's parents."

Aiden, bless him, smiled and shook hands. "It's nice to
meet you," he said pleasantly.

They chatted briefly until Denise noticed Ryan's family
approaching. "I think we're needed," she said. "Please excuse us."

After they were gone, Laurel let out a breath. "One
down," she murmured, and Aiden gave a low chuckle.

"They seem like nice people," he mused. "Do you miss
them?"

"A little. I don't think I realized how much until now.
They were so good to me." Indeed. They'd been looking
forward to grandkids. Laurel wondered if they still did,
and if Dan and Ryan had any plans . . .

It wasn't any of her business now.

"That's normal, I'd think." Aiden responded to her words about Tony and Denise. "Who do we tackle next?"

She grinned up at him. He seemed totally unfazed by it all and it helped to steady her. "How can you look so calm and collected?" she asked.

"I'm a cop. We deal with awkward and strange situations all the time. Most people aren't happy to see us, you know."

"I guess I never thought of that." She couldn't imagine not being happy to see Aiden. Then again, on the day of her robbery, he was the last person she'd wanted to talk to.

How things had changed.

They mingled in the group, and she greeted several former coworkers. Some were simply happy to see her; others were more assessing in their looks, particularly with Aiden by her side. When she explained that she owned the garden center off the highway, she often got looks of surprise and once or twice people actually looked patronizing, as if her new venture was some sort of pet project or something. She'd gotten so self-conscious at one point that she'd hid her hands, worried that she had dirt from the garden beneath her nails. By the time five to two rolled around, she was exhausted from her painted-on smile and forced perkiness.

"Do you want to sit down?" Aiden's voice was soft in her ear.

"More than anything," she replied, ready to stop the small talk and get the ceremony over with. There'd be even more socializing after. She wondered if Aiden hadn't been right after all. Maybe they should have called it a day and just gone home.

They found seats on the left-hand side and Laurel crossed her legs, draping her full skirt over her calves.

More and more people found chairs and the hum of conversation lowered in expectation. Dan's parents sat in the front row, and Laurel watched as Ryan's mother and sister sat with them, though his father was conspicuously absent. The whole thing felt surreal.

Then the officiant came forward, dressed in a suit that seemed like it might be quite hot for the day, and took his place on the platform. Everyone looked toward the back of the seating area and there were Dan and Ryan, coming forward together, dressed in matching tuxedos. The only music was that of the birds and the breeze in the leaves, and they walked up the aisle together, stopping in front of the Justice of the Peace.

It was a nice ceremony, but Laurel found it difficult. The promises Dan was making right now he'd made to her. He'd known they were false even as he'd spoken them. He'd admitted that much to her. And yet he'd said them anyway. He'd vowed, in a church, in front of a minister, and their families, and their friends, that he loved and cherished her. That they'd be together forever. She'd been happy to go along with his idea of a big church wedding when she'd really wanted something more like this—intimate, outdoors, with friends and family and flowers. Instead she'd had a huge gown and three hundred guests and a reception in a ballroom. A big show that had signified nothing.

Now he was making those same promises to someone else, in a park under a June sky. Irrational anger bubbled up inside her. Those years felt so wasted. So pointless. And somehow she felt like she should have known it wasn't right. Why was it she couldn't tell when someone was lying to her, for Pete's sake? Was she really that gullible?

"You okay?" Aiden leaned over and whispered in her

ear. She realized she'd been holding his hand in the folds of her skirts, gripping his fingers tightly.

She nodded quickly, but there was an uncomfortable bitterness inside her. She didn't want to have these feelings; didn't like feeling as if she were not a very nice person. She shouldn't feel robbed, because she wouldn't have wanted to stay in a marriage based on a lie. So why couldn't she just let it go?

Thankfully, the ceremony was brief, and she was glad when it seemed things were wrapping up. The rings were exchanged, pronouncements made, and she started to relax the tension in her shoulders. An hour. She could make it through an hour, couldn't she? A cup of tea or lemonade or whatever, nibble at some fancy finger sandwiches and cookies, and be on her way? Today Dan was making a new start and maybe it was time she really did, too.

She glanced over at Aiden. Did she want to make that new start with him? For real? She swallowed against the lump in her throat. Wanting something was very different from reality. She liked Aiden a lot. She had fun with him. The sex was spectacular, but more than that?

She wasn't sure she believed in promises. And if she did, she wasn't at all sure she'd trust them. Didn't that put her in a bind?

The ceremony ended and she sagged in relief, but it was short-lived. Dan and Ryan turned to the crowd and then, on their way back down the aisle, they stopped. At the end of her row. And her heart pounded painfully in her chest. *No*, she thought. *Dear God. Just move on . . .*

But they didn't. They paused and Dan smiled at her and reached out his hand. What the hell? Being here wasn't blessing enough? Putting out several hundreds of dollars' worth of plants didn't show her support? Grossly uncomfortable, she put her hand in his and stood, knowing she wouldn't—couldn't—cause a scene. He reached in for an embrace and she smiled as gracefully as she could muster and hugged him back, and then hugged Ryan, too. The whole time her anger built. He hadn't warned her at all. No, he'd just assumed that she'd be okay with this display of magnanimity. Because that was what she did. She smiled and said it was okay when it really wasn't.

She sat back down and calmly arranged her skirt. Today was just the limit. The Ladybug was the first thing she'd done that *she* wanted, and the sideways looks pissed her off, like she'd made a strange and bad decision. She liked being in the dirt, she liked the stupid golf shirts that they wore, and she liked being outside. She didn't miss the office or the lunches out or the prestige or even the salary. But opening the garden center had been a quiet act of defiance, really. She hadn't said one word about her personal dissatisfaction . . .

As the wedding guests all clapped and smiled, she figured she really could use that yoga day at Willow's. She was wound tighter than a spring and finding a little inner peace might be a good idea.

As the couple went to the bridge for pictures, Laurel turned to Aiden. "What do you think? Shall we drink their champagne?"

Aiden wasn't quite sure what to do with the woman beside him. He'd hoped she'd relax once they sat down, but she'd nearly broken his fingers during the ceremony. Her smile had been pasted on her face, but he could see the strain behind it. She was here today and it was costing her on a personal level. Costing her a lot. He remembered that look. It was the same one she'd had on her face the day she'd found out he'd taken her parking on a bet. Anger and hurt bound up in one.

Now she was standing up because her ex-husband had made a big show of acknowledging her on his walk back down the aisle. Hell, Aiden was embarrassed for her and he didn't even have a horse in this race. How oblivious could the guy be? Couldn't Dan see what this was costing her?

"What do you think? Shall we drink their champagne?" Laurel turned to him and met his gaze. There was a fire in her eyes he remembered well enough; in the past it had been directed at him. She was angry. Well, good. She should be. He'd thought this was a crazy idea in the first place. Who went to their ex's wedding, anyway? After four years, he was pretty sure that he was the last person in the world Erica would ask to attend her wedding. If she were married. He had no idea if she was or not.

"You can drink as much of their champagne as you like," he said with a nod. "I'm driving."

"Not too much. Ask Willow. Alcohol has another name, you know. Truth Juice." She smiled up at him. "And I don't think you want me to go there today."

"Thanks for the warning," he said. "Come on. I hear corks popping over by the tent."

The caterers hired for the day were opening bottles and pouring fizz into slender glasses. Aiden snagged one off a tray and handed it to Laurel, then ordered a club soda for himself. There was a brief toast and then Dan and Ryan were called away by the photographer for pictures on the bridge.

"Laurel!" They both looked over toward the voice and Aiden saw a middle-aged man waving at Laurel.

"Friend of yours?"

She smiled. "Old boss. He's harmless. Do you mind?"

"Not at all. I'll get us a refill. Do you want some food?"

"I'd love some. I haven't eaten since breakfast."

He'd just bet she'd been too nervous to eat earlier. He watched her greet her ex-boss and let out a breath. Did she know how beautiful she was? He could tell that her smile right now was genuine. The edges of it were soft and sweet, and the way she rested her fingers on the man's sleeve showed her level of comfort. She'd done something with her hair, making the dark strands extra sleek and soft looking, and that dress showed the curves he knew so well. Hell, he'd been proud to walk into the park with her on his arm. He wasn't sure he'd ever known a stronger woman.

"Scone with cream, sir?"

He turned to see the server balancing a silver tray. Good Lord. Scones with jam and cream, little triangles of sandwiches that looked like something a Great-aunt Mildred would eat. Was this really a thing? The last reception he'd been to that was remotely like this had served finger foods like mini-sliders and shrimp skewers and his personal favorite, fried macaroni and cheese balls.

"No thank you," he replied.

When he'd turned his attention back to Laurel, he saw that Dan was walking away from her, back to the bridge and photos, and her smile had that brittle, forced look again.

He was going to get her out of here.

On his way over he snagged another glass of champagne and when he reached her, he slid his arm around her waist. "You look thirsty," he said.

"Oh, thanks!" She smiled brightly, and as she turned toward him a little, said, "Your timing is impeccable."

He held out his hand to the man she'd been talking to. "Hi. I'm Aiden Gallagher."

"Pctcr Murphy," the man replied, shaking his hand. "Laurel worked for our firm in Burlington. We sure miss her around there."

"I'm sure you do. Your loss is definitely Darling's gain," he replied, giving her waist a little squeeze. "The garden center closed a few years ago. Laurel's brought it back to life and it's doing a booming business. She's a smart cookie and a hard worker."

"You don't have to convince me."

"Aiden's a police officer," she filled in, looking up at him. "But I knew him in high school. I hadn't seen him in years until we had a break-in and he responded to the call."

"Sounds romantic."

He and Laurel both laughed, which he knew gave a further impression of intimacy. He'd said earlier that he was here to support her. If she wanted to make their relationship a real "thing," particularly to her old coworkers, he was perfectly fine with that. However she wanted to play it.

"I should get back to my wife," Peter said, giving a nod. "Laurel, it was really great to see you."

"You too, Pete."

When he left, she took a huge drink of champagne. "Rough one?" he asked.

"Pete? God, no. He's lovely. Dan stopped over for a moment."

"What did he want? I saw him walking back to the bridge."

"He wants me to do a picture with him and Ryan."

"You're fucking kidding me."

She elbowed him. "Aiden."

"Well, really? Come on. You didn't say you'd do it, did you?"

She shrugged. "What was I supposed to say?"

"How about *no thank you*? Or, *that's a little awkward, don't you think*? Or even a *go to hell, Dan*."

She sighed. "It'll be fine. I'll be fine. Don't worry about it."

And that was just it with her. Aiden had been watching her for weeks now, and when it came to people she cared about, she put herself last, like her needs and wishes didn't matter. Today's flowers were a prime example. And the wedding. What, she was supposed to be all nice and accommodating because Dan had had a hard time? What about how betrayed she'd been? Wasn't she entitled to that? He knew now that her divorce had shaken her beliefs in love and trust, and for some reason people expected her to just *get over it*.

Meanwhile, who was there to stand up for *her*?

It seemed to him that everyone expected Laurel to just do, and when she didn't it was a personal affront. Like with the promotional picture on the bridge. He'd heard from Claire that they were grumbling at the town hall, wondering what the big deal was anyway.

Laurel, he realized, was one of those nice people who got taken for granted because she didn't want to hurt anyone's feelings.

"I'm going to go grab some cake," she said. "Do you want to come?"

"I'll be there in a minute," he said.

"Okay. But I can't promise to save you any icing."

When she was gone, he made his way over to where Dan and Ryan were posing for pictures. They were standing in the middle of the bridge, looking ridiculously happy, the photographer snapping away. And Aiden didn't want to mar their happiness, but his first thought right now was for Laurel. Just because they were happy didn't mean they had to be callous. And asking her to pose for a photo was pretty damned callous.

When the photographer stepped back for a moment, Aiden caught Dan's eye and inclined his chin. It was enough of an invitation that Dan excused himself and came over, a small frown pulling his brows together. "Hi. You must be Aiden."

Aiden held out his hand. "Aiden Gallagher. Congratulations, by the way." No sense being confrontational. He could be a pretty patient man—on the outside.

"Thanks." Dan's grin was brilliant. "And Laurel . . . she was such a help today. She's quite a woman."

"She is. Which is why she's not going to do a picture with you today."

Dan's smile faded. "I don't understand."

Aiden wondered how a person could be so oblivious. "Dude. You asked her to the wedding. That was awkward enough, but then you asked if she'd help out. Then you made a spectacle of her when you pulled that 'down the aisle hug' thing. . . . Did you even run that past her beforehand? But Laurel wouldn't say a thing to ruin your day. That's not her style. Now you've decided a photo is a good idea? How many kinds of 'you have my blessing' do you need? Let her go, man. Just let her go."

"I don't think you . . . I've known her a lot longer." Dan's chin jutted out.

"Oh, I don't think so, my friend." Aiden smiled through his teeth. "I kissed her right on this bridge when we were only five years old. And I hurt her, too. I know what that looks like. And right now you're hurting her to make yourself feel better. So you don't feel guilty for turning her life upside down."

Dan's dark eyes cooled. "I see. You know, Laurel could have simply told this to me herself."

"Only she wouldn't. And if you know her at all, you'd know that."

Dan nodded briefly. "Fine. No picture."

"I appreciate it."

Aiden started to turn to walk away when Dan put his hand on his arm. "Hey. Despite what you may think of me, I care about Laurel a lot. Take care of her. She's a good woman."

"Don't worry. I'm the last person who wants to hurt her. You can count on it."

He walked away, but he'd only gone about twenty feet when he saw Laurel watching him, disapproval flashing in her eyes and her lips a thin, angry line. She was holding a plate with cake and he wondered if he'd made a misstep by interfering.

Then he stopped second-guessing himself. Someone had to stand up for her if she wouldn't stand up for herself.

He went over and smiled down at her. "Hi. That cake looks delicious. Is it lemon?"

"What did you say to Dan?"

Her voice was condemning. Her mouth had a set to it that he recognized and he knew he had to tread carefully.

"It's no big deal," he said, trying to make his words sound breezy. "I just saw that the idea of having your picture taken made you tense up. I got you off the hook."

"I really wish you hadn't done that."

"It's no biggie. I'm sure they can manage their wedding photos without a shot of the ex-wife." He looked down at the cake. "Are you going to eat that? The cucumber sandwich didn't really fill me up."

"Help yourself. I'm not hungry anymore." She put the plate in his hand and stalked off.

What the . . . ?

He went after her, pausing to put the plate down on a vacant table. "Hey, Laurel, wait up." But she didn't slow down. The bright blue shoes walked faster and the fluffy skirt swayed with each step.

"Laurel! Hold up!" He jogged after her, feeling like he was about to step on a land mine but knowing he couldn't just let her walk away.

He caught up with her and refrained from grabbing her arm. Instead he matched her steps and put his hand lightly along the small of her back, so it maintained the look of equanimity.

"Laurel, slow down. Let's talk about this."

"I don't want to talk about it."

"You mean you don't want to listen."

"Whatever. It wasn't your place to speak to Dan. It wasn't your place to speak for me."

"Someone had to. You weren't speaking for yourself."

"Oh my God. Tell me you didn't just say that." She finally stopped walking and faced him.

He really was in a minefield. There was probably nothing he could say now that would be right. And yet . . . he had to say something. It wasn't fair how people just assumed that she would be okay with everything.

"Laurel. You were upset he asked. You were upset about the hug in the aisle. I was trying to help. And trying to save you from having to have that awkward conversation."

"But it wasn't your place." Her gaze darted around the reception area. "And now there's a scene. And this thing."

"Sweetie, there is no thing. This is their day, not yours."

Her mouth dropped open. *Shit.*

"That's not what I meant." He scrambled to find the right words. "What I mean is, this is their day and they're focused on each other. They probably won't even remember there was even an issue."

He took her hand. She let him, but she didn't clasp his fingers in response. "You never want to hurt anyone's feelings. You do things for people and put yourself last. Do you think I don't see it? Even with your folks. You still do dinner just about every Sunday, even though I bet you'd rather have a few hours to yourself to unwind sometimes."

"It would hurt their feelings if I stopped going."

"That's just the sort of thing I'm talking about. When do you do anything that's just for Laurel?"

She held his gaze for a moment, and he thought he was getting through. But then she turned away. "I'd like to go home now."

"Okay." It was better than working this out in public. "Things are pretty much over anyway. No need to stay for any of the speeches."

She walked away from him and he sighed before following. At her car he got out the keys, unlocking the doors and holding hers before going around to the driver's side. When he got behind the wheel, he noticed that she was sitting stiffly in the passenger seat, staring front.

He had no idea what to say next. Instead he started the car and began the short drive back to her house.

The silence was excruciating. And he still didn't understand exactly why she was so angry. All he knew was that he cared about her. He wanted her to be happy and it drove him crazy when someone hurt her—even unintentionally. She'd donated stuff to the scholarship fund. She ran a business and was dedicated to wonderful community service. She'd forgiven him and she'd hired a homeless man out of the goodness of her heart, when most in the town had simply looked the other way.

She gave to others, taking nothing for herself, and damned if he didn't love her for it.

In her driveway, he put the car in park and sat, speechless, trying to reconcile himself with his last thoughts. He loved her. He hadn't planned on it. He'd known they needed to go slowly. He didn't do love. He wasn't built for it . . .

What a time to realize how deeply his feelings ran. Just when she was furious with him. Erica had told him that he was only in it for fun and didn't take love seriously. She'd been wrong. He'd just been young and not ready.

He looked over at Laurel. The past month had shown him something completely different. For the first time in his life, he felt like putting someone else's needs ahead of his own.

"Laurel," he said softly.

CHAPTER 16

Laurel twisted her fingers in her lap. She didn't know what to think right now. The day had been just one big mess of emotions. Most of all, she was starting to realize that she had a lot of anger that she hadn't dealt with yet.

"Now's not the time to go through this, Aiden."

"When would be a good time?" His voice was quieter now. And she thought she sensed a hesitation in it. The whole atmosphere of the car was one of trepidation and uncertainty. Like either one of them was only a breath away from saying something they couldn't take back.

"I don't know. I'm mixed up, okay? Part of me knows that you're right. I've been too nice. I've said yes to things because I wanted to be the understanding, supportive one but I ignored my own feelings along the way and now it's all catching up with me." She sighed. "Oh, Aiden, it's not fair to drag you into all that."

"Are you saying you want to break up?"

She looked over at him. "Break up? That would mean that we were . . . are . . . a couple."

"Aren't we?"

Oh God. She was feeling more and more trapped as the day went on. Everything was all off-balance. "I don't know. We said no labels, remember? Day by day. Nothing serious . . ."

"We're sleeping together, Laurel. I don't just do that without some feelings being involved, despite what you and some other people might think."

She was relieved to hear it, but it scared her, too. Because she felt the same way. She could never have had sex with him if she didn't care about him. He'd been kind, gentle . . . constant. He hadn't given her a single reason to doubt him.

"Okay," she said. "Okay. Maybe that's true. We're involved. I wouldn't have taken you today just as arm candy, no matter what we said."

Silence dropped for a minute, and she wondered if they were both thinking about what to say next. She didn't know how to do this. Dan was really the most relationship experience she'd had, and it had all been based on a lie.

"What are you really angry about?" he finally asked, turning in his seat and pinning her with a steady gaze.

"I don't know!" Her voice lifted and she felt her lip quiver. The stupid thing was, she had all the emotions bubbling inside her and she couldn't sort through them all on the spot.

She wanted to believe in him. Wanted to trust in their feelings for each other. But she wasn't there yet. "I'm getting sick and tired of smiling for everyone and acting like everything's okay, okay?" Her voice rose. "I knew that Dan was struggling so I felt like I had to be kind and generous and supportive, and it's not like I wasn't those things sometimes, but I shoved down all the other things I felt. I felt duped into a marriage that shouldn't have happened in the first place. I felt robbed of the future I'd envisioned and the hopes for children we might have had. I'm so sick of swallowing down my disappointments, Aiden. Sick and tired of it!"

She was nearly yelling at the end. Aiden calmly looked at her and asked, "Do you feel a little bit better?"

She didn't. All her rant had done was pop the cork on all the emotions she'd held back. And she did what she hadn't done yet. Not once. She burst into tears. Big, gulping tears that were full of sadness and frustration and loss.

"Shhh," she heard, and felt the seatbelt give way from around her hips. Aiden had unhooked it and let it retract, then pulled her as close as he could. Her outer thigh was pressed uncomfortably against the console and gear stick as his arms came around her.

"Let's get you inside," he whispered, his breath warm on her hair. "Come on, sweetheart."

She nodded mutely, and he gave her a squeeze before pulling away and opening the car door. She was sniffling as he opened her door and took her hand, the flood of tears only partially staunched. Overall there was just a feeling that things were unfair. And as Aiden shut the front door behind them, she looked at her foyer and living room and realized she lived here but it wasn't her home. There were no pictures on the wall or bits of herself in the décor. There was nothing of her life because most of her life contained things she'd rather forget. The thought made her sad all over again, and the tears spilled once more. She'd never been one for waterworks . . .

Aiden tugged on her hand and pulled her over to the sofa, where he sat down and put her on his lap. It felt so good and safe in his arms. She let it all in, finally: the hurt, the disillusionment, the guilt. Yes, there was guilt, too, for harboring such awful feelings and knowing she probably wasn't a very good human being because of it. He'd asked her once if the garden center was a consolation prize. She didn't want it to be, but in some ways it was. She'd been so determined to do something positive after the divorce. And she did love it. But there was still a definite sense of slinking home with her tail between her legs after her failed marriage that still, months later, fed the gossip mill. Particularly thanks to Dan deciding to remarry at that stupid, stupid bridge.

She took a deep breath and a mighty sniff. "The last thing I need is for you to come riding to my rescue. I'm on my own now, don't you see? I've got to fight my own battles."

"Who says?"

"What?" She looked up into his eyes.

"Who says you're on your own? You have your parents and Willow and me . . . and that's just a basic start."

She pushed up out of his arms a bit. "Maybe what I should have said was that I need to fight my own battles."

"Everyone needs help from time to time."

"Help means then that you owe somebody something. Or that you can't do it yourself. I can. I know I can."

"But if you don't ever allow anyone to help, you don't trust them, either," he countered.

Why was he being so tough on her? One moment he was cuddling her in his lap, offering sympathy, and in the next it truly felt as if he were blaming her for something.

She'd disappointed him, too. She could tell, in the thin line of frustration in his voice and the way he held himself back just a bit. What the hell did he want from her?

"Trust?" she countered. "Bah. Where has trusting people

ever got me? Oh sure, I was brought up in this great home where there was all sorts of love and security. And then I quickly realized that life isn't really like that for most people. I trusted because I didn't know any differently. Today's a prime example of what happens to people who trust blindly. Heck, I trusted you, Aiden. Did you know you were the first guy to break my heart? All because I trusted that what I heard and what I saw was the truth. And I was so wrong."

She felt him pull away. Not a lot, but it wasn't hard to sense that she'd hit him where it hurt.

"I thought you'd forgiven me for that."

"I did. It doesn't mean I've forgotten it."

He cursed a little, nudged her off his lap, and stood. "Really? You're really going to bring this up again? My God, Laurel, it was high school. Get over it already. Know what I think?"

His tone both surprised and provoked her. She rubbed at her wet cheeks and lifted her chin. "What do you think, oh wise one?"

"I think you're pulling up that old thing again because you're scared. Today reminded you of how things went so very wrong. And then there I was. Someone you could have a real chance with. Someone who was willing to go to bat for you even when you weren't able to do it for yourself. And that scared the shit out of you because you want it and you don't trust it. Is it me you don't trust, Laurel, or yourself?"

"Wow. That's ballsy, coming from you," she snapped back. "Really, you think this is all about you?"

"I don't know what the hell it's about at all. If I did I wouldn't be standing here not knowing whether I want to hold you or try to knock some sense into that thick head of yours. Don't you get it, Laurel? I love you. Scared or not, pushing me away, falling apart in my arms . . . I love you. All of you. Maybe I always have, even if I haven't always shown it in the right ways."

It was like he'd shot her right between the eyes, she was just that stunned by his pronouncement. "No," she whispered. "You can't. You don't."

"Why? Because you say so? It doesn't work that way. If you want to know why I spoke to Dan today, it was incredibly simple. Someone was trying to take advantage of someone I love. Someone was trying to take advantage of your good heart. And that heart should be cherished, not taken for granted."

"Don't," she murmured again. Love. Not love. She wasn't ready for love. She hadn't even given it a thought. Panic strangled her lungs, tightened her chest. What she and Aiden had was fun. It was friendship, and some really hot sex, but it wasn't love. Love was . . . indelible. Irreversible. It was the ultimate label in a relationship she wanted to keep fluid and unnamed.

All love had ever given her was a kick in the teeth.

"You don't believe me," he said, standing back. "Wow. That's . . . wow."

She took a moment to catch her breath before looking up into his face. "I believe you think you love me, but it's not real, Aiden. It's too soon. And we've just been having fun."

She wished she'd looked away rather than see the hurt in his fallen expression. "I'm not trying to be cruel," she added. "I just think that you're caught up in, I don't know, the newness or something. You're not in love with me, don't be silly."

"Don't be dismissive of my feelings," he replied, the

words tight. "At least respect me enough to not throw them back at me. I take it you don't feel the same way."

Did she? There had been moments when they'd been together that she'd been stupidly happy. But she hadn't delved too deeply into analyzing her feelings. She hadn't wanted to. The very concept of love was overwhelming, let alone have it be a real possibility.

"I can't," she answered honestly. "I am so not in that place. I thought you knew that."

"I thought things might have changed. You know, since we started dating. Spending time together, talking, making love." His gaze locked with hers. "Don't deny that, either. I was there. It wasn't just quick, meaningless sex. Not for either of us. You don't do casual and neither do I."

"Stop," she said, putting her hand against her forehead. Everything was so mixed up. "You're mad at me and I'm mad at you, and I'm pissed at Dan and so confused, and you're just making it worse."

"That's me. I make things worse. Of course, maybe it's not me. Maybe if you'd let me explain years ago things would have been different. Know why I said what I said today? Because the last time I messed up, I tried to talk to you and you wouldn't listen to a word I had to say. I learned from that, Laurel. I wasn't about to let you silence me again. So do with it what you will. If you don't love me back, let's just get it out in the open."

Panic fluttered in her chest. He was talking about breaking things off completely. How had this even started? By her being angry he'd spoken to Dan about a stupid photograph? She couldn't say she loved him. She knew she couldn't. But she didn't want to lose him, either. Which . . . wasn't fair. To either of them.

"What are you going to do?"

"You mean, if you say you don't? It's pretty obvious, isn't it?" He ran his hand through his hair. "Let me tell you something, Laurel. Today is not easy for me. I'm not the guy who puts feelings into words. When I was twenty-one years old, a woman dumped me because she wanted to get married and start a family and I wasn't ready. Know what I did? I didn't have the courage to break up with her, so I let her 'catch' me fooling around with another girl at a bar. She left me just like I wanted. I was off the hook. I didn't understand her side of things until today. Now I know how hard it is to stand in front of someone and tell them how you feel and what you want in your life, only to have them not be on the same page. I never thought I'd empathize with Erica, but there it is. Now I know how she felt."

"M . . . marriage? And children?"

"I wasn't ready. Truth was, I would never have been ready, not with her. Isn't that just a kick in the ass?"

Because he'd been waiting for Laurel. She didn't need to hear him say it to know that was what he meant. No, no, no.

"I'm sorry," she murmured, a horrible, heavy weight settling into her stomach. "I can't give you what you want. I don't believe in promises, Aiden. Or forever. I used to. I'd only hurt you in the end."

"You're hurting me now."

"Better now than later, when we've . . ." Her throat tightened, preventing her from completing the sentence.

"Before we're married, have a house, start planning a family? You don't want to do to me what Dan did to you?"

"If he'd been honest from the start, this all might have been prevented. So I'm being honest with you now. It's for the best."

He gave a short laugh. "For the best. I see."

"You don't, but you will. I promise."

He stood there for a few moments more, and then gave a nod. "Okay then. Right. I guess . . . I guess I'll be going."

She heard him struggle with the words and it left a bruise on her heart.

"I'm so sorry," she said again.

"Forget it," he said. "You haven't dealt with your divorce yet. I suspected it and let it go. Maybe once you do that, you'll come find me again."

He turned on his heel and left. That was it. No last plea, no last goodbye. Just walking out her door and shutting it with a quiet click. The muted sound of his truck starting up and fading as he drove away.

The house was so quiet that the only sound was the hum of the refrigerator.

Laurel got up and went to her bedroom. She kicked off her shoes and threw them in the closet, stripped off the dress and left it in a heap on the floor, a minty-green confection of disappointment. She ripped the headband from her hair, pulled on an oversized T-shirt and pair of cut-off sweat shorts, and curled up on her bed.

The bed where they'd made love. Where she'd felt beautiful and strong and like she could do anything.

She knew, in all likelihood, that she'd just made the biggest mistake of her life.

She pulled up the blanket and cried it all out.

She hadn't expected him to be that stubborn.

As the days passed, she kept expecting him to stop into the garden center. Drop by the house with a pizza, call her when he was off shift. There was nothing. Not a text. Not a call, not a wave as he drove by in his cruiser. Not that she could see if it was him bchind the wheel from the greenhouse, but still.

Nothing.

Right now she was thinning out her carrots, a job she detested. It seemed so wasteful, somehow, pulling out the delicate stems that would be food in a matter of weeks. Yct if she didn't thin them out, none of them would grow properly and they'd be scrawny and crammed together. With a disgusted sigh, she bent to the job once more.

Aiden was proving a point, she supposed. It drove her crazy and she admired him for it all at the same time. And maybe it was better this way anyway. She knew he was right; she hadn't dealt with all those emotions. She'd sucked it up and pretended it didn't matter.

And he'd said he loved her.

Ah, that one stopped her up every time.

The back gate creaked and she closed her eyes. She really didn't want company right now. "Wil, can we hang out later?" she called out. "I really want to get this done."

"It's not Willow," came a familiar female voice.

Laurel turned her head. "Mom. Oh my gosh. What are you doing here?"

Her mother smiled at her, a soft, sad smile if Laurel was reading it right. "It's Sunday night and it's seven o'clock. You missed dinner. You didn't answer your phone. I was worried."

"I left my phone inside. The last time I had it in my pocket while I was gardening, I pocket-dialed Willow five times." She stood and brushed her hands off on her jeans. "I'm sorry, Mom. I got working and forgot all about dinner."

Her mother came closer, looked at Laurel's face, and

frowned. "Oh, sweetie. You are not happy. Does this have anything to do with Dan's wedding? With Aiden?"

"What about Aiden?"

The words came out sharply, and a heavy silence followed in their wake.

"Something did happen, then," her mom said. "Oh, honey."

"I'm fine." Laurel flashed a smile. "Dan's wedding's over and I'm relieved. I'll admit it was harder than I expected, but I'm fine."

She half-expected her mom to just let it go. They'd been close but not super-close. They'd never been the kind of mother and daughter who could read each other without speaking. But when her mom came over and took her hands, a bittersweet pang touched her heart. Sometimes a girl really did just need her mama.

"You're not fine. Leave the carrots be for a while and come talk to me."

"I want to get this done tonight." She pulled her hands away, but the look aimed her way was shrewd and knowing. Her mom wasn't going to let her off the hook.

"You're stubborn like your father. Oh, I probably should have pushed for this conversation months ago, but I figured if you wanted to talk about it you'd come to me. Denial is more than a river in Egypt, you know."

Laurel chuckled. She'd heard her mom use that saying before. "Ha, ha."

"I brought leftovers. Have something to eat. Tell me what's going on."

She didn't want to, but she also knew that if she didn't, her mom would fuss and worry and start hovering. Besides, maybe she needed an objective ear. Moms always took their kids' sides, right? But she'd kept her family deliberately distanced from the situation. Maybe her mom might have a clearer perspective.

"Let me wash up, then. Come on inside."

She dumped the thinned carrots in the compost bin on the way by and took off her shoes at the door. She washed her hands, but no matter how hard she tried, she never quite managed to get all the dirt from beneath her fingernails. Giving up, she turned off the tap and dried her hands. By the time she made it to the kitchen, the microwave was running and there was a glass of iced water on the table along with a knife and fork.

"What was for dinner tonight?" she asked, reaching for the water.

"Stuffed pork chops and twice-baked potatoes."

"Damn." She smiled. Two of her favorite dishes and she'd missed out. "Did you make the green beans, too?" Whenever her mom made the pork chops, she did green beans with little bits of bacon and red pepper. Delicious.

"Of course." The microwave beeped and Laurel went to get her plate. "Thanks, Mom. I really am sorry I forgot."

"You're a big girl. I'm a mom. I live for family dinners, but maybe I shouldn't expect it all the time. You have your own life to live." She sat down across from Laurel. "I just like having you back in town again."

Laurel scooped up a bit of potato. "This is so good."

"Do you like being back home, sweetie? Really? Be honest."

It said something that Laurel had to stop and think about it. "Yeah, I do," she admitted. "I was good at accounting, but I love running the garden center. It's fun. It's long hours but it's fun. My staff is awesome. It's more than numbers in columns. It's beauty, and smiles on people's faces, and nice smells. It's hard to be gloomy around flowers and fresh air."

"I'm glad. It suits you in a way that office never did."

Laurel paused cutting into her chop. "You never said."

"You're an adult, making your own decisions. If that was what you wanted . . . besides, what would you have said if I'd voiced my opinion?"

Laurel popped the morsel into her mouth. "I would have denied it," she admitted, then continued chewing and swallowing.

"Right. Now, about Dan . . ."

The food turned a little tasteless at the change in conversation.

"Dan's off living his life. Good for him." The last thing she expected was for her mom to chuckle. "What's so funny?"

"You sound annoyed. It's about time." When Laurel merely stared, she continued. "You were so understanding when Dan came out, and that's to your credit. He's not a bad guy. And I know it had to be horribly hard for him. But I can't help feeling that he's taken advantage of your good nature. Maybe I was just angry on your behalf, but when it was all about Dan I kept thinking, 'What about Laurel?' What about what you wanted? Are you ready to fight for that now?"

"Not you, too," Laurel grumbled, and she cut through the potato skin rather savagely.

"Oh?" Her mom's eyebrows went up. "Who else has been sharing the same wisdom?"

Laurel didn't answer, just huffed out a frustrated breath and continued eating to avoid answering.

"Let me guess. Aiden Gallagher."

Laurel looked up. That was all.

"Oh, I'm glad. I always liked Aiden. I heard you guys were seeing each other. Though I kind of hoped you'd be the one to tell me."

"We're not anymore, so don't get too excited."

"How come?"

"Because he wants me to deal with my *unresolved issues*." She put every ounce of sarcasm she could muster into those last two words.

"And are you? Or are you just torturing tiny carrots, hoping it'll go away?"

Damn.

She put down her knife and fork; her appetite was diminishing anyway. "It's not the best strategy, is it?"

Her question was met with a shake of a head.

"Oh, Mom. I'm such an idiot. All my life I've hated hurting another person, especially deliberately. I've always kind of regretted the day I poured the milkshake over Aiden's head. Even though he deserved it. It just wasn't like me to do something like that."

Her mom laughed. "It's a good thing it was out of character. I had to convince the principal not to suspend you."

"He lied to me, mom. Aiden lied. And it hurt. Then I got married and my husband lied to me, too. Does everyone lie? Or is it just me?"

"Sweetie, Aiden was a kid who buckled to peer pressure. And Dan . . . I can't imagine what it was like for him. It doesn't excuse them, not by a long shot. But it's not you. I promise."

"Are you sure? Because sometimes I think I wear a sign on my back that says 'bleeding heart' on it. I didn't want to make things worse for Dan so I bottled it all up. I don't want to be that person who is bitter and craps all over their ex, but I'm . . . I'm . . ."

"Angry?"

"Yes."

"Disillusioned?"

"Maybe some of that, too. I wanted babies, Mom." She came right out and said it, and it was a huge relief. She'd wanted a family so much. "We'd talked about it but the time was never right for Dan. He wanted us to have a few years working. A chance to pay off all our student debt. Then I thought we were good and it was the down payment on the house. Waiting, waiting. For the perfect moment, he said. So when he said we had to talk, I was so excited. I was ready to flush my birth control down the toilet and I started planning a nursery in my head."

She looked up. Her mom had big tears in her eyes. "See? Now you're crying. I didn't want for any of this to happen."

"Tears are a part of life, Laurel. Go on. Get it out."

"He told me the truth and I was just . . . numb. It wasn't babies. It was divorce, and his coming out, and that he'd been having an affair. . . . It all just jumbled together and turned into one big mushroom cloud of . . . broken dreams. Oh hell, what a cliché."

"You feel cheated. And not only from the affair, but . . ."

"But from the life I wanted and thought I was going to have."

Silence fell over the kitchen. Laurel knew her mom was being wise by staying quiet, because pieces started to fall into place. "He stole my dreams. My future."

"And you're mad because now he's living it and you're not."

"And I hate myself for it," she admitted. "Because it's not nice. And I'm always nice, you see?"

Her mother got up from the table and returned with a

plastic dish. Inside was a helping of brownie pudding. The chocolate sauce was still warm. "You could use this."

Laurel laughed. "Thank you, Mom. For letting me vent."

"Did you say these things to Aiden?"

She shook her head and reached for the spoon. "Not all of it. I was too mad at him for seeing things a little too clearly. I pushed him away because he stood up for me when I was too weak to stand up for myself. I should have thanked him. And now . . ." She felt her cheeks heat. "Now I have too much pride to admit I was wrong."

"Now *that* sounds like the Laurel I know. For a while I thought that sweet side was outweighing the stubborn independence I admire. And Aiden Gallagher is a nice guy, no question, but he needs someone to keep him on his toes."

"Mom!"

"All men do." They shared a wicked smile. "So what are you going to do now?"

"Eat brownie pudding. Wallow."

"And then?"

She thought about it. What did she want to do? Take control of her life back? How?

"I don't know where to start."

"First of all, you have to realize that the life you want is still within reach. Just not the way you planned. Not with Dan. You can still go after what you want."

"And get let down again?"

"Maybe. But maybe not. I'd hate to see you become a bitter old maid, dear. And being a coward isn't the same as revenge. The best revenge is living well."

"I don't want revenge!" The whole idea left a bad taste in her mouth. "Revenge isn't my style. Not since . . ."

Not since Aiden had taken that milkshake cup and

thrown it across the cafeteria. She knew now that what she'd wanted was for him to talk back. To argue. To commit some grand gesture in some seventeen-year-old, impossibly dramatic sort of way. In some small way she'd wanted him to prove her wrong. But he hadn't. He'd been furious and he'd left her standing there, feeling like an ass. That victory had been horribly hollow and all this time her pride had been telling her it was justified while her head and heart told her it was just . . . stupid.

"I don't want revenge. I just want to be happy."

"Then be happy. Stop letting what happened control your decisions. I'm not saying you need to run back to Aiden and leap into a serious relationship if you're not ready. But find a way to make a first step toward what you want."

It was damned good advice. She looked over at her mom and felt a wave of love. "I don't think I've ever given you enough credit," she whispered. "I love you, Mom."

"I try to be there when it counts. You've always done such a good job of standing on your own two feet. This time I just thought you needed a little nudge."

Laurel pushed over the dish of pudding and they ate out of it together for a while. Laurel was still sorting out all her thoughts. What first step could she make? If she really wanted to start over, where did she begin? And it wasn't the greenhouse. It had to be something more personal than that.

Just like that, it hit her. "I've got it." She sat back in her chair and smiled, impressed at the brilliance of it. "I'm going to go to the chamber of commerce and tell them I'll do the photo."

"What photo?"

"You know the one that they've used for years? Of Aiden and me at Aunt Suzy's wedding?"

"Sure."

"They want to do a remake, of us now that we're older. Update the photo with the same models. I refused, because I was still mad at Aiden. And I couldn't stand the thought of putting on a wedding dress. It made me sick to my stomach. But I think I can do it now. If nothing else, I'll prove to myself that I can put on a wedding gown without feeling like I'm gonna throw up."

"It's a small commitment. A baby step, I guess." Her mom didn't sound convinced.

"No, it's perfect! Aiden called me on it right at the beginning. I made all sorts of excuses except for the real one—that I hadn't dealt with my divorce yet. Maybe, if I can do this, I can really start over, you know?"

"If it makes you this excited, it's probably the right thing. I say go for it."

"I'll call Oaklee first thing in the morning. She'll be thrilled. I don't think she's ever had to take no for an answer before."

Once the decision was made, Laurel felt about ten pounds lighter. She tidied up the kitchen, had a less-heavy chat with her mom over a cup of tea, and vacuumed through the house before heading to bed.

After she called Oaklee, she'd have to tell Aiden. That would be a tougher conversation, but for right now, she felt she could take on the world.

CHAPTER 17

Aiden took a sip of his coffee and wandered down Main Street. He was on duty later, but he hadn't been able to sleep. He'd got up and had a shower around seven, then made breakfast, and actually tidied up the apartment. Wouldn't Rory be surprised at that? Of course, he'd made sure to put things away in slightly wrong spots just to get on his brother's nerves. He wasn't that far gone with his broken heart.

And then the phone had rung and it had been Oaklee, asking if he was still available for the photo shoot. Apparently Laurel had changed her mind. He'd agreed because he couldn't back out now, could he? What was Laurel trying to prove by agreeing now? Because she hadn't so much as sent a text since he'd walked out of her house. He was fairly certain that he'd never understand women.

Now it was nearly ten, he was drinking coffee and wandering around aimlessly, wondering if he should stop by the Ladybug to ask or just wait it out. He wasn't generally a patient sort of guy, but there was nothing "usual" about the situation with Laurel. He'd gotten in over his head, and now he was paying for it.

His phone buzzed again against his hip. He reached for it and stared at the number. It was Laurel, calling from work. Maybe she wanted to tell him the news herself.

He stared at it long enough that it went to voicemail. Damn.

And then it buzzed again.

He frowned and hit the button to answer. "Hello?"

"Oh, thank God. It's Laurel. Are you working? Have you seen George this morning?"

His brain switched gears. "No. I'm in town, off duty, but I haven't seen him at all. Why?"

"He was supposed to be to work at eight, but he never showed up. I didn't worry too much until nine, but it's very unlike him. I called the shelter and they said he left at seven-twenty, the usual time. I'm really worried, Aiden."

"I can tell. I can take a look around."

"Can I come with you? I'm going to go crazy sitting here."

"I'll be there in five."

"Thanks, Aiden." She didn't even say goodbye; just hung up the phone.

Aiden frowned as he turned around and headed back to his truck. George could be unreliable, sure, but things had been different the last few weeks. Plus, George really liked Laurel, and despite his issues, Aiden didn't think he'd leave Laurel high and dry. Something felt off.

A few minutes later he was at the Ladybug and Laurel was at the gate, purse over her shoulder, ready to go. He didn't even have time to get out of the truck; she hopped in the passenger side and reached for her seatbelt. "Let's

drive the route from here to the shelter," she suggested.
"Then go from there."

All the focus was on the current problem. He was okay
with that. There'd be time for them to talk later. He drove
them down the main drag toward town center, going a
good ten miles an hour below the speed limit so they could
get a look at the sidewalks and curbs along the way. Neither of them saw anything. Going through the business
district was the same, and on the other side, where the
lots got bigger and more residential, there was no sign of
George, either. The shelter was just west of the main road,
off in a cul-de-sac by an auto repair shop and a window
and door warehouse.

"Let me go in and check to see if he came back," she
said. He hated seeing the strain on her face. She was so
worried. She cared. Not just about George but about people.
She always had. It was one of the things he'd always liked
about her.

"I'll wait."

She hurried out of the truck and into the waiting area
of the combined shelter and food bank. Moments later
she came back out, shaking her head. "No sign of him,"
she said, and slumped into the seat. "What now? Call
the station?"

"He's a vagrant and it's only been a couple of hours.
They'd keep their eyes open, but not go looking." He hated
what he was about to say, but knew it had to be said.
"George has a history of just up and going sometimes.
He'll take off to Montpelier or somewhere. He'll hitchhike
and we won't see him here for weeks or months. I'm sorry,
Laurel. I thought maybe that wouldn't happen once you'd
hired him."

And typical Laurel, she shook her head. "I don't think so. He wouldn't do that. If you could see the change in him . . . he would have told me. I know it."

"You always think the best of people. Maybe that's why you keep getting disappointed."

She turned to him, her jaw set in a stubborn line and her eyes flashing. "It's not a quality I'm ashamed of. And someday, maybe someone will live up to those expectations."

Ouch. Now if that didn't hit him square in the pride. He was about to say that he hadn't walked but had been pushed away, when he thought he saw movement in the trees, only fifty yards or so from the drive.

"Laurel." He spoke firmly and she instantly quieted.

He undid his seatbelt and pinned her with what he hoped was a don't-argue-with-me stare. "Stay here. I'll be right back."

He got out of the truck and jogged toward the trees. There it was again, a little bit of movement, the flash of a red shirt.

Train tracks ran through this part of the property, not used anymore, with weeds growing up between the rails and ties. Aiden stepped over them and into the underbrush. "George? Is that you?"

All he got in response was a groan.

Aiden's pulse quickened as a familiar kind of adrenaline shot into his system. "George? Hang tight. I'm coming. Stay still."

He shoved through the brush and tall weeds and found George, trying to stand. "Jesus, buddy. Hold on."

There was blood all over. It streaked his face, over a split just above his eye and beneath his nose, which sat at an odd angle. His skin was pale and Aiden could see he was struggling to breathe. "Hold still," he ordered. "Can you sit down? I'm going to call for help. You're hurt."

"Work." The word came out more like "wok," followed by a harsh gasp. "Back . . . kid."

"Don't try to talk," Aiden commanded. "Stay right here. I'll be right back." He'd left his phone in the cup holder of his truck, and he jogged back as quickly as he could so he could call for help.

Laurel had her door open as he approached. "Hand me my phone," he said, slightly breathless. "It's him. He needs an ambulance."

Laurel grabbed his phone and shoved it into his hand. He hadn't even punched in the numbers when she was dashing across the train tracks.

He joined her only moments later. She had George resting, propped up against a tree. "Don't try to talk now," she said gently. "You're going to be okay. Help's on the way."

Aiden did a quick check. Legs and arms seemed okay, but when he lifted George's shirt there was already some bruising and when he gently touched ribs, George cried out. It was worse when he touched his abdomen, on the left, and Aiden wondered if he had some internal injuries. He'd had the shit beat out of him for sure, and Aiden fought down a surge of anger that someone could treat another human being in this way.

He heard sirens approaching. "Not long now, buddy. Hang in there."

"Shosh." George closed his eyes and his swollen lips formed the sound. "Shell."

"Hush," Laurel murmured, smoothing his forehead. "There'll be time for that later."

"Up." This sound was clear and George struggled to

brace his hand somewhere so he could rise. The ambulance pulled up right behind Aiden's half-ton and Aiden waved them over. "Up," he demanded again, glaring at Aiden through his swollen eyelids.

Aiden went over and put his arm around George's back. If the man wanted to meet this head-on, then Aiden would help him. He got the sense that there was some sort of pride at stake here. That George was, despite being hurt, terribly pissed off at being a victim.

And then George cried out; a sharp wail full of pain. The paramedics were just approaching when George went limp against Aiden's arm, and Aiden scrambled to catch the rest of the man's weight so he wouldn't fall.

"Shit," he barked, his arm quivering beneath the weight. George wasn't a small guy, and he'd put on some weight in the last month. "A hand here?"

In no time flat they'd got George on a stretcher and immobilized, then moved to get him out of the woods and back to the ambulance. Laurel looked as though someone had struck her, she was so pale, and Aiden reached for her hand and helped guide her out as they followed the team.

"He's still unconscious," she whispered, her fingers clinging to his.

"I know," Aiden replied, and with the same worries. George hadn't just blacked out from pain; he would have come to already if that were the case. He had some serious injuries. And someone had done this to him. It was no accident.

"We can follow them to the hospital." They got to the other side of the railroad tracks and he stopped, put his hands on her shoulders. "Are you okay? Do you need a minute?"

"I'm fine. I'd like to go be with him. He doesn't have anyone else."

Aiden felt the same way. He helped Laurel into the truck—her hands were still shaking—and got in the other side. As the ambulance pulled away, they turned on lights and sirens. Aiden swallowed against a lump in his throat. George was harmless, and now he was seriously hurt.

"Aiden?"

"Hmm?" He pulled a U-turn and hit the gas, pulling in behind the ambulance as they headed for the highway and the hospital.

"He won't have any insurance."

"He'll be cared for. Don't worry."

They drove in silence to the hospital, and parked while the ambulance pulled into the emergency bay. By the time they'd hurried inside, he was already being triaged.

"Are you family?" the clerk asked.

"Emma. You know we're not." Aiden frowned. "We found him. He . . . helps out at Laurel's garden center."

"He lives at the shelter," Laurel added, her voice quivering. "I don't . . ." her voice caught. "I don't even know his last name."

"Have a seat," the clerk said, gentler now. "I'll let you know as soon as I have any news."

They sat. Aiden made a few phone calls to the station and then went for coffee while Laurel checked in at the garden center. Minutes passed, then an hour. Then two. He heard Laurel sniff beside him and he put his arm around her, pulling her close. "No news is good news," he said quietly. He didn't believe it, but he didn't know what else to say.

It was past noon when Emma finally beckoned them over. "You can have five minutes," she said. "I'll take you back."

They went through the sliding doors to the trauma room. It was quiet inside, except for the beep of machines. A nurse was checking an IV bag and smiled at them. "The doctor will be right in."

"Thanks," Laurel said. There were no chairs, so she stood beside the bed. "He's so bruised. I don't want to touch him in case I hurt him."

"I know."

"He was beaten very badly, Aiden."

"I know that, too. There'll be an investigation." He looked down into her eyes. "Maybe we don't know his last name, but he's not nobody."

Her gaze warmed and they shared a moment where it felt like they were on exactly the same page. God, he loved her. Even though she was mixed up, even though she drove him crazy, she had such a good heart. She cared about people and was loyal to a fault. Anyone would be lucky to have a champion like her backing them up.

And he'd driven her away, after he'd promised they could take it slow. What a fool.

The doctor bustled in, her fresh blue scrubs rustling as she moved briskly. "Good morning. You're here to see our George Doe." She smiled at them.

"I'll get to work on a last name," Aiden said. "I'm a cop with the Darling police force."

"You might be interested in his personal effects, then," she said. "Check at the desk."

"It's evidence in any case," Aiden replied. "How bad is it, doctor?"

She sighed. "He was beaten pretty badly, but he's going to be okay. Broken nose, facial lacerations, and a concussion are going to have his head hurting for a good while. We'll monitor that closely, because the last thing we want is a bleed. There's bruising on several parts of his body, and he's got four broken ribs on the left. There's significant bruising there, too. I suspect he took a big boot to the side."

Aiden saw Laurel pale. "You okay to hear this?" he asked.

She nodded. "I'm fine."

"He lost consciousness but regained it en route, which was a big relief. But one of his ribs caused a collapsed lung. He'll be in here for a few days at least, and then he'll be out of commission for at least three to four weeks as his ribs heal."

"But he's going to be okay?"

The doctor nodded. "Yes. We did some imaging to rule out any spleen injury or other internal bleeding. If there aren't any complications from the concussion, he'll be on his way to a full recovery before long."

Laurel wilted against him. "Oh, that's such a relief."

"We're going to be moving him to a room soon. Do you want to be notified?"

"Yes," Laurel answered quickly. "I'll stay with him. I don't want him to wake up and be alone."

"You're sure?" Aiden squeezed her arm. "I can come and spell you, but I have to clock in for work in another hour and I'm not off until late tonight."

"No, I'll stay," she repeated, and he knew that look. When Laurel made her mind up, nothing would shake it. "I'll have the staff close up for the day."

"Great." The doctor touched Laurel's arm lightly. "He's sleeping right now. We've given him something for the pain. We'll be monitoring the concussion, but he'll wake up. Relax."

Laurel smiled a little. "Thanks. Seeing him faint was scary."

"He was lucky you two came along."

Aiden looked down at Laurel. It hadn't been any accident they were there. She'd been determined to find George. She'd been the one to save him.

When the doctor left, Aiden guided her out of the trauma room and back to the waiting room. There was a corner where no one was sitting, and he led her there, sat beside her on the vinyl seat. "Just so we're clear, George owes this to you. You're some woman, Laurel."

"I just knew he wouldn't take off."

"You believed in him. More than anyone, me included." He put her hand in between his. "Don't change. I know I gave you a hard time. I know I walked away. But don't change who you are. You care about people even when they let you down, and at your own expense. That's not something to be ashamed of. It's honorable as hell."

"Aiden . . ."

"I heard you agreed to do the photo."

"Oaklee beat me to it. I was going to tell you today, and then George didn't show up . . ."

"Why did you change your mind?"

"Because my reasons didn't hold up anymore. It wasn't because I hated you, even though I thought I did when I first moved back. And it wasn't because I was too busy with the garden center, even though I'm working long hours. The truth is, I couldn't face putting on a wedding dress again. It felt like such a farce. I stopped believing in the symbol of it. For me, a dress like that was a fraud. But it wasn't really the dress, it was me holding myself back. And I need to move forward. If I can put on a silly satin gown, maybe there's hope for me to get on with my life and stop feeling sorry for myself."

Did that mean there was hope for them? Aiden wanted

to ask, but with everything that had happened today, he didn't want to push too much. "Good for you," he replied. "It'll be fun. If we can remain civil to each other for an hour or two?"

Her eyes delved into his. "I think I can manage that."

"Me, too." An hour or two, or a lot more than that. But maybe what Laurel needed was baby steps.

"You want to know the ironic bit?" She was smiling at him now. He was glad. He hated how they'd ended things, and had missed that note of warmth in her voice.

"What?"

"I always wanted a simple wedding in the park, like Dan had. Just some flowers and people I cared about, and a simple but pretty dress, and maybe a backyard barbecue for a reception. Instead I had a big, fancy, uber-official-looking event that was the real deal. And now I'll be in a dress and standing on the bridge, just the way I always dreamed, and it's all pretend." She shook her head and laughed. "Oh well. I'm trying to learn to roll with the punches a little better these days."

She couldn't know how much her simple little speech had touched him. The whole time she'd been at Dan's ceremony, she must have been thinking about the wedding she'd wanted and hadn't had. And there her ex had been, having it, and going on with the life they'd planned but with someone else. No wonder she'd been so upset. Dan had stripped away just about everything.

But maybe, just maybe, he could give her some of it back.

"Laurel." Aiden reached out and touched her face. "I really am sorry. I promised you we could go slowly, and then the day of the wedding I pushed."

She shook her head, and he saw her throat bob as she

swallowed. "I wasn't ready to hear all that, you know? It was a hard day and I was overwhelmed, and I took it out on you. When you said you loved me . . ."

She bit down on her lip, and his heart squeezed a little bit. He reached out and took her hand.

Her gaze met his as she continued. "I wasn't ready to feel what I was feeling. I'm not sure I'm ready now, either. But it wasn't just fun for me, Aiden. It was much, much more. I just get so scared when I hear the 'L' word. It hasn't really worked out for me in the past, and I'm not sure I can take having my heart broken again."

He rubbed his thumb over her hand. "You're not the only one to have your heart broken, you know."

"Your ex? What was her name?"

"Erica?" He gave a short laugh and shook his head. "No, not her. You, Laurel. I have never felt about anyone the way I feel about you. I can't think straight. I keep replaying that conversation and wishing I'd handled it differently. But I was scared too. And I wanted you to hurry up and move on already, so we could have a shot."

Her voice quivered as she said, "I broke your heart?"

He thought about how irritable he'd been lately. How he'd hated getting out of bed in the morning, how the days seemed pointless. "Yeah. Nothing's been the same. I can't eat, I sleep too much, I snap at everyone."

"I'm sorry. I never wanted to hurt you."

Her eyes filled with tears and the ache in his heart intensified. "Don't cry, okay? We'll figure it out."

She nodded. "I need to tell you something. I mean . . . we've talked about the divorce, and me getting over what happened, and you were one hundred percent right about that. But it's not just Dan's affair, you see? It's much bigger than that. We had this life planned, Aiden. A life that included children—a whole future. He kept putting it off, but we're only in our twenties. I wanted to start a family but the clock wasn't exactly ticking yet, you know? So when he told me about Ryan . . ." She let out a long breath. "I thought he was going to say he was ready for babies. He crushed all of my dreams that night, and ever since I've been too scared to dream again."

Children. His stomach clenched and he stared at her. Babies. This was big territory he was wading into. He remembered Erica talking about marriage and babies and how it had terrified him. Now, though, the terror rushing through his veins wasn't the urge to run. It was bigger. Different. It was the earth-shaking fear of being a father, and all that came with it. Fatherhood was huge. And then he thought about Connor and Ronan and wondered how their kids would look, his and Laurel's. And something new rushed through him. Something wonderful and scary.

"You should dream," he said quietly, wanting to gather her into his arms but holding back, considering they were still in a hospital waiting room. "You should always have dreams."

"You were right about the consolation prize. I love the Ladybug, but it really was a 'since you can't have the life you wanted, take this instead' thing."

"And now?"

Her fingers tightened around his. "And now I'm starting to think that coming home and opening that place was the best decision I ever made."

He smiled. She was wearing her Ladybug golf shirt and no makeup and her hair was held back by a simple band, but to him she was the most beautiful woman he'd ever seen. There wasn't a single thing about her that was false.

"Aiden?"

He met her gaze.

Her lip trembled a little. "I feel the need to say something here, and I don't want you to read too much into it, okay? But I think you need to know that I love you, too. I knew it this morning when I couldn't find George and I called you. It wasn't because you're a cop. It's because you were the first person I wanted to turn to when I was afraid. You make me feel safe, even when we're not even speaking. I love you. Maybe we can start there, and start over?"

She looked so scared, and yet so gloriously defiant as she said the words. Everything in his chest seemed to expand as hope slammed into him.

"Thank God," he murmured, and ignoring the public setting, he tugged on her hand. She slid over and onto his lap.

"What? You're not worried someone will see you?" he asked.

She shrugged. "It's time I stopped caring about stupid stuff and focused on being happy."

He held her close, closing his eyes and soaking up the moment. After a minute or two, he lifted his chin. "So, what happens now?"

"You mean, where do we go from here?" She gave a little laugh. "I don't know. I suppose we can start with the picture on the bridge. Let's get that out of the way first, and get George on his way to recovery."

"If that's what you want."

She nodded and he felt the movement against his temple. He lifted his head and kissed her, just a brief kiss but on the lips. "God, I feel horrible this has happened to George but so happy that it led to this."

"Me, too." She smiled down at him. "Oh, Aiden. It feels good to be excited for the future again." She kissed his cheek. "I stopped going after what I wanted. Maybe I felt I didn't deserve it. Or the universe was telling me I didn't. But here you are. And it feels right, doesn't it?"

He would have answered but the clerk called them over again. When they approached the desk, Emma looked directly at Aiden. "I've got George's things here, but there's a bit of a problem."

Aiden's brow furrowed. "What sort of problem? George really didn't have much to speak of, and as far as I know his backpack stayed at the shelter."

"Can you come back here with me, please?" She opened the door and ushered them into a little triage desk area. "I know you called the assault into your station, Officer Gallagher. We're waiting for them to arrive before we hand over the personal effects."

"Because they're evidence?" he asked.

She nodded.

"What sort of evidence?"

"He had a plastic zip bag in his pocket. It's got the name of the Ladybug Garden Center on it."

"May I see it?"

"Just don't touch anything," Emma replied. She gestured to the articles on a small table. "The problem is, it has pills in it. Do you know if he was using? Maybe dealing to local kids or anything?"

Aiden felt as if he'd been punched in the gut. "Pills? Not George. He's not a user or a pusher. I'll stake my badge on it."

"But the bag is one that I use to keep the cash float in at night," Laurel said, sounding shaken. "It doesn't make sense."

"Well, I'm sure once he wakes up it'll be explained just fine." Emma's smile was polite, and Aiden felt like saying,

"You're not sure at all. I know that smile." He looked at the other items. No bills, but a little loose change, a stubby pencil, and a receipt from the corner store deli were all that was on the table along with the bag.

"Wait," he said. "George always wore a black bracelet. It's not there. Would he still be wearing it?"

"We would have taken it off," she replied, frowning. "Maybe he didn't wear it today."

Laurel shook her head. "No, I noticed it, too. He'd show up to work and always have it on. I kept meaning to ask what it meant, but George is pretty private. I didn't want to stick my nose in. But I've never seen him without it on, not that I can remember."

Emma shrugged. "I don't know what to tell you."

"Thanks, anyway. And for showing us. Maybe we can help put the pieces together if we remember anything."

They left the room, escaping as far away from the triage desk as they could. "He wasn't using or dealing," Laurel hissed. "I've never seen him high. Ever. And I can't imagine him selling."

"Me, either. He's got a story but that's not it."

"Then you don't believe it, either. Oh, I'm so relieved."

He squeezed her hand. "Look, I hate to do this. I'd rather spend the whole day with you, but I have to show up for my shift. Can someone come pick you up? Do you want to go back with me and pick up your car?"

"I'm staying," she said firmly. "He'll wake up soon, and he'll be hurting. He should see a familiar face. I can always call my mom if I need to."

"I'll come back as soon as I'm done."

"Okay."

"Text me if there's any change or you need anything, okay?"

"Okay."

There was a moment of hesitation where he knew he had to go and wasn't sure what to do. He knew what he wanted. He wanted to take her in his arms and hold her close. He wanted to kiss her lips, lingering for a few moments so he could take the taste of her with him. Instead he dropped a kiss on her forehead, closing his eyes briefly. "I'll call you on my break to check in," he promised, and then cleared his throat.

She stood on tiptoe and pressed her lips to his, giving him a sweet, sweet kiss. "I'll be here," she assured him. "Be careful, okay?"

A warmth filled his chest at her quiet caution. "I'm always careful. And Laurel?"

She raised her eyebrows in response and he really wanted to call in sick. But he wouldn't, because he wanted to get to the bottom of what was going on. "We're gonna work it out, you'll see."

He gave her one last smile and then stepped out of the hospital into the summer sun.

CHAPTER 18

Laurel was fairly sure that her bottom was now the precise shape of the hospital chair.

To her relief, George had awakened twice. Both times he'd been groggy, and she knew he likely wouldn't remember her speaking to him or taking his hand at all. His right hand, she noticed, had split knuckles. He'd managed to get a few shots in on his attacker, it seemed.

Now it was eight p.m., the shadows outside the window were getting longer and she was feeling dozy. Willow had stopped in around seven with some curry lentil soup and fresh bread, as well as a bottle of her home-concocted vegetable juice that she swore would have George up and going again in no time. Aiden had checked in, too, around six-fifteen, but she'd had little to report and he hadn't heard anything, either.

A groan sounded from the bed and she perked up, leaning forward. "George? It's Laurel."

"Lorl." Her name was cumbersome on his lips, but recognizable. She got up and moved to the bed, perched on the very edge. She moved carefully, not wanting to disturb him. He had to be horribly sore.

"I'm here. You're in the hospital, George."

He opened his eyes. Or at least the one eye that wasn't completely swollen shut. "Ow. Bad."

Her throat tightened. "You've got a concussion, a broken nose, a few stitches in that pretty face of yours, and I'm afraid you've got some broken ribs."

He swore. That word she recognized, plain as day. She grinned. He'd never cursed in front of her before.

"I'm going to call the nurse. Do you want some water?" There was a plastic cup on the table beside the bed. At one point it had had ice in it. The ice had melted but the water was still cool.

"Yuh."

She called the desk and then held the cup and bendy straw for him as he took a long pull. "Ahhh," he said, closing his eyes for a second. "More."

She let him drink some more and then put the cup down as the nurse came in. She spoke to him in quiet tones and asked if he wanted more medication.

"No. Soon. Want to talk first. Put me to sleep again."

"Okay. I'll get Ms. Stone to buzz when you're ready."

George looked at Laurel. "Hurts all over. Hurts to breathe."

She nodded. "Your lung collapsed because of your ribs. They're going to hurt for a while, I'm afraid."

"Not first time," he said, laboring.

He reached for the cup again and she noticed his gaze falling on his arm where the hospital bracelet was fastened. "Bracelet. The black one?"

"We couldn't find it."

He swore again. Well. She smiled. "George. Such

language," she teased. It was such a relief to have him awake, but she was also so very sad at how badly he was hurt and how the loss of the bracelet seemed important.

"Punk ass kids," he said, quite clearly.

That got her attention. "Can you tell me what happened, George? If you want to wait, that's okay. I don't want you to strain yourself."

"Waking up more now. Water helps." He tried to smile, but his lips barely moved. "Ow."

"Take your time."

He sighed. "Left for work. Usually walk along the tracks, you know? Couple kids came out. They had paint . . . spray paint. I guess one recognized me 'cause he started calling out stuff about the bum and . . . well, you know."

He paused. That much had been difficult. She waited while he prepared himself again. "They started pushing me around. I knew I was going to be late. I tried to leave but the bigger one . . . he's got a mean right hook." George's tongue snuck out to wet his lips. "Once I was down they started kicking me. Then they just left."

"Did you recognize either of them?"

He nodded slightly. "Son of a bitch, my head hurts."

"Do you want your meds now?"

"In a minute." He took a slow, cautious breath. "Mitchell kid."

She sat back in surprise. "Brent Mitchell's kid? The mayor?"

"Seen him around town before." His dark, bloodshot gaze met hers. "See lots when you're invisible."

Oh, now that made her heart ache. "So," she said slowly, "it was Brent Mitchell's kid who attacked you, as well as someone else?"

"Kid he hangs around with. Dark hair. Stubby nose." George grimaced. "Big boots."

"George, did you take any of the zippy bags from the store? You know, the ones that I put the deposit and the float in?"

He frowned, his brows pulling together. "Never saw you use those bags. I'm not there at night."

Right. Because the deposit was done up after close and so was the float for the next day.

"I'll get the nurse to bring your pain meds. And maybe something to eat, some broth or something, if you're allowed."

She stood up from the bed.

"Lorl."

The way he said it made her heart ache all over again.

"Why are you here?"

"Because you're my friend," she stated simply, and escaped the room before he could see the tears in her eyes.

She stopped at the nurse's station and gave an update, and then went to the quiet waiting room down the hall and called Aiden. When he didn't answer, she figured he must be busy on a call. It was only another few hours until he was off, anyway.

She waited for him, sitting on the more comfortable sofa in the waiting room. She must have nodded off, because she felt a hand on her shoulder and she lifted her head. Aiden was looking down at her, and her heart gave a big thump in response. He'd come straight from work, still in his uniform. He looked so strong and formidable and . . . safe, dressed like that. The shirt was short sleeved and she could see the curve of his biceps just below the hem. His tattoo, however, was covered. She remembered tracing it with her fingertip one time while he was sleeping, and wondered when they'd get to that point again. She wasn't going to rush it. Their relationship was too important. They had to find their balance first before they took any big steps.

"Hey, sleepyhead," he said softly, and it was all she could do to keep from standing and walking straight into his strong embrace.

"Hey," she replied, and smiled a little. "I guess I fell asleep."

"Long day."

"Sofa was more comfortable than the chair in the room."

Aiden came around the sofa and sat down beside her, put his wide hand on her knee. "How is he?"

"He woke up. Told me some things that might help you figure out who did this."

"Oh?"

She nodded. "Of course, he's had lots of drugs, but I don't think there's any reason to not believe him. He said it was Brent Mitchell's kid and a friend who beat him up."

"Oh, man. Brent's a good guy. If it's true, this'll kill him. What'd he say?"

"That he and another kid started making fun of the 'bum.' And he's missing his bracelet. He also said the bag wasn't his. Don't know why it'd be on him, though." She frowned.

"I'll talk to George. If I get the same story as you, then we'll know it's not the drugs talking and get going on it."

"He said something that made me really sad, Aiden." She sighed. "When I asked how he knew who the Mitchell kid was, he said that when you're invisible you notice a lot. That's not right."

"I agree with you." He reached over and took her hand.

"I'm going to pop into the room and see if he's awake. You get some rest. I'll take you home soon."

"Okay."

He got up and walked out to the hall. She watched him go, immeasurably glad that they'd talked. Nothing had felt right without him.

He came back twenty minutes later, his face looking considerably more weary. "I got the same story as you. Looks like we'll have to check it out. Is it wrong of me to hope George is mistaken? Brent's a good guy."

"Sometimes you don't know what's happening behind the scenes," she said, sighing. "Maybe they're having some troubles with the son. Those teenage years are difficult." She stood and put her purse strap over her shoulder, preparing to leave. It was nearly midnight. "I guess I always think about it as having gone through it as a kid, not as a parent. Do you think we were that much trouble for our parents?"

They began walking to the elevator. "I don't know. Probably. My mom could likely tell stories that'd curl your hair." He sent her a sideways grin.

The doors opened and they stepped inside the car. "I remember my brother having lots of arguments with my dad," she confessed. "Of course, he was on the debate team. I guess it served him well, now that he's working in the governor's office."

Aiden grinned. "I see Ethan struggling with the boys already. I'm thinking we were more trouble than our parents let on."

She smiled, feeling a strange sort of nostalgia, paired with a familiar longing. She knew Ethan had lost his wife, but she envied him those two little boys. They were precocious and darling.

"Aw, they're just busy, like little boys are supposed to be."

The elevator stopped and they got out on the main floor. "Connor's the oldest," he commented. "He takes the lead. And he gets into the most trouble. But Ronan . . . he's different. He watches. He reminds me of me a bit, I suppose."

"Why?"

He shrugged. "Believe it or not, I tried to stay under the radar. Ethan was the oldest and man, is that guy bull-headed. Then there was Hannah, and she had all the girl hormones. Rory was . . . well, he loves order and everything in its place, enough that he'd throw a fit if something wasn't just right. And the twins came along and were a total handful. I just tried to never make waves. I didn't want to cause anyone worry."

"So you covered your feelings with jokes and smiles." A lot of things started making sense now. He'd been care-free and charismatic, but not troublesome. Even when he'd gone to parties and such, he'd been the guy to look after others, not the one puking in the bushes. His choice of profession didn't seem quite so odd now.

"Pretty much."

"You've started sharing a lot more of your emotions lately, big guy."

He chuckled. "Don't let that get around. I have a reputation to uphold."

"Your secret is safe with me," she answered, reaching for his hand as they continued walking to the truck. "Thank you for telling me, Aiden."

"It still doesn't come easily, Laurel. But maybe now you understand why what happened between us, back in school, was so difficult. I'd made a huge mistake, and everyone knew it. And then you called me on it and I just felt so guilty. I had no right to even talk to you after that. I'd disappointed my parents—they got a call about it, you know. And I'd disappointed you and myself, too."

He opened the door to the truck and closed it behind her once they got in. After he started the engine, he looked over at her. "Laurel, I really admire you. Particularly today. You're a loyal friend. You stick by the people you care about, even when it hurts." His gray-blue eyes locked with hers. "I could take a lesson."

She was touched, and looked away before he could see what had to be a stupid, sappy look on her face. "I think you're doing just fine," she whispered, and rested her temple against the window as he backed out of the parking space.

That was the last thing she remembered until she heard him say her name and felt his wide hand shaking her shoulder ever so gently.

"Laurel. We're home."

She lifted her head and hoped to God she hadn't drooled. "I fell asleep."

He chuckled. "Yes, you did. Before I even got to the street."

She rolled her shoulders, trying to ignore the tingles she felt when he spoke in that low, smooth voice that teased along her nerve endings. Memories slammed into her, of coming home with him, going inside, making love. It was love, she knew now. The way she felt in his arms, the connection they shared in those moments . . . it was more intense than anything she'd ever felt. Ever.

She wasn't quite ready to go all-in yet, but after today, at least it seemed like a possibility.

"I should get inside. Thanks for driving me home."

He left the truck running. She wasn't sure if she was relieved or disappointed he wasn't going to walk her to the door.

"Of course. I'll keep you posted, okay?"

She nodded. "I'll go back to the hospital tomorrow. I'll do the same."

He unbuckled his seatbelt and leaned over. "Can I kiss you?"

That he even asked touched her heart. He was truly letting her take the lead and she loved him for it. He touched his lips to hers, moving them slowly, drawing her into a deeper, more intimate kiss. It was sweet, and hesitant, and . . . new. When he moved back, her heart was pounding against her ribs and her breath came in shorter gasps.

She opened the door and stepped out into the cool summer air. "See you later, Aiden. Thank you for everything."

He lifted a hand in farewell. But he sat in her driveway and waited for her to go inside and turn on the lights before he finally drove away again, leaving her feeling empty and alone without him.

Driving into Brent Mitchell's yard in any official capacity was not a job that Aiden looked forward to. He was seated in a cruiser with another officer, Tracy Holbrook, and neither of them said much.

This morning, they'd visited George and took an official statement. By that time, they'd also found out that the zippy bag contained Molly, a refined form of Ecstasy, and that George's fingerprints were *not* on it.

They'd discovered something else, too. His prints showed up as being in the military database. More specifically, an army sergeant out of Fort Hood.

He was a damned veteran and he was living on the

streets. There was just something so inherently wrong with that.

Holbrook pulled into the Mitchells' drive. By Darling standards, it was a heck of a house. Aiden's dad had been one of the contractors on the development and they were considered "estate houses." Big homes centered on one-acre lots that were groomed to perfection. Brent's BMW sat in the driveway, next to an Acura 2-door with a DHS Devils football sticker on the back window.

"This's gonna be a poor-little-rich-kid routine, isn't it," Holbrook said, sighing.

"Probably."

"Great."

They got out of the car and walked up to the front door. Aiden knocked, firmly, then stood back.

It was Brent who came to the door. "Oh. God. Was there an accident or something?"

Aiden smiled. "Nothing to panic about, Brent. We were just wondering if we could have a few words with you and your son."

"With Josh?" His face registered surprise. "Has he done something?"

"We don't know for sure," Holbrook said easily. "Something came up and we need to ask him a few questions, that's all."

"He's upstairs. He took a nasty hit in practice yesterday morning."

Aiden looked over at Tracy. He'd bet any money that the nasty hit was courtesy of George. He whipped out his phone and did a quick check of a website while Brent disappeared upstairs.

He came back down with Josh, who was dressed in sleep pants, a T-shirt, and a scowl. A purple bruise covered the crest of one cheek, and his eye was puffy and blood-shot. He shoved his hands into the pockets of his flannel pants and stood a few steps behind his dad.

"That's quite a shiner you've got, Josh."

He shrugged.

Aiden looked at Brent. "There was an assault yesterday, Mr. Mitchell. A witness puts Josh at the scene, along with another boy that he didn't recognize. Dark hair, big build."

"Corey. He and Josh are playing summer football to-gether. Right, Josh?"

Josh gave a quick nod. "Yeah."

"Where were you yesterday morning, around seven-thirty, Josh?"

"On my way to the field." He pointed at his face and scowled. "Duh."

"Josh." Brent's voice was sharp.

"What time was your practice?"

"Eight. Ask Corey. He'll tell you."

Aiden nodded. "You ever do drugs, Josh? Smoke a little weed? Pop some Molly?"

Brent's face paled. "What the hell? Aiden, I can't imag-ine what would make you ask these kinds of questions." He looked over his shoulder at Josh. "I'll admit we have our teenage moments, but Josh isn't a user."

Aiden felt sorry for Brent at that moment. Josh was standing there, looking like a cocky asshole. Like he was untouchable. God, if Aiden had gone home with a shiner like that, his dad would have kicked his ass right after he'd had a long lecture from his mom. Brent was a good guy, but he was busy. His wife commuted to Burlington each day. The house was a testament to electronic babysitters with a big-screen TV and the latest gaming system. Not to mention the car in the driveway.

Aiden kept his face neutral. "Yesterday, a homeless man was attacked just outside the shelter. He's in hospital and has identified Josh as one of his attackers."

"Jesus." Brent's mouth dropped open. "That's not possible. You heard him, he was on his way to practice."

"You practice at the high school field, right?" Aiden aimed the question at Josh.

He nodded.

Aiden brought up the last website in his browser on his phone. "The high school field is closed for maintenance this week. There was no practice yesterday." He looked at Josh. "You want to tell me where you got that black eye?"

Josh looked at his dad. "This is bullshit."

"Watch your mouth. And answer the question, Josh."

Josh crossed his arms and adopted a sullen expression. And kept his arrogant little mouth shut.

But the motion, so reflexive, also showed his hands, and Aiden saw the marks. "You want to show me your hands, please?"

"Dad, he can't make me, can he?"

"Show him your hands, Josh." Brent's voice was tight.

Josh hesitated, but then finally slid his arms out of their folded position. The knuckles on his right hand were cracked and scabbing, the knuckles swollen. And there was black spray paint on his fingertips, like he'd tried to wash it off but hadn't quite succeeded.

Aiden thought back . . . to the break-in at the garden center, to the tagging at the school and in Memorial Park, and the rude graffiti on Laurel's fence. That was annoying but not the same as physically beating on another human being.

Then he noticed the black band on Josh's left wrist.

He stepped forward and grabbed Josh's arm in a firm grip. "Hey! Ow! What the hell, get your hands off me!"

"Where'd you get that bracelet?"

Aiden could hear the anger in his own voice and fought to keep his cool as he released Josh's arm. The bracelet looked just like the one George wore. What a punk. It took a special kind of arrogance to beat on a homeless guy and then wear a souvenir as if he'd never get caught.

"I found it."

Aiden wiggled his fingers in a "give it to me" motion, and Josh sighed but slipped it off his wrist. Aiden read the inscription: SSGT IAN MERCK SC ARMY. Below was a date in 2004, and three devastating letters: KIA.

Aiden's hand shook. Josh stepped back, a smile playing on his lips, while Aiden fought to hold on to his temper. What he really wanted to do was wipe that smirk off of Josh's lips.

"Found it. Shit. Josh." Brent's face was full of suppressed anger. "What the hell is wrong with you?"

"It's bullshit. Come on. You're the mayor, Dad. All you've gotta do is say the word and this goes away, right? It's bullshit."

"Go upstairs. Get dressed. And don't even think about not doing it or standing there and mouthing off to me, you got it? Do it right now."

"But it was Corey's . . ."

"Go!" Brent barked out the command.

Josh made a dismissive sound and slumped off toward the stairs.

"Dammit," Brent said the moment Josh was gone. "Officers . . . I don't know what to say." He ran his fingers through his hair, shook his head. "I never thought . . . Do you need him for questioning?"

"Yeah, we do," Aiden said. "Brent, I'm sorry, man. I know he's your kid. And it's got to be hard. But I think he might be involved in the break-in at the Ladybug Garden Center this spring, as well as the acts of vandalism going on around town."

Brent sighed. "He's angry. We've known it and tried to convince ourselves that he'll outgrow it. I'll have him to the station within the hour. I'll bring counsel, too. I expect you'll lay charges."

Holbrook stepped in. "Yes, sir."

"The homeless guy . . ."

"George."

"He's in the hospital?"

"Yes. He's been working for Laurel Stone here and there. When he didn't show up yesterday, she went looking."

"Is he okay?"

"He will be, but I won't lie to you. They really did a number on him."

Brent's shoulders slumped. "I'll see you within the hour."

Aiden found Laurel sitting on George's bed, feeding him soup and chatting away. He nearly laughed at the sight. George was bruised and looking rather put out at being spoon-fed, Laurel looked as if nothing was out of the ordinary. "That's a man who looks like he needs a steak, not some watery old broth," Aiden said, stepping into the room.

George made a motion as if to laugh, caught himself, winced, and let out a groan.

"Sorry, dude." Aiden went the rest of the way in, tried not to stare at Laurel and how pretty she looked today in a casual flowered skirt and blue knit top. "No steak in here. Figured you got your teeth rattled. They still loose?"

"A little."

Aiden reached into the paper sack he was carrying and took out a container. "Willow from The Purple Pig sent along a dish of her rice pudding. She said the fresh cinnamon makes all the difference. I thought it might have some substance while being mild enough you can handle it."

George lifted his hand and wiggled his fingers. "No more soup," he commanded, and Laurel laughed.

"Fine," she said, sitting back.

"Can you feed yourself, George? Or are your fingers too sore? Next time use some boxing gloves, huh?"

George took the container and spoon and tried a bite. "Better than soup."

"Good. You look like hell, my friend. Or should I say . . . Sergeant."

The spoon stopped mid-air.

"We tested your fingerprints. They came up in the database. Good news is, yours weren't on the bag they found. And we arrested Josh Mitchell and his friend. They were charged with assault, vandalism, breaking and entering, and theft." He looked over at Laurel. "The bag was from the Ladybug. Once he realized his dad wasn't going to step in and fix everything, he fessed up to it all. He broke in and took what was in the safe. Mummy'd cut off his allowance that week and he wanted to score."

"Goodness." Laurel looked shocked. "He can't be more than sixteen."

Aiden shrugged. "Old enough to get in trouble. You were right, Laurel. You never know what's going on within a family, do you?"

He reached into his pocket and took out the bracelet. "Now, I think this belongs to you."

Aiden fastened it around George's wrist, just above the hospital bracelet. "Someone special?"

George looked up, tears in his eyes. "Brother and best friend."

"I'm sorry."

"Me, too."

Aiden looked over at Laurel, and she shook her head a bit. He agreed with her. Now wasn't the time to go poking around into George's past. There'd be enough time for that later.

"I should probably go. Let you get your rest."

"Okay." George frowned. "After this . . . I don't know . . . where to go. What to do."

Aiden stepped up to the foot of the bed. "Do you want to go back to the shelter? Is there family we can call?"

A pause, and then George shook his head. Looked at Laurel. "I want to go back to work. But I can't until this is better."

That was all Aiden needed to hear. "Let me do some digging, okay?"

Laurel nodded. "My brother's got some connections, too. If you want to get back on your feet again, we'll help you."

George sniffed. "I'm not very good at accepting help."

"Not many people are, brother. But sometimes you just have to. And then down the road, you can help someone else. That's how it works."

George nodded. "We'll see."

It was as much of a commitment as Aiden had ever heard pass his lips. He was satisfied.

"We'll be back later. I won't let her bring you soup."

"Thanks."

Laurel looked up at Aiden as they walked out together. "It's really true? Brent's kid was responsible for it all?"

"It looks that way. He was waiting for Daddy to bail him out. It didn't happen. I don't think he'll be driving the new Acura in the driveway anytime soon, either. Brent's beside himself."

"No kidding." She laughed a little. "You know, we did some stupid stuff as kids, but I don't remember anyone who would have gone past graffiti. Theft, assault . . . that's a big deal."

"Well, they've owned up to it now. It'll be interesting to see what comes of it. If it were my kid . . ."

"You'd what?" She was rather interested in this response. He hadn't been a troublemaker, but he hadn't been straight and narrow, either.

Straight and narrow. Funny, she remembered now, that was what the other cop had called him that night on the golf course.

"I'd make him work to pay for all the damages. Then he'd have to do a crapload of community service. Volunteer with vets, or at the shelter or the food bank. He could spend his spare time painting over graffiti. Contributing to society rather than considering it his personal consequence-free playground."

"You'd make it a hell of a teachable moment."

"Hardly. A judge will have his say, particularly for the assault. But there are other lessons to be learned, too. That's what my dad would have done."

"Mine, too." She looked up at him. "I know there were

just two of us, whereas there were six of you, but I think
we had similar upbringings."

"Me, too."

They stopped outside the hospital doors. The day was
warm and the breeze perfumed with the scent of nearby
planters and flower beds. Laurel inhaled deeply and sighed.
"Oh, it's nice out here. It's too bad George is stuck inside."

"His name's George Reilly, by the way." Aiden looked
over at her. "The fingerprint ID gave us his details. He's a
veteran of Enduring Freedom."

"I wonder how he went from there to being in Darling
on the streets." It made her sad just thinking about it.

"Well, it's a new start for him. Not a great beginning,
but we'll help him get back on his feet again." He touched
her arm. "It wouldn't have happened without you, you
know. You giving him that job gave him more pride and
confidence than anything I ever did or said."

Her heart swelled at his words, but she just shrugged.
She'd never had a moment's regret about it.

They both had their own vehicles, so when they said
goodbye this time it would be a real parting of the ways.
She thought of the photo session coming up and figured
they'd better at least chat about it a bit. "So, this picture
thing . . . ?" Now that they'd made up, she wasn't entirely
sure how to proceed. She wasn't ready to jump back into
a relationship with him, despite her feelings. Now that it
was all "out there," the idea of being together, of making
love, was overwhelming. It took some getting used to, and
she was scared.

He nodded. "Oaklee said they were hoping for the first
Saturday in August, weather permitting."

"Two weeks away. You can bet she's going to have me

looking for the right dress to wear and driving me crazy." The idea sent little butterflies of apprehension through her stomach.

"Enjoy it," he suggested. "Think of it as . . . getting to dress up in a special dress and have your hair done and not have to pay for any of it. Oaklee said they're footing the bill for the expenses. Dress, tux, flowers, hair and makeup. What the hell, right?"

"We can do this, right? And then we'll talk about us?"

He held her gaze for a long time, then smiled a little. "It's going to be a very long two weeks, but I'll wait, because I want you to be sure. Because I love you."

A lump formed in her throat. "I love you, too, Aiden."

"Do you mean that?"

She was almost in tears as she nodded. She did love him. It scared her to death, but she did. The last few days had showed her that he would be there when it counted, even when she didn't necessarily deserve for him to be. She'd called and he'd come. And he was respecting her boundaries so perfectly it was painful.

"Okay, then," he said softly. "Two weeks. I'll see you at the Kissing Bridge."

He started to walk away.

"Aiden, I—"

"The Kissing Bridge," he called back, grinning, walking backward for a few steps before turning and jogging to his truck.

Two weeks. One wedding dress. And perhaps an acting ability she wasn't sure she possessed, because she had no idea how she was going to be able to pose with him and not want it to be the real thing.

CHAPTER 19

Oaklee and Willow met up with Laurel at Blushing Bridals at two o'clock on Tuesday afternoon. Laurel was nervous as anything. She shouldn't be. It was just a dress for a photo shoot. But after all her distress about even thinking of wearing one again, and then her growing feelings for Aiden, her nerves were a little on edge.

She didn't want to feel like a bride. She had to keep remembering that they were taking their relationship slowly. She was a model. Except she wasn't a model, she was the owner of a garden center and the whole thing felt surreal.

"You made it!" Oaklee greeted her with her usual energy and enthusiasm. "Here, let me snap a pic." She whipped up her phone and took a shot. "Perfect. Hang on." She used her thumbs and typed something quickly, then looked up with a triumphant smile. "First tweet of the new campaign: *All set to say yes to a dress! #somethingoldsomethingnew.* See? That's our official campaign hashtag for the shoot."

If Laurel had any romantic ideas, they totally fled in

that moment. This was business. Full stop. Willow was behind Oaklee, and rolled her eyes.

"Get it?" Oaklee continued on, undaunted. "The old photo and the new. This's gonna be great. I'll go get Tricia and tell her we're ready to start."

When she was gone, Willow came over. "You ready for this? Oaklee looks ready to steamroll you."

"That's why I have you along. I know it's just a photo, and the dress is only on loan, but I don't want to be shoved in something horrendous and so blinged out I can hardly walk."

Willow laughed. "Gotcha. Don't worry. I've got your back." She took Laurel's hand for a moment. "Are you sure about this?"

"Yes," Laurel replied, determined. "It's time I got over the past."

"But you and Aiden . . ."

Laurel hoped she wasn't blushing. "We've made our peace. We'll both be fine."

Oaklee came back, the saleslady in tow. "Everyone, you know Tricia, right? She's going to help us pick out a dress today."

"Hello, Laurel. This is going to be so fun, right? All the great bits of shopping for a dress, without any of the pressure." She threw Laurel a wink. At best guess, Tricia was in her early forties and had left her wedding day long in the past. Her huge diamond winked in the light as she moved her hands.

"I want something pretty simple," Laurel said, being clear from the start. "I know it's not real, but I still want to be comfortable. I've never been into a lot of flashy sequins or beads or any of that stuff. "

"Perish the thought. You're what, a size six? Eight?"

She assessed Laurel's figure with a keen eye. "Good figure, though you hide it a bit. We can find something to bring out those assets while keeping it simple and classic, yes?"

"Oh God," Laurel whispered to Willow. "I forgot how crazy this is. My assets?"

"Oh, shut up and have fun." Willow ran her fingers over a rack of bridesmaid dresses. "Be pretty and girly for once."

Oaklee and Tricia got busy and within what felt like seconds they were back with an armload of dresses. "Okay, dear. Here's your dressing room. Do you want me to help you?"

"Sure, I guess."

"You ladies take a seat. We'll be out with dress number one in no time."

The first number was plain satin, strapless, falling to the floor in a simple column. A single beaded belt created an empire waist. Laurel couldn't believe she was going to say it, but it was too plain.

"Honey, let's put your hair up in a little bun. Then we can play with some headpieces and such because a dress never looks finished without it."

Laurel sighed and grabbed the hair elastic from around her wrist. She gathered her hair into a messy knot and Tricia added a little tiara to her head. "What do you think?"

She didn't, but she'd let Willow and Oaklee see, at least.

She stepped out of the change room and Willow's gaze met hers, amused, while Oaklee immediately shook her head. "That's too simple, Tricia." She blushed a little. "Oh gosh. I should have asked how you like it, Laurel."

"I actually agree with you. It's not . . . me."

"Okay, let's try number two."

Number two was a strapless fit and flare with asymmetrical ruching. The beadwork was pretty but simple along the edge of the bustline, and the satin folds of the skirt were pretty. A miniature train followed behind her. She liked it better than the last, but it still wasn't right. A step outside the change room got the same response. Oaklee liked it much better, but Willow shook her head. "It doesn't really say 'romance in the garden,' which is what the bridge is, right? Laurel's more about nature. This is pretty, but it's more 'walking down the church aisle,' don't you think?"

That was it precisely. "I agree with you, Wil. I wasn't sure why it wasn't working for me. It's very pretty and fits great. It's just . . . not right."

Oaklee and Willow exchanged glances.

"So I should try number three?"

And so it went on. The mermaid was a definite no-go. The sheath style was pretty but the super-low back made her uncomfortable. The princess fluffy skirt dress made her collapse into giggles, along with everyone else.

It was Willow who finally disappeared and came back with a dress on a hanger. "I know it has a sash, and you might not like that, but try this one."

Laurel looked at it. On the hanger it was nearly shapeless, and it had an overlay of lace that she thought looked old-fashioned and busy. But because Willow had grabbed it, she dutifully put it on.

And fell in love.

The lace fell over lustrous satin, dropping in elegant folds to the floor. The bodice was more modest than the others, with a scalloped lace V-neckline leading to lace straps just over an inch wide. The sash was a pale, pale periwinkle, like the softest of the lilacs in her mother's garden. She looked at herself in the mirror and got a lump in her throat. The lace wasn't busy at all. It was perfect. Soft, romantic, nostalgic.

"You need a veil," Tricia murmured, a reverent tone in her voice. "Something long. Hang on."

She came back in a flash, carrying a simple veil that was attached to clear plastic combs. She anchored it just above Laurel's knot, and then spread it wide over her back and shoulders. Laurel looked around; the veil went nearly to the floor. Oh heavens.

"Come on, what's taking so long?" called Willow.

Laurel slipped into the shoes she'd brought—her original wedding shoes—and took a breath. "I know I'm not even getting married," she whispered to Tricia. "But I feel very bridal."

"You look bridal. Let's take you out."

She stepped outside of the dressing room and there was silence.

"Don't you like it?" she asked, stepping up on the dais.

"Oh," Willow said. "Sweetie. It's perfect."

She looked down and gathered the skirt in her hands. "Do you think?"

Oaklee's eyes were wide. "Holy shit. That's the perfect dress. It's stunning on you. Good job, Willow."

Laurel met Willow's gaze. "You know me pretty well, huh."

"What are best friends for?"

"Now, here's an idea," Tricia said. "The original picture has a sage-green sash on your dress. Should we match it, instead of the periwinkle?"

"We can do that?" Oaklee's eyes lit up.

"Sure we can."

Oaklee looked at Laurel. "So this is it? This is the dress for the photo shoot?"

Right. The photo shoot. Not a wedding. After all her self-talk to remember that, she'd conveniently forgotten. Right about the time that Tricia had expertly tied the sash.

"This is the one." She looked down at the tag. "Oh my stars. I'm glad it's on loan. I promise not to get a thing on it."

"Don't worry about that."

Oaklee nodded. "It's publicity for the shop, too. A bunch of local businesses are helping out to get a stake in the promotion."

Once again with the hard business. It made her feel a little bit better about wearing a dress that was so expensive. "Oh?"

Oaklee was on her phone again. "Of course. Laurel, you're going to need hair and makeup done. We've got that covered at Sally Ingram's salon. New shoes from Stepping Out. Flowers from Buxton's Blossoms. Oh, and you need a ring. On loan too, of course." She smiled brightly. "The jeweler is next."

"A ring? For a picture?"

"What happens if you lift your left hand and there's no engagement ring on it? People notice that stuff. Good heavens, have fun with it. I know I am. Maybe I should have been a wedding planner instead of doing social media."

She looked up from the phone. "And. . . . tweet number two. *We have a dress. No peeking until the big day! #somethingoldsomethingnew.* Can't forget to use the hashtag every time."

Laurel had a feeling that by the end of the day she was going to tell Oaklee what to do with her hashtag.

Tricia had one of the seamstresses come in and measure for a few alterations, and it seemed like no time at all and they were out on the bright street again, squinting against the sunlight. At the jewelers she picked out a gorgeous princess-cut diamond with diamond accents down the sides and milgrain detailing. Once more she goggled at the price tag, but since it was on loan, she started breathing again. The jewelry store would hold on to it until the morning of the shoot; then it could be picked up.

"This is really, really strange," she commented, as the trio then went to Buxton's Blossoms. "I feel like such a fraud!" It also felt incredibly real, and she had to keep reminding herself that it wasn't.

"Don't be silly." Oaklee grinned at her. "We're thrilled you and Aiden are willing to do the shoot. It's going to be awesome. The then-and-now thing is going to be a dynamite angle for the press release."

"What about flowers, Laurel? What do you like?" asked Willow.

She frowned. "Last time I had roses and calla lilies and it was all very elegant and fine. Not that there's anything wrong with that, but it's not who I am. Even if it's pretend, I think it'd be neat to have something I like. I mean, I'm not out to please a mother-in-law this time." She snorted a little. "Or a fiancé. Dan had definite ideas about the flowers."

"So you can get exactly what you want. Are you more a wildflower girl?"

"I'm a . . . a backyard garden kind of girl," she said. "How about lilacs?" She brightened. "And peonies. Oh my, yes. Purply lilacs and blush-colored peonies and something white. Baby's breath? It'd have to be delicate around those other blooms. Peonies can be really showy. And just enough fern to go with the sash on the dress."

"What do you say?" Oaklee asked the lady behind the counter. "Can we do something with lilacs and peonies?"

The woman pulled out a catalog, went to a page, and pointed at the arrangements there. "We can swap out these flowers for the ones you want. It'll be a little fuller—lilac and peonies are a fuller flower than lavender and roses, but the colors you mentioned would work beautifully."

Willow leaned over and looked at the page. "We can get the sash from the gown and match the ribbon."

"Oooh!" Oaklee's smile was wide. "Girls, I think we've got a good handle on this. Laurel, you go ahead and set up the appointments you need for hair and makeup at Sally's. Oh, and Sally also agreed to bring you in on the Friday for some pampering. Facial, manicure, the works."

"Oaklee, it's too much."

"Hush." She leaned over. "You know, you're the town sweetheart these days. You brought the garden center back to life, and then you helped that homeless guy . . . George? And now you've agreed to do the picture. Believe me, everyone's eager to help."

"You're sure . . ."

"It's done. Compliments of . . . the town of Darling."

"I doubt it was the mayor's idea," she muttered. "I doubt I'm on his list of favorite people these days."

Willow put a hand on her arm. "Brent doesn't blame you. I'm sure of it. He probably feels horrible about what happened."

"We're all good, right, ladies?" Oaklee looked up from her phone once more. "I've got to get back to the office. I'll be in touch, Laurel, to firm up details. But for now I think you're set. I'm leaving the shoes to you." She grinned. "Just have them bill me at the office."

"Thanks," she said, and after Oaklee was gone, she let out a big breath.

"Well. That was something. I feel like I've just been spun out of a tornado."

Willow laughed. "Come on. Let's go get tea. You can tell me what's going on with you and Aiden." Willow had left the café under the care of a supervisor, something she rarely did. "Let's go to the tearoom," she suggested. "We'll have tea and scones in the garden and little cakes and girly things."

"You don't want to check in at the Pig?"

"Even I like to have something different once in a while."

They went to the tearoom and were seated in the English garden in the back. The scent of roses was heavy in the air, and Laurel took a deep breath. "You know, it's kind of funny. I work around flowers all day long, and I don't actually have a lot of time to stop and enjoy them. This is nice."

They were brought tea—the real stuff, loose leaf—and milk, honey, and sugar. That was followed by a tray of scones, clotted cream, little sandwiches, and tomato and goat cheese pastries. They switched to a pot of Earl Grey and nibbled on lemon poppyseed cake and strawberry tarts.

"Oh my gosh. I'm so full." Laurel sat back and patted her tummy. "Little things add up to big things, apparently."

Willow bared her teeth. "Okay, you're my best friend. Tell me if I have poppyseeds in my teeth."

Laurel burst out laughing. "God, we're classy."

"Hey. I am so." Willow grinned. "Okay, enough tea already. I've been more than patient. Time to get down to business. What's happening with you and Darling's Finest?"

Laurel looked down at her plate. "Oh. Well . . . I don't know."

"That's . . . ambiguous."

She smiled. She couldn't help it. "We broke it off, you know, before George was hurt."

"After the ex-wedding."

She chuckled. "Yeah. Why I thought I'd be able to breeze through that, I don't know. It was harder than I expected."

"It's tough when you finally have to face some things."

Laurel put down her tea cup. "That's just it. I wasn't facing it. I was pretending and swallowing all my anger and disillusionment. We broke up because Aiden had the balls to call me on it."

"Let me guess. You didn't like it."

Laurel smiled, feeling a bit sad and a bit sheepish. "Would you?"

"Not likely."

They sipped tea for a few minutes more. Then Laurel looked at Willow. She was so kind. Funny, but sweet. Tough as nails, but fragile, too. Laurel liked that Willow, for whatever reason, wasn't quite perfect. It made it easier for her to say what came next.

"Know what I realized, Wil? When Dan and I split, I mourned the life I wanted more than I mourned the man. And that's not right. I mean, I loved him. I did. But it's . . ."

Her throat closed over. Damn. Why did even thinking about Aiden make her so emotional lately?

"It's not like the way you love Aiden?" Willow asked gently.

She met Willow's gaze. Hesitated. Then shook her head.

"No," she whispered, "it's not. Maybe it's always been him. It sounds crazy, but . . ."

Willow reached over and put her fingers on Laurel's. "Love hardly ever makes sense," she answered, squeezing. "I've seen you and Aiden together. There are just sparks there, you know? It's like you both light up. Even when you don't want to."

Laurel's lower lip quivered. "I think we sort of made up. But we're holding off until after the shoot. When George was in the hospital, we talked. We agreed to do the picture, you see. I couldn't bear to even think of wearing a wedding dress before then. But it's just a dress. I was so hung up on that and not the hearts involved. I've been such a blind fool."

"You've been hurt, and you had to work through it. Don't be so hard on yourself."

"Well, I have something to prove. I can put on a dress and pose for a silly picture. And I think I'm smart enough of a businesswoman to realize that Oaklee is right. Having the initial photo with the two of us as kids and then twenty years later . . . it's publicity gold."

Willow's eyes shone. "You bet it is. And today was fun. Once it's all over, maybe you and Aiden can start again."

Laurel sighed. "I want to. I think he wants to. We've . . ." her face heated a bit. "We've said the word, Wil."

"The 'L' word?" Willow put down her tea cup. "Oh, yay! It's about time."

Laurel smiled softly. "I know. And it's great, and it's complicated, so we're taking our time. Which is what I thought I wanted. But he's only called me twice since George got out of the hospital, and both times it was about George's living arrangements. Nothing personal at all."

"Maybe he's waiting for you to make the first move."

Laurel sent Willow a wry glance. "You mean, go jump his bones or something? That's not usually my style. The thought's crossed my mind, though."

"I'm like that, too. About asking someone out, not jumping Aiden's bones," Willow corrected with a smile. "Which is probably why I'm perennially single. I don't do the asking and I think most of the men in this town don't quite know what to think of me."

"You mean with the pink and purple hair and the nose ring and the organicness?" Laurel grinned. "And let's not forget the meditating and yoga. You're new age, baby. You probably scare them to death."

"Pssh," Willow replied, her eyes sliding away from Laurel's. "I'm about as harmless as you can get. Like a cute and fuzzy kitten."

"Even kittens have claws," Laurel advised. "I don't know, do you think I should call him?"

"What exactly did you guys decide? After all the I-love-yous and stuff?"

Laurel played with the edge of her napkin. "I guess we just . . . I said . . . oh hell. That I loved him but needed to take my time."

"So he's giving you the space you asked for?"

Willow was right. She'd been the one to put on the brakes. "Maybe he knows exactly what he's doing," she answered, letting out a frustrated sigh. "He's given me what I wanted and it's driving me crazy. I think about him all the time."

Willow laughed. "You've got it bad. And I think it's awesome. You know what? I think you should just knock his socks off in that dress. I know the wedding isn't real or anything, but it'd be a hell of a story to tell the grandkids someday."

"You're not saying it should be official, are you?"

"Of course not." Willow looked away and bit into the last tart, then brushed crumbs off her lips with her napkin. "But it'd be a beautiful way to start over. You in a pretty dress, and Aiden in a tux. It's romantic as hell."

It was. And maybe, just maybe, after it was over they could pick up where they left off, but without the weight of all their baggage. The idea was so exciting that she was ready to tackle the last errand of the day. "So what do you say? Hit the shoe store and then call it a day?"

"Sounds like a plan."

They were back out on the street again when Willow stopped and put her hand on Laurel's forearm. "Hey, Lor?"

"Yeah?"

"Promise me that if the chance for happiness comes your way, you'll reach out and grab it?"

Laurel frowned. "Hey, where's that coming from?"

"Just someone who wants you to be happy. Who thinks you deserve it lots."

"Same goes for you, then." Laurel stopped and gave Willow a hug right in the middle of the street. "We both deserve it. And don't let anyone tell you differently."

They went to the shoe store then, but Laurel couldn't shake a strange feeling that Willow was hiding some sort of sadness. It wasn't like her to get sentimental like that.

Chapter 20

Aiden adjusted the sage-green necktie once more and looked in the mirror. This was the craziest thing he'd ever done, and he was nervous as hell. Terrified. It could all go so very wrong.

But if it went right, Oaklee would have one hell of a press release to send out on Monday.

Rory came into the bathroom, holding Aiden's tuxedo jacket in his hand. "There. I think I got all the cat hair off. Sorry."

"Hazards of living with a veterinarian," Aiden said. It wasn't Rory's fault the kitten had crawled through the gap in the zipper of the garment bag. "How do I look?"

"Dashing. Sick to your stomach."

"Correct on both counts."

"She doesn't know?"

"Not a thing. At least, that's what Willow says, and she had tea with Willow the other day. And Oaklee's backing her up. I can't believe everyone's kept this a secret."

"Particularly Oaklee," Rory said, frowning. "God, that woman talks and talks and talks."

"Apparently she's discreet. Jesus, Rory." Aiden's knees went weak. "What if Laurel says no?"

Rory grinned. "My money's on you. You can be downright charming when you put your mind to it. Besides, she told you she loved you. And you love her. Believe in that."

"Why don't I feel better?"

"It's time to go."

"I need to sit down."

Rory laughed. Aiden was serious. His hands were shaking, for Chrissakes.

It took nearly five minutes for him to get his gumption up again. "Okay. The shoot's at two. It's one thirty. I have to be there in ten minutes if I'm going to arrive before she does. God."

"Let's go. I'll text Willow and tell her to stall."

Rory was the one behind the wheel, thank God. Aiden's heart pounded almost painfully. It had been two weeks of crazy, hectic planning. Willow had been in on it from the start, and so had Oaklee, who in particular had seemed to enjoy the secrecy and surprise elements. He couldn't have pulled it off without her. Maybe Rory didn't appreciate Oaklee's efficiency, but she gave orders and got stuff done. Today was hopefully going to be the wedding day that Laurel had always wanted. And even though it had been nerve-wracking, he'd loved the idea of spoiling her silly.

He patted the pocket of his jacket. The ring was inside. Oaklee had told Laurel that because of the cost, the ring would be in the possession of a town officer until the moment it was required. The town officer, of course, was him.

"The weather's playing nice," Rory said, finding a spot along the curb. "Look, Aiden. Wow. There are people here and everything."

"Any update from Willow?"

"Hang on. I've been driving, you know." He shut of the car and then reached for his phone. "She says to text when we arrive. I'll tell her the coast is clear." He tapped in a few words and then looked over at Aiden. "Jesus, buddy. You've got about five minutes. Get yourself together."

"I might be sick."

Rory laughed. "Sucker. If you wanted sympathy, you should have asked Ethan to be your best man. He's been through this before."

"He has his hands full with the boys," Aiden replied. "Besides, Bruh . . ." He and Rory had lived together. Shared a lot. He really didn't want anyone else beside him.

"I know. And it's gonna work out, so I'm going to say it now: congratulations."

"I need to get out there."

"Yes. You do."

He got out of the car and immediately saw Oaklee bearing down on him. "Oh Aiden . . . you're so handsome! And that tie is perfect. Here. I have this for you." She whipped a little box out of her enormous handbag and before he could blink she was pinning a sprig of lilac on his lapel.

"Is she here yet?"

"On her way. How're you holding up?"

"I'm a wreck."

Oaklee met his gaze, and her eyes were soft. "I think this is the most romantic thing I've ever heard or seen, so buck up, big guy. You got this."

He laughed. He couldn't help it. And he was laughing

when he saw Laurel's car pull up and Willow coming around the side to open the door.

And then the laughter died on his face.

She was the most beautiful woman he'd ever seen.

This was the most real, honest moment of his life. He couldn't breathe. It felt like his heart stopped beating.

She was walking toward him, smiling. Smiling! And holding a beautiful bouquet of lilacs and something else that was fluffy and pale pink and her dress was perfection. She even had a veil, and it swirled on the breeze, waving behind her just a little bit.

This was the day she'd wanted only she didn't know it yet. He just prayed she would be right there with him. Ready to take the leap.

"Well, don't you clean up nice." She was grinning up at him. "Quite the production, isn't it? And chairs and people! I guess Oaklee was determined to have some real atmosphere, and not just the two of us for the shoot. Is the photographer ready?"

"Laurel." His stomach turned over and over again, his throat tightened. He had to get a grip. "Before any pictures, can we talk for a minute?"

Her smile faded a bit. "You look so serious. Is it George? Is there something wrong?"

Oh, bless her heart. She really didn't have any idea. And she cared about George so much. "No, it's not George. It's about today."

Her eyes looked worried. "What is it?" She bit down on her lip. "Have you changed your mind?"

"No," he said, "but you might. Though I hope you don't."

"I don't understand."

"Then just listen, okay? Hear me out." He reached for

her hand and pulled her over to the side. He knew Oaklee and some other people were watching and he tried his best to ignore them. For heaven's sake, her parents, brother, and his family were all over on the other side of the war memorial, waiting for the all-clear. In all his life, even in the worst police situation, he'd never found himself more afraid than he did at this moment.

"You remember after Dan got married, and you told me about your wedding? That it was a big affair, but what you'd really wanted was something like Dan had had? Simple, outdoors, a few family and friends . . ."

"Ye . . . es," she answered, hesitation in her voice.

"Laurel . . ." He held her fingers tight, while she clutched her bouquet in the other hand. "You're always thinking of other people. I've seen it time and again. You listen and you try to make people happy, whether it's choosing the right plants for their stupid backyard, or showing up for their wedding, or going looking for them when they're missing. And know what else I've noticed? Your wishes take a backseat. Well, not today. Today you're going to get the wedding you always wanted . . . I hope."

"I don't understand." Her eyes were wide and her lips were open just a bit. He got the feeling she did understand and either didn't quite believe it or didn't want it. God, he hoped it was the first.

"All this . . . it can be more than a photoshoot. It can be real, Laurel. All you have to do is say the word."

"Real . . . What are you saying, Aiden? What word?"

He reached into his pocket. "Say yes."

He held out the box and opened it. Nestled inside was the ring she'd picked out at the jewelers. It sparkled in the sunlight and he watched as her mouth dropped open.

"That . . . but Oaklee said . . . it's only on loan."

"No, it's not." He lowered his hand, still holding onto the box. "Oh, God. You know I'm not good at expressing my feelings, but today . . . with you . . ." He took a deep breath. "It's all real, Laurel. I knew the day we took George to the hospital and you said you loved me. I love you, so much. I probably always have, and you scare me to death, but I'm man enough now to tell you and be at your mercy. This is the most terrifying, amazing feeling and I'm so scared you're going to break my heart. But I just . . . I want to be with you. Forever. And I want to give you the wedding of your dreams. I want to make you feel special, and seen, and heard." His voice caught. "I want to make all your dreams happen."

Her lip wobbled. "You did this?"

He smiled, nodded. "I had some help. I wanted you to be able to pick things out just the way you wanted them, without a bunch of pressure." He reached out and touched her face, skimming his fingers ever so gently along her jaw. "You said once that you just wanted something simple with a backyard barbecue or something afterward. I listened, you see. I heard you, Laurel. Today when the photographer takes our picture on that bridge, it doesn't have to be us posing for the camera as Aiden and Laurel, the two kids from the last photo. It can be that ring bearer and flower girl, now husband and wife."

It felt as if his heart was right in his throat, his pulse was pounding so hard. He knelt down, held her hand. "Marry me, Laurel. I'm pretty sure now that there's never been anyone for me but you. I screwed it up when I was seventeen, but I'll spend the rest of my life making it up to you."

He waited for her answer. And while he did, he saw two tears slide past her mascara and down her cheeks, and her lower lip trembled.

Laurel was still reeling in shock from Aiden's pronouncement. Marriage? That was what he was asking? He was kneeling on the ground before her and she couldn't say anything. Her throat wouldn't work and she glanced around frantically. People. Chairs. A minister. Oh, God, a minister.

And that was a real diamond ring.

She didn't want to cry, but she couldn't help it. Willow would cuss her out for ruining her makeup.

"You did this?" she repeated. "For me?"

"It's all for you, Laurel. My heart and my soul. Like the night I kissed you, remember? It was like all the layers were peeled back and it was just you and me and this chemistry we couldn't avoid. But it's more than chemistry. It's your heart I love. I know I've made mistakes. I'll make more. I'm human. But I promise that they'll always come from a place of loving you."

More tears. No one had ever done anything like this for her before. When she'd married Dan, it had been about what was appropriate and right and suitable. She'd had very little input. In some ways her life had been that way up to this point. A useful degree. A good job. A husband, a good home, money in the bank. Secure and boring and a life full of shoulds rather than coulds. Safe rather than full of possibilities. Now she could do what she wanted. And she had someone in front of her who cared enough . . . who listened enough . . . to give her the one day she'd wanted and had missed out on.

She'd said that when they were kids, she'd just wanted a grand gesture to show he cared. Well, he'd certainly got that right this time. This was the granddaddy of all gestures. And even though he'd set it up in secret, the power to decide her future was completely in her hands. He had put himself at her mercy. On his knees.

"Aiden," she murmured, sniffing back a few tears. "Get off your knee, you big goof."

That he did as she asked, without question, surprised her. And it said something about the seriousness of the moment. The gravity.

"You want to share my life."

"All of it."

"We'll fight."

"And make up." A ghost of a smile flirted with the edges of his mouth.

"I'm insecure."

"I'll hold you tight."

Oh, damn. That was a good one.

"I want babies, Aiden. I want a family."

"I know that. And I do, too. Maybe a few months to chase you around the house naked first."

"You want kids?" Did most guys in their mid-twenties think about starting a family? "You don't want to wait until we're more financially stable, or our jobs are more secure, or . . ."

"Laurel." Oh, the way he said her name just sent a shiver of delight down her body. His eyes were deep and serious as his gaze held hers. "I have nothing to hide. I love you. I want to marry you. And I'm filled with awe at the thought of you carrying my baby. I wasn't ready before. It wasn't a flaw. I know that now. It was the wrong person at the wrong time in my life. But this is right. I know it . . . in here." He pressed his fist to his heart, right below the lilac pinned to his jacket. "Believe in me, Laurel. I swear I won't let you down."

She wasn't sure how a heart could break and heal all at the same time, but those words seemed to accomplish it. There was a bittersweet-ness to them that touched her in her most vulnerable places. His words . . . they gave her hope like she hadn't known in a long, long time.

A leap of faith.

It was time.

She put her bouquet in her right hand and held out her left. It was shaking. So was her voice as she said, "Put the ring on, Aiden."

His face blanked. "Really? You're saying yes?"

"I'm saying yes. I love you. I think I always have. I'm tired of making choices with my head. This time I'm going to follow my heart. And my heart is here, with you."

He didn't slide the ring over her finger at all. Instead he swooped her up in his arms and held her close. "Oh my God," he whispered in her ear. "I was so afraid you'd say no. And you made me wait, dammit. What am I going to do with you?"

She was crying now. "Make an honest woman out of me?"

"Damn right." He set her down and they laughed, their laughter thick with emotion. Then he finally took out the ring and slid it on her finger. A quick kiss and he turned to the crowd. "She said yes!"

Cheers went up and Laurel started to laugh again. This was all so surreal. Conversation buzzed all around them now as everyone came to offer their congratulations. Her mom and dad came up, dressed in their Sunday finest, beaming at Aiden. "Aiden Gallagher, you are full of Irish blarney," her mom chided, grinning from ear to ear. "Well done."

"Do I get to call you 'Mom' now?"

"You'd better."

He shook hands with Laurel's dad. "I won't let her down, sir."

"About time," was all her dad said, and they went off to find their seats.

She looked up to see George hovering around the fringes. Her heart warmed at the sight. "Aiden, look."

George had on a suit. And a tie. The bruising on his face was almost gone, and he smiled a little as he came forward, still moving gingerly.

"Oh, George. You came! And you look so handsome." She looked up at Aiden. "Maybe I've just said yes to the wrong guy."

George chuckled and then put a hand to his side. "Laughing still catches, dammit."

"Then can I hug you? Gently? I'm so glad you're okay. And the new place? You're settling in?" They'd lined up some VA assistance and he was in a place of his own.

"It's good," he responded. And he came forward and gave her a small hug. "Thank you for saving me," he said quietly. "Both of you."

"You're welcome. And I expect to see you at work as soon as you're ready. Got that?"

"Yes, ma'am." He looked up at Aiden. "She's bossy. You've got your hands full."

"I hope so," Aiden replied.

After George moved on, Oaklee was Johnny-on-the-spot with Sally Ingram in tow. "You need a makeup fix. Sally's got the emergency kit. You come with us. Aiden, you get to the front. Rory's waiting for you and the minister has some last-minute details to discuss."

Laurel was tugged along to a bench beneath a tree, where the light was slightly more consistent. "There's not much damage," Sally said, giving her face a quick look and digging into the cosmetic bag. "I had the girls use the waterproof stuff. It's important for weddings."

"Thank you, Sally," Laurel said, smiling at the older lady. "For yesterday too. Nails, toes, my facial . . . Oh my gosh. It feels like the whole town's been in on my wedding."

"Most excitement we've had in a long time," Sally decreed, giving Laurel's lashes a swipe of mascara. "Here, stop talking. I need to fix your lips."

Oaklee was tapping on her phone again. "Laurel, this is so amazing. Look." She held the screen out for Laurel to read. The tweet read, *She said yes! #somethingoldsomethingnew #laurelandaiden.*

There was something about seeing their names paired together that way that gave Laurel a silly thrill.

Oaklee adjusted Laurel's veil and then Willow came around the corner. Laurel gasped, delighted at the sight.

"Every woman needs a Maid of Honor," Willow said. "I hope you don't mind. I just assumed . . ."

"Of course! Oh, you look beautiful!" Willow had changed into a flowy, wispy dress in a slightly paler shade of green than Laurel's sash. She carried a matching bouquet of lilacs and peonies, and there was a just-blossoming peony in her hair, right next to the pretty pink stripe.

"Happy?" Willow asked.

"Shocked. Happy. Overwhelmed."

"You love him?" Willow's eyes were dark and serious. "You need to be sure."

Laurel caught her breath. "Willow, when he walks in a room I just get this feeling. I can't explain it. I can talk to him. I can argue with him. He's . . . and don't take this the wrong way . . . he's my best friend. I've cared for him for so long. We've both made mistakes. But he's a good man, and he loves me, and he makes my heart glad every time I see him." She felt like crying again and held it together, barely. "He wants a family. It's just . . . it's right. I feel it right down to my bones. I fell in love with him this spring. I just spent a lot of time fighting it because I was scared."

"You're not scared anymore?"

She shook her head. "I'm terrified, but golly, it's a beautiful kind of terrified. Besides, you told me that if I had a chance at happiness I'd better take it. Oh my Lord. You knew. You sneaky thing."

Willow came forward and hugged her. "Be happy, my friend. I'm so excited for you."

They pulled apart and Laurel smiled. "Okay, I think we've made him sweat enough. Should we go out and do this thing, Maid of Honor?"

"Why yes, I think we should . . . Bride."

Oaklee led the way and made sure everyone was in position. Near the front, a single guitar started playing softly, something simple and beautiful that suited the atmosphere perfectly. And there was her dad, waiting to escort her up the aisle.

Willow smiled and started her slow walk to the front, where Aiden and Rory waited with the minister.

Laurel took her dad's arm and began the walk over the grass to where her future husband waited, smiling at her as if she were the only woman in the world, then tucking her hand inside his as she reached the front and they faced the minister together.

And her heart healed that last little bit when Aiden said, "I, Aiden, take you, Laurel . . ."

CHAPTER 21

The main event of the day was to have been the photos on the bridge, but now, as Laurel sat at a table in the Gallaghers' backyard, she realized the pictures had been rather anticlimactic. She remembered group shots, and laughing, and kissing Aiden while he held her bouquet. Then they'd been ushered into someone's borrowed Cadillac and Ethan had driven them out to the house.

Aiden sat beside her, enjoying a glass of champagne, watching the kids run around with their shirttails untucked.

"You remembered everything," she said, shaking her head. "I said I wanted a simple wedding, then something in a backyard that was casual and with all our favorite people there. And you did it. You did it all. That's pretty amazing."

"I had a lot of help. Mom looked after this, with some help from Willow's staff. Oaklee is a dynamo. Everything else was just simple. Not a lot of fuss. You'd already looked after the flowers and I did the rings."

She held out her hand. Her diamond engagement ring

was now nestled next to a matching band. And he was wearing a plain band of his own.

"What would you have done if I'd said no?"

He laughed. "Spent a lot of time returning things around town."

"You paid for all of it. Oh God, Aiden. I didn't watch what I spent because it was supposed to be on loan."

"I've got it covered," he said, putting his arm around her. "I've been working and living with my brother for a while now. I consider this a solid investment in my future."

She leaned over and kissed him. It was meant to be a quick, sweet kiss, but it turned into something longer and lazy. Delicious.

"How late do we have to stay?" she asked. "And speaking of roommates, have you thought about the housing situation? Would you like to move into my place? Or do you want to find something together?"

"After all the work you've put into the garden? Sweetheart, all your place needs is a family to liven it up and make it a home."

"I couldn't agree more."

They drank more champagne, and ate cake, and spent a crazy amount of time chatting and laughing. Around seven Laurel was getting tired, and she wanted to go home with her husband and sort through the craziness of the day. She found Oaklee and suggested that she throw the bouquet so they could make their escape.

Before the bouquet, though, came the garter. Among jeers and catcalls, Aiden reached up beneath her skirt and pulled off the lacy strip of elastic. He smoothed his fingers over the soft flesh of her thigh on the way down, sending tingles along her skin. "Naughty," she whispered, looking forward to the night ahead.

All the bachelors were pushed onto the stone patio as Aiden stretched the elastic and sent it flying. It landed right on top of Ethan's glass of beer.

There was lots more hollering and teasing going on, and Ethan's scowl was made deeper by the blush on his cheeks. Then he gave a sheepish smile and everyone relaxed a bit more.

Laurel turned her back on the gathered single women and counted down. "Three . . . two . . . one!" She sent the bouquet flying over her head and, if she aimed right, down the left side of the group. A shout went up and she spun around to see Willow holding the bouquet in her open hands.

Just as she'd wanted.

Next they made Willow sit while Ethan was supposed to put the garter on her leg. He got it up to her calf and then made the mistake of looking up. Laurel nearly laughed. Both of them were blushing furiously, and Ethan backed off right away. Maybe Laurel wanted Willow to find her true love next, but it was highly unlikely it would be determined by a bouquet and garter toss. Ethan and Willow were far too different. She saw Oaklee with her stupid phone out again. Probably sending out another tweet or something.

"Well, Mrs. Gallagher, shall we go?" Aiden's voice was warm in her ear.

"Yes. Let's go home, Aiden."

Rory did transportation honors. Aiden and Laurel cuddled in the backseat as he drove back into Darling and straight to Laurel's house. There was finally quiet now, and a settling that had the both of them coming to terms with the day and pausing before stepping into their future together.

Rory got out and opened Laurel's door. "Congratulations. I really don't need another sister, but if I have to have one, I'm glad it's you."

"I see flattery runs in the family," she responded, and kissed his cheek. "Thank you, Rory. For everything."

Aiden and Rory had a quick man-hug before Rory got in the car and left them standing there on the sidewalk outside her house.

"Well, Mrs. Gallagher?"

He scooped her up in his arms and she gave a little squeak. She dug out her key from her tiny purse and opened the door, and he stepped inside and put her down in the tiny foyer.

"Welcome home," he said softly. "It doesn't feel real."

"I know. But it is. We did it. For better or for worse."

"Remember what I said about how what your place needed was some touches to make it into a home?"

"Mmm-hmmm." She was busy at the moment, nuzzling at his neck, reaching for his neck tie. It had been a long day. And they'd hardly seen each other in three weeks. She was ready. So ready. And this dress would take a few minutes to get out of . . .

"Laurel, turn around."

She did. And pressed her hand to her chest.

There, above the mantel, was the original picture of the two of them. Straight out of the town hall, it was now above her fireplace. Lord, he'd been adorable, all gingery curls and impishness. He was holding her flower-girl basket and she was leaning forward, planting a kiss right on his lips, wearing a white dress with a pale green sash.

And there, on the table next to it, was a new picture. One from this afternoon, done so quickly. . . . How had he arranged it?

"Your mom," he said, answering her unasked question. "She had a key. The photographer rushed to print it, and I had the frame already. It's my wedding gift to you."

This picture was nearly identical to the first. She still wore a white dress with a sash, and he was holding her flowers as she leaned in to kiss him. But they were older, wiser, less innocent, but far more hopeful.

She leaned back against his chest. "I never thought I'd really find this, you know," she said softly. "I thought it wasn't meant for me. That I'd come as close as I ever would."

"But?"

"But I didn't plan on finding somebody like you. Or rather, you finding me."

"But I did. We did."

"And you didn't give up."

"Nope."

She sighed, unbelievably happy. "I think we've always been moving toward this moment, you know? And I know I said I wanted time, but I discovered something before the wedding."

"What's that?"

"I wanted you more than I wanted space."

He nuzzled at her ear. "Know what else?" he whispered.

She tilted her head back against his shoulder. "What?"

He smiled against her cheek. "It's time you stopped talking."

She turned around and wrapped her arms around his neck. Then kissed him, and kissed him, and kissed him, until they were both breathless.

And then he loosened his tie, and she put down her bouquet of flowers, and they began their journey . . . as a family.

Don't miss the next two novels in the Darling series by
Donna Alward

Someone to Love

Somebody's Baby

Coming soon from St. Martin's Paperbacks